WITH

ONCE UPON A
TOAD

ALSO BY HEATHER VOGEL FREDERICK

The Mother-Daughter Book Club

Much Ado About Anne

Dear Pen Pal

Pies & Prejudice

Home for the Holidays

Spy Mice: The Black Paw

Spy Mice: For Your Paws Only

Spy Mice: Goldwhiskers

The Voyage of Patience Goodspeed

The Education of Patience Goodspeed

Hide-and-Squeak

ONCE UPON A
TOAD

HEATHER VOGEL FREDERICK

SIMON & SCHUSTER BOOKS FOR YOUNG READERS

NEW YORK LONDON TORONTO SYDNEY NEW DELHI

SIMON & SCHUSTER BOOKS FOR YOUNG READERS
An imprint of Simon & Schuster Children's Publishing Division
1230 Avenue of the Americas, New York, New York 10020
SIMON & SCHUSTER BOOKS FOR YOUNG READERS is a trademark of
Simon & Schuster, Inc.
For information about special discounts for bulk purchases, please contact Simon
& Schuster Special Sales at 1-866-506-1949 or business@simonandschuster.com.
The Simon & Schuster Speakers Bureau can bring authors to your live event. For
more information or to book an event, contact the Simon & Schuster Speakers
Bureau at 1-866-248-3049 or visit our website at www.simonspeakers.com.
Book design by Krista Vossen
The text for this book is set in Aldine.
Manufactured in the United States of America • 0312 FFG
2 4 6 8 10 9 7 5 3 1
CIP data for this book is available from the Library of Congress.
ISBN 978-1-4169-8478-8
ISBN 978-1-4169-8707-9 (eBook)

For Jami and her girls,
Kylie and McKenna

CHAPTER 1

"Are we there yet?" My little brother pulled his index finger out of his mouth, sounding anxious. Geoffrey's not quite four and doesn't like car trips.

Without taking his eyes off the road, my dad reached over the back of his seat and stuffed the finger back in. It works kind of like a safety plug. Geoffrey's nickname in our family is Barf Bucket.

"Not much longer, buddy. Hang in there."

I was well out of range, sitting in the very back of the minivan next to Olivia. If you can call being braced against opposite car windows sitting "next to" each other. There was practically a force field between us. My stepsister and I are not exactly best friends.

I'd just arrived from Houston, where I live with my mom for most of the year, and was on the way from the airport to my dad's house in Oregon. Usually, I only spend vacations with my father: Thanksgiving or Christmas, take your pick;

plus half of spring break and a month every summer.

This time, though, was different. This time I was moving in for three months, smack-dab in the middle of the school year. Well, almost the middle. April 1, to be exact. What choice did I have? It's not like I could stay at home with my mom. She was in outer space. Literally. My mother is an astronaut.

"It's either go to Portland or stay with your great-aunt Abyssinia," she told me when she broke the news that she'd been selected to go to the International Space Station. Obviously, there was no way she could take me with her. Not that I didn't beg her to anyway. Anything would be better than sharing a room with Miss Prissy Pants Olivia Haggerty.

Well, almost anything. The prospect of staying with my great-aunt Abyssinia was marginally worse, I had to admit. Great-Aunt Aby is my mother's only relative. She lives in an RV with her cat, Archibald, and spends her time travel-ing around to all the national parks. Our refrigerator back in Houston is plastered with her postcards: "Greetings from Yosemite!"; "Having a grand time at the Grand Canyon!"; and my personal favorite, "Chillaxin' at Glacier!" All of them are signed "ABYCNU"—the stupid little jingle she and my mother use when they say good-bye to each other. "Abyssinia!" my mother always hollers as Great-Aunt Abyssinia drives away. "Not if I be seeing you first!" my great-aunt hollers back, and then they both laugh their heads off. They think this is just hilarious, for some reason.

Once, a couple of years ago when I was still in elementary school, my mother and I flew out to meet my great-aunt at Mount Rushmore for a week. It was kind of cool staying in the RV, but Great-Aunt Aby is weird. She's scatterbrained and disorganized, and she has some strange hobbies (her snow globe collection is about ready to take over the RV) and even stranger ideas about food. I was in my "I don't eat anything but fish sticks and peanut butter" phase back then, and her refrigerator had neither, just pickled eggs, kimchi, and about a hundred bottles of this disgusting green gloop that she drinks for breakfast. Her cupboards weren't any better. Who eats dried seaweed? If it's stinky or looks like it should be thrown in the trash immediately, you can be sure it's on my great-aunt's list of top ten favorite foods. I nearly starved to death on that trip.

Dad was thrilled with the idea, of course. Not me starving to death, but me coming to live with him. Ever since he remarried and became the proud owner of a brand-new family, he's been dying for us all to turn into the Brady Bunch.

Like that's ever going to happen.

It wouldn't be so bad if it weren't for Olivia. My half brother, Geoffrey, is actually really cute, except for the barfing, and my stepmother isn't like one of those fairy-tale stepmothers, the ones who secretly hate their stepdaughters and make them sleep in the scullery or something. Iz—her real name is Isabelle, but everybody calls her Iz—is awesome. The two of us actually have way more in common than she and Olivia do. For instance, Iz loves the outdoors and she loves classical music, which are my two main passions in life. Sometimes she takes me to the symphony when I visit, just the two of us, and leaves Olivia home to babysit Geoffrey. Olivia hates it when that happens, even though she can't stand classical music and she has all the rest of the year to do stuff with her mother.

No, it definitely wasn't Iz. The real reason we'd never become the Brady Bunch was Olivia. My stepsister is a major pain.

If Olivia went to my school back in Houston, there's no way we would ever be friends. She tap-dances; I'm a tomboy. She's into arts and crafts; I break out in a rash at the sight of a tube of glitter. And I play the bassoon, while she still plays with Barbies. Olivia gets really mad when I say this—"I don't *play* with them, they're *props*," she insists. Yeah, right. Whatever. My stepsister wants to be an interior designer when she grows up, and her room is crammed with boxes she's decorated to look like rooms from magazines. They're wallpapered and painted, and there are curtains made of scraps of fabric from Iz's quilting basket, and carpet samples on the floors. Inside, the Barbies lounge around, reading on their little sofas and cooking in their itty-bitty kitchens and talking on the phones in their miniature offices. It's creepy.

It would be so much better if Olivia and I didn't have to share a room. My dad's house is way different from our supermodern high-rise condo back in Houston. It was built in 1912, for one thing, and for another, it's tiny. I mean *teeny* tiny. It's cute and everything, but it's designed more for Goldilocks or Thumbelina or somebody like that. Not for real people. It's like living in one of Olivia's Barbie dioramas.

My dad and Iz are really proud of their house, though. They call it their Northwest Honeymoon Cottage, and they're always going on about how much character it has, and swooning over the hardwood floors and the tile work around the fireplace and the stained-glass window on the landing of the stairs. Maybe that's where Olivia gets her

passion for decorating, I don't know. What I do know is that
I'd trade character for a few modern conveniences any day
of the week. Another bathroom would be nice, for starters.
There's only one for all five of us, which is totally ridiculous.
Didn't anybody ever have to use the bathroom back in 1912?
I guess nobody had clothes back then either, because the
closets are minuscule too. Olivia loathes having to share her
closet. She doesn't like having to share anything, especially
with me, and especially her room. Stuffing the two of us in
there is like throwing a lighted match onto a pile of wood
shavings. *Kaboom!*

Dad and Iz have been talking about fixing up the attic
into a master bedroom suite and giving me their room, but
this trip came up kind of suddenly. There wasn't time for a
remodel. Mom was a last-minute replacement for one of the
other astronauts, who broke his ankle a week before launch.
She was up and into space so fast we didn't even get a chance
to celebrate my birthday. I had to go stay with my friend A.J.
and his family instead.

My mother and I had been planning a special trip over
spring break, just the two of us. Dad had even agreed to let
me skip my usual week in Oregon so that Mom and I could
have more time together on our "mystery trip," as she called
it. She wouldn't tell me where she was taking me. Not that it
mattered now. When she got the news about the space mission, we had to cancel.

I was still brooding about this fact as we pulled off the
freeway onto the winding road that led up into Portland's
West Hills. We were almost home. Unfortunately, it didn't
happen soon enough for Geoffrey.

"Gross!" shrieked Olivia as the car swerved and my dad pulled off onto the road's narrow shoulder. "Couldn't you have held it for five more minutes, you little twerp?"

Geoffrey started to cry. My father frowned at Olivia, then turned to him and said gently, "It's okay, buddy. We'll get you cleaned up in a jiffy. Just a little April Fools' Day joke, right?"

Some joke, I thought, holding my nose and catapulting out of the car. I sprinted past Olivia, waiting until I was safely out of range of eau de barf before taking a deep breath of fresh air. I love the way Oregon smells. Like evergreens and moss and clean earth. It rains here a lot, especially in the winter and spring, which keeps the air crystal-clear, unlike downtown Houston. And unlike downtown Houston, everything in Portland is incredibly green. I've never seen so many shades of the color before in my life.

My dad is a wildlife biologist, and he loves taking me hiking when I visit. I swear he knows every trail in Oregon. And in Portland, too. His house is on the fringes of the city, tucked into the woods up near Forest Park. He loves to brag that he lives on the edge of the biggest city park in the United States, and he loves the fact that the Wildwood Trail passes right by our house. I've always thought it was cool how you could hop on it and be out in the middle of nowhere one minute, then downtown the next.

I glanced back at the car. My father was changing Geoffrey's clothes. Olivia was lounging nearby, fiddling with her cell phone. She'd spent the entire drive home texting madly. She was probably telling her BFF, Piper Philbin, what a loser I was and how I'd completely ruined the rest of the school year for her by coming to Oregon.

Not that I really cared what she said, especially not to Piper Fleabrain.

I think it says a lot about a person, who they pick for their best friend, and the fact that Olivia picked Piper didn't exactly boost my opinion of my stepsister. Piper is one of those empty-headed popular girls that my middle school back in Houston is stuffed full of. Texas, Oregon—it doesn't matter, they're all the same. I swear they're made with cookie cutters in a bakery somewhere. All they care about is clothes and boys and makeup, and they talk in these high, squeaky voices that get higher and squeakier whenever someone male is nearby. It's enough to make a person, well, barf.

My best friend, on the other hand, may be a total nerd, but he's also the nicest guy on the planet. A.J. D'Angelo is the smartest kid in my school, and possibly in the whole state of Texas. He's a computer geek, which isn't surprising because both his parents work for NASA. Not as astronauts, but doing computer stuff. The whole family is scary smart. They live in the same building as my mother and I do, only we're on the seventeenth floor and they're on the fifteenth. I've known A.J. since the day we moved in, when I was six.

"All clear!" called my father.

Olivia and I climbed back into the van, still holding our noses, and a few minutes later we pulled into the driveway. My father tooted the horn to let my stepmother know we'd arrived, and the door flew open and Iz came running down the front steps, her long, curly blond hair bouncing behind her.

"I'm so glad you're here!" she said, throwing her arms around me, and for a brief moment I was glad too. Such was

7

the power of Iz. Then Olivia ungraciously set my suitcase down on my foot, and all of a sudden I would have given anything to be back in Texas.

My stepmother planted a kiss on the top of my head. "You grew again," she said. "At least an inch."

I smiled up at her. Iz knows that my greatest ambition in life—besides playing bassoon for a major symphony orchestra or doing something involving the outdoors—is to be taller. I'm really, really short. Vertically challenged, as A.J. puts it.

"Sorry I couldn't be at the airport to meet you," Iz told me. "I had a shoot up on Mount Hood and I couldn't reschedule."

My stepmother is a nature photographer. Even though deep down I still sometimes wish that my parents would get back together again, I have to admit that Iz and my dad are kind of a match made in heaven. The two of them have a whole lot more in common than my parents ever did.

My mother always tells me that what happened between her and my dad isn't my fault and it isn't my business, either. My business is just to know that they both love me more than anything and always will. I suppose she's got a point, but still, sometimes I wish things could have worked out differently.

"That's okay," I told my stepmother. "I don't mind."

This was true, and Iz knew it. She smiled and gave me another hug. "Wait until you see some of the shots I got. The mountain was out in all its spring glory this morning."

Mount Hood is amazing. There's snow on it all year round, and you can see its white-capped peak from all over the city. It's like Portland's trademark. One of our traditions when I come here during summer vacation is to drive up to Timberline Lodge and take the ski lift to the snow line. Iz takes our picture for the family Christmas card, and then we have a snowball fight. I love telling my friends back in Houston about this. They can't believe there's someplace that has snow in July and August.

Olivia really gets into the snowball fight—big surprise there, especially since I'm always her prime target—but that's about the only outdoor activity she likes. Nature is not Miss Prissy Pants's favorite thing. And Geoffrey's still at the stage where he wants everybody to carry him, so the two of them get left at home a lot when there's an outdoor adventure planned.

"Olivia, why don't you help your sister take her things upstairs?" Iz prompted.

Stepsister, I thought automatically.

"While you girls are getting settled in," she continued, "I'll get dinner on the table."

"Um, someone needs a bath first," said my father.

My stepmother plucked Geoffrey from his arms. "Bathwater's drawn and ready," she said, and gave Geoffrey a kiss too, even though he still smelled faintly of barf. Mothers are amazing that way. "How about I scrub the G-Man while you set the table?"

"Deal," said my dad.

Iz nudged Olivia, who glared at me as she picked up my suitcase again.

I followed her warily into the house.

CHAPTER 2

Upstairs, the first thing I noticed was that Olivia had redecorated. Again. Everything was blue this time, her favorite color. The second thing I noticed was that she'd stuck a line of duct tape right down the middle of the floor. Was this another lame April Fools' Day joke?

Apparently not.

"This is your half of the room, and this is mine," she said, stating the obvious. She heaved my suitcase onto my bed, which I noticed she'd moved to the darkest corner of the room, by the wall. All part of the redecorating plan, apparently. "I don't know where you're going to put all your stuff. The closet is really full."

Big surprise there.

"Mom asked me to clear a couple of dresser drawers out," she continued ungraciously, "but I couldn't find any place else for all my art supplies."

"Fine," I snapped. My stepsister might as well have hung

up a big sign on the door that said KEEP OUT! "I'll just leave everything in my suitcase." I didn't bother to add, *That way I'll be ready to leave at a moment's notice,* but I'm sure that was obvious too.

Olivia gave me a poisonously sweet smile and flipped on the radio. She knows how much I hate pop music, so I knew right away that this was another phase of her campaign to torture me into going home early. As she hummed along to some inane pop star warbling, "Gimme gimme all your luuuuuuuuv," I heaved a sigh and took my iPod out of my backpack. Slipping in my earbuds, I turned the volume way up on Bach's Cello Suite no. 1 (the version featuring Yo-Yo Ma, one of my heroes) to block out the noise. I hung my bathrobe on a hook on the back of the door—amazingly, Olivia had left one free for me—slipped my pajamas under my pillow, and wedged a handful of things into the drawer of my bedside table. That pretty much took care of things in the unpacking department. The rest of my stuff I just left in the suitcase, which I shoved under the bed. I was itching to tell Olivia exactly what I thought of her, but Mom had made me promise not to pick a fight on my first day here.

"Dinner!" Iz called a few minutes later.

We held hands around the table while my father said grace. Olivia's fingertips barely grazed mine, and she whipped her hand away the second we said "Amen," but Dad held on a little longer, giving me a warm squeeze. "It's really good to have you here, Kit-Cat," he said, beaming.

I gave him a crooked smile. My father is the only one who calls me by that nickname. He's called me that since I was a baby. My real name is Catriona, but nobody calls me that except Great-Aunt Abyssinia. Everybody else just calls me Cat.

Olivia thinks Cat is a stupid nickname, of course, but I like it. It suits me. Short and sweet, my mother says. I don't know about the sweet part—I try, really I do—but she's right about short. Being small is the bane of my existence. I'm barely five feet tall, shorter than anyone else in the family. Olivia is five foot eight already, plus she's three weeks older, which gives her the upper hand, or at least she thinks it does. She loves to introduce me to everyone as her little sister. Which is so ridiculous.

Iz dished me up some of her homemade lasagna. She always makes it the first night I get here because she knows how much I love it, and how much I love the garlic bread she fixes to go with it. Dad passed me the bread basket, and I reached in and tore off a piece and took a bite. I had to close my eyes it was so good, all warm and crusty and dripping with garlicky butter.

"I think it's wonderful that you came in time for the spring talent show," my father said, his voice brimming with enthusiasm. "Did Olivia tell you she's going to do a tap dance routine this year?"

"No," I replied, turning to my stepsister and crossing my eyes at her. Olivia glared and looked away. She knows what I think of tap dancing.

"She's now officially a Hawk Creek Tapper!" Iz said proudly.

"Great," I murmured, trying to sound sincere.

After we finished our meal, I started to clear my plate.

"Hold on, honey," Iz told me, jumping up and heading for

the kitchen. A moment later she poked her head around the door and grinned. "One, two, three!" she called, then sailed back in carrying a cake platter. She and my father burst into a chorus of "Happy Birthday." Olivia mumbled along half-heartedly until Geoffrey banged his spoon against his booster seat and hollered, "Cat! Cat! Cat!" Then she stopped singing and glared at me again.

My little brother doesn't say much. In fact, he only says three things: "Are we there yet?" "With a G!" (whenever any-one says his name), and "Cat." This last one makes Olivia furious, especially since he doesn't say her name yet.

I can tell that Dad and Iz are worried about Geoffrey, but my mother says they shouldn't be. "Einstein barely said a word until he was four," she assured me. "And he turned out okay."

Iz set the cake down on the table in front of me. Twelve candles blazed brightly atop the chocolate frosting.

"Thanks," I said, truly surprised. I hadn't been expect-ing anything—my birthday was last weekend, the day after Mom flew to Kazakhstan to catch a ride aboard a Soyuz rocket to the International Space Station. I was staying with the D'Angelos, finishing my last week of school before our spring break. A.J.'s family had a little party for me, and Dad and Iz had called, and sent a present and everything—the new iPod I'd been listening to up in Olivia's room.

My dad reached over and squeezed my hand again. "I know how disappointed you were about postponing the trip with your mother, Kit-Cat," he said. "She says you've been a really good sport about it."

I lifted a shoulder, not sure if the mini-tantrum and

weeklong sulk really qualified me as a "good sport."

Iz opened a drawer in the sideboard behind her and took out two small, brightly wrapped boxes. "We have another present for you," she said, handing one of them to me. "There's one for you, too, Olivia."

Uh-oh, I thought, glancing at my stepsister. I could tell by the expression on her face that she had a bad feeling about this too.

I pulled the paper off slowly, then opened the box. Inside was a silver ring. There was some engraving on it: SISTERS ARE FOREVER FRIENDS. Between each of the words was a tiny aquamarine, the birthstone I shared with Olivia. Looking across the table, I could see that her ring was identical.

"I saw them in the gift shop up at Timberline this morning and instantly thought of you two," my stepmother said happily. "Aren't they adorable?"

I didn't want to burst Iz's bubble, but for one thing Olivia wasn't my sister, she was my stepsister—big difference—and for another, forever friends? Was Iz completely clueless? Maybe this was an April Fools' Day joke too.

But it wasn't, of course.

"How do they fit?" she asked, and Olivia and I reluctantly slipped them on. "Oh good, they're just the right size."

Iz looked so sincerely delighted that I knew there was no way I'd be able to take my ring off. Not as long as I was here in Oregon. It would hurt her feelings, and I loved Iz too much to do that. Unfortunately, that meant I was stuck wearing the thing for the next three months.

"Two beautiful rings for our two beautiful girls," my father said, smiling at us. Olivia kicked me sharply under the table as he added, "Aren't you going to blow out your candles and make a wish, Kit-Cat?"

I closed my eyes. *Please let me open them and be back in Houston!* No such luck, of course. I blew for all I was worth, but I was still at the dining-room table across from Olivia, who stared sourly first at me and then at her new ring.

"What did your mother give you for your birthday, Cat?" asked my father. "Last time I talked to her, she said she had something special for you."

I reached into the collar of my T-shirt and fished around for the charm on the thin gold chain of the necklace I was wearing. "This," I told him, pulling it out.

"Nice," he said, peering at it over his glasses.

"Nice?" said Iz, leaning in for a closer look. "It's gorgeous! Look at the detail." She reached out and traced the design on the flat gold disk. "That's meant to be a sprig of juniper, isn't it, Tim?"

My dad inspected it. "Indeed it is, berries and all."

"The ancient symbol of protection," Iz mused. "The necklace looks really old, Cat—is it a family heirloom?"

I shrugged. "I don't know. It was under my pillow when I woke up on my birthday." I didn't tell her about the note I'd found in the box, which was weirdly formal for my laid-back mother: "For Catriona Skye Starr on the occasion of her 12th birthday."

"There's something written on the other side," said Iz, flipping the charm over. I didn't have to look to see the two words she was talking about: HOLD FAST. "Do you know what it means?"

I shook my head. There'd been no explanation with the note.

"Well, you'll have to find out more when your mother returns from her mission."

I grunted, slipping the necklace back under my T-shirt.

Iz gave me a sympathetic look. "Too bad she couldn't be there to celebrate with you. But I'm sure she'll do something special to make up for it when she gets back home."

I shrugged again, wishing she'd change the subject. My birthday was still a bit of a sore spot.

"I called the school the other day and spoke with Mr. Randolph, the principal," she continued briskly, cutting the cake and passing out slices. "He said he didn't see any reason why you two girls couldn't be in the same homeroom. Isn't that wonderful?"

Olivia shot me a look. One that said, *It's not wonderful at all, and if you weren't here, it wouldn't be happening.*

I knew exactly how she felt, because that was exactly what I was thinking too. Stuck in the same room at home *and* school with Miss Prissy Pants for the next three months?

Life couldn't possibly get any worse.

CHAPTER 3

Yes it could, as it turned out.

"Mrs. Bonneville doesn't take any guff," my new home-room teacher announced, right after she called out "Catriona Starr" and I said "Present."

I had absolutely no clue what guff was, but I dutifully replied "Yes, ma'am" anyway. In Texas everybody says "ma'am" and "sir," but I guess they don't all that much here in Oregon, because every head in the classroom swiveled around to take a look at the weird new kid.

"And, um, it's pronounced 'Katrina,'" I added. Mrs. Bonneville had called me "Ca-tree-oh-na," the way it's spelled. "But I just go by Cat." I didn't bother trying to explain that the odd spelling was Scottish, or that I'd been named for my great-great-grandmother. Well, for her and for an asteroid, too. Can you believe there's an asteroid named Catriona? My mother said she couldn't resist, what with her being an astronaut and all.

But the asteroid wasn't something I wanted to bring up on the first day at a new school. Not unless I wanted to assure myself a spot on the bottom rung of the popularity ladder.

Mrs. Bonneville frowned. "Mrs. Bonneville doesn't like to be interrupted, *Cat*," she continued, and proceeded to enlighten me on the rest of her list of rules. "Mrs. Bonneville doesn't like chewing gum, or tardiness, or cell phones in class, and most of all Mrs. Bonneville doesn't like sass."

Great. My new teacher was the kind of person who referred to herself in the third person. Hawk Creek Middle School was not off to a very good start.

"Mrs. Bonneville doesn't think you should sit here," said Olivia a few hours later in the cafeteria.

Piper Philbin burst out laughing. So did all the rest of Olivia's friends. I just stood there by the lunch table feeling stupid. Even the knowledge that my lunch bag held an Iz special—peanut butter and honey sandwich, carrot sticks, an apple, and a homemade chocolate chip cookie—didn't help. Not that I should have expected anything else from my step-sister, but still, it was my very first day at this school, and you'd think she'd make at least a tiny effort to make me feel welcome, like any other normal person on the planet.

But noooo, not Olivia.

I turned away quickly so that she wouldn't catch me blinking back tears. As I moved through the cafeteria, it struck me that it wasn't all that different from the one back home in Texas. It's strange how once you get to middle school, everybody splits up into different groups. In elementary school nobody cares whose table you sit at, but the minute you hit sixth grade—*wham!* I spotted the table with all the jocks right away because they were the loudest, and I already knew where the popular kids sat—with my stepsister, naturally. Drama kids (green fingernail polish, weird hair), check. Nerds (busy trading Elfwood cards), check. Skateboarders (baggy shorts and hoodies), check. Finally I spotted my people: the band kids.

The only bright spot in my morning so far had been band. When I'd walked into the music room, I'd instantly felt at home.

Mr. Morgan, the band director, practically swooned when I played my bassoon for him.

"Now, that," he exclaimed when I finished, clasping his hands to his chest dramatically, "is *music*!"

I could tell right away I was going to like Mr. Morgan. He was young and energetic and funny. Whenever anyone hit a sour note, which was pretty often—this was middle school band, after all—he'd cry, "Oh, my delicate, shell-like ears!" and clap his hands over them protectively. Then he'd smile right away, to show us he wasn't really mad.

After band practice Mr. Morgan took me aside and asked what kind of musical experience I'd had back in Texas. His eyebrows shot up when I told him I played with the Houston Youth Symphony.

"Too bad you got here so late in the year," he said. "The Portland Youth Philharmonic is just finishing up their season. We sure could use you in Hawkwinds, though."

"What's Hawkwinds?"

"A wind ensemble I started last year for some of the more advanced musicians," he explained. "They're playing in the talent show next week. The trio could happily become a quartet, if you'd like to join. We could use a talented bassoonist."

I signed up right then and there.

"You'll like the other kids in the group," Mr. Morgan told me. "Rani Kumar plays the flute, and her brother, Rajit, is our oboist. They just moved here last summer, so they're still pretty new to the school too. And Juliet Rodriguez is our clarinetist. You should get to know them."

I spotted the three of them at the band table and crossed the cafeteria to where they were sitting.

"You're Cat, right?" said a pretty, dark-haired girl, smiling up at me.

I smiled back. The little knot in my stomach that Olivia and Piper Fleabrain had put there started to untie itself, and I took a seat. "And you're Rani and you play the flute, right?"

"Uh-huh." She pointed across the table at a boy who could almost have been her twin. "This is my brother, Rajit. He's in eighth grade, so he thinks he's better than the rest of us."

A glint of mischief danced in Rajit's eyes. "That's because I am."

The girl sitting on the other side of Rani started to laugh. Leaning forward, she waved and said, "Hi! I'm Juliet Rodriguez." Her shiny hair was dark like Rani's, but she wore it really long instead of to her shoulders. My hair was somewhere in between theirs in length, and plain old boring brown by comparison.

"Are you going to join Hawkwinds?" Juliet continued. "I saw Mr. Morgan in the hall a few minutes ago, and he said you played with the Houston Youth Symphony."

I nodded shyly, taking my sandwich out of my bag.

"Cool."

"So you're from Texas?" said Rajit.

I nodded again. "I came to live with my dad. I'm Olivia Haggerty's stepsister."

The table fell silent. Rani's smile vanished. "Oh," she said cautiously, exchanging a glance with Juliet. "That's nice."

Now it was my turn to laugh. I knew exactly what they were thinking. "Don't worry," I told them. "We're nothing at all alike."

Rani flashed me a grin. "That's a relief," she said. "Olivia is, well—"

"Annoying?" I suggested helpfully.

"Big-time," she agreed.

Now that the ice was broken, the four of us started to chatter away.

"Mr. Morgan said you guys are pretty new to Portland too?" I said to Rani and her brother.

"Yep," said Rajit. "We moved here from L.A. at the end of last summer."

"Our parents are originally from Mumbai, though," added Rani, answering my unspoken question.

"India! Wow. Have you ever visited?"

They both nodded. "Our grandparents still live there, and a bunch of our aunts and uncles and cousins," said Rani. "We're going back again this summer."

"How about you, Juliet?"

"Native Oregonian," she mumbled through a bite of tuna fish sandwich. "They call us Webfeet. Because of the rain, get it?" She pointed to the cafeteria window, which was streaked with droplets.

They asked about my family, and I told them about my dad and Iz. Their eyes widened when I explained that my mother was an astronaut.

"Really? No kidding?" said Rani.

"She's on the International Space Station right now. That's how come I'm here in Portland."

"Wow," said Rajit. "That is totally awesome." He flashed me another smile, and I smiled back. "How long will you be here?"

"Through the end of the school year."

"That's a long time to be away from home," said Rani.

I glanced across the cafeteria at Olivia. "Tell me about it."

Rani and Rajit and Juliet wanted to know all about NASA, and how I liked living in a high-rise building. I took my cell phone out of my backpack and showed them some pictures of our condo, and of my mother in her astronaut suit, and of my friends.

"Who's that?" asked Rani, pointing to a boy with reddish hair and a gap-toothed grin.

"A.J. D'Angelo," I told her. "He's my best friend. He lives two floors down from us back in Houston."

"Does he play in the youth symphony, too?"

I laughed. "Nope." A.J. might be a computer genius, but he couldn't carry a tune in a paper bag. Not that he didn't try—he played trombone in our middle school band.

By the time the bell rang a few minutes later, I was on my way to having three new friends.

"What classes do you have this afternoon?" asked Rani as we cleared away our lunches.

I pulled my schedule from the pocket of my jeans and consulted it. "Uh, PE and then science."

Her face lit up. "Me too! Come on, I'll show you where the lockers are."

I followed her out of the cafeteria feeling a lot more cheerful. It didn't even bother me when we passed Olivia and Piper in the hall and I noticed them whispering. Who cared what they thought?

The cheerful feeling lasted right up until the moment when Ms. Suarez, our PE teacher, blew her whistle.

"Okay, girls!" she hollered. "Let's beat those rainy Monday blues with a little hoops fun. Team captains—Olivia Haggerty and Taylor Brown."

My heart sank. Basketball? How about a slam-dunk game of humiliation instead? When you're barely five feet tall, basketball rarely qualifies as fun. I was about to go down in flames.

And my stepsister was happy to shove me into the fire.

Olivia and Taylor flipped a coin for first pick, and Olivia won. She looked straight at me and smiled. It was not a nice smile.

"Rani Kumar," she said.

Rani gave me a regretful look and crossed the gym to stand beside my stepsister. I steeled myself for torture, Olivia-style. It was uncanny the way she knew exactly how to bug me the most in any given situation. By picking the first friend I'd made at school all day, she was hanging me out to dry. There was no way Olivia was going to pick me for her team, and the other girl, Taylor, didn't know me from a hole in the ground, so no way would she pick me either until she was forced to. And since she was picking second and there were an even number of girls, that meant not only would I not be on the same team as Rani, but I would also be the absolute last person picked.

Which I was.

"You should go home to Texas," Olivia whispered to me in the locker room afterward.

Can I please go home to Texas? I wrote that night in my daily e-mail to my mother. *The D'Angelos said I could stay with them.*

The answer was no, of course.

Pull up your socks, she replied. *You're a star—and a Starr! Things with you and Olivia are bound to get better, once you settle in.*

But they didn't, and the rest of the week pretty much went downhill from there. Tuesday and Wednesday were no different. Olivia kept up her campaign to send me packing, and the only bright spots at school were band and Hawkwinds practice. Especially Hawkwinds practice. I slipped into the trio-turned-quartet effortlessly, and Mr. Morgan found us a new piece to play for the talent show, a Bach fugue that was one of my favorites.

But even that couldn't make up for Olivia's Reign of Terror, as A.J. had dubbed it. My stepsister talked about me constantly to her friends behind my back and made a big show of giving me the cold shoulder whenever she could, which was often, since we were in the same homeroom and most of the same classes.

Life at home wasn't any better. Because it had been raining nonstop since my arrival, I couldn't even escape outside for a walk. In order to avoid Olivia, I was forced to spend most of my time in either the kitchen or the living room, where Geoffrey would pounce on me to play LEGOs with him. He'd been following me around like a puppy ever since

ONCE UPON A TOAD

I arrived, which was cute and everything, but sometimes a person just wants to be alone, you know?

The problem was, there was no place to do that in a house as tiny as my dad's.

If I went upstairs to our room, Olivia would inevitably be there talking about me on the phone to Piper, or worse, sitting there with Piper in person, the two of them making loud, snarky remarks about my clothes (what was wrong with jeans and a T-shirt?), my hair (why should I have to brush it more than once a day?), my lack of makeup (who wanted to smear that goop all over their face?), and everything else they could think of. Oh, and forget practicing my bassoon. I had to barricade myself in my dad's office if I wanted to do that, otherwise Olivia would moan about it hurting her ears.

On top of everything else there were the stupid dioramas. My bed was an island in a sea of art supplies, as Olivia's stuff had soon crept over into my half of the room. Iz had spotted the duct tape on the floor that first night and made Olivia take it off, but it quickly reappeared in the latest Barbie vignette—an exact replica of our bedroom. On one side of the decorated box a Barbie meant to be Olivia (I could tell by the curly blond hair) sat on the bed with her arms folded, staring across the room at the other Barbie—actually a vintage Skipper, Barbie's little sister, thank you very much, Olivia—who was standing by the door with a suitcase in her hand. From it hung a luggage tag that said HOUSTON, TEXAS. Above the Skipper-who-was-me's bed hung a little poster of a red circle with a slash through it. The word inside the circle? "CAT."

Nice.

I got even by sneaking another Barbie into the diorama—this one with dark hair just like Piper's. I placed her by the tiny window in her underwear, looking out. Then I gave her huge red lipstick lips and taped a sign to her back that said FLEABRAIN LOVES CONNOR.

Olivia and Piper's other favorite pastime, besides torturing me, was swooning over Connor Dixon, the boy next door. That's another big difference between my stepsister and me—she's boy crazy. Our bedroom was at the front of the house, and the window had a perfect view of the Dixons' driveway, where Connor and his older brother, Aidan, spent a lot of time playing basketball. Olivia and Piper were always spying on them. Well, on Connor, mostly. They both had a huge crush on him. I knew Connor from the times I'd visited before, and also now from band, since he played the saxophone. Technically, I supposed he qualified as cute—I never really paid much attention to that stuff—but I didn't think he was worth all the fuss the two of them made over him.

Olivia shrieked when she saw what I'd done to her diorama, but she couldn't tell Iz, of course, without her mother seeing the rest of it. Instead she snapped a picture of it with her cell phone and sent it to Piper. Both of them were spitting mad at school the next day.

Funny, but hardly likely to help improve matters, my mother wrote back when I e-mailed her about it. *Focus on the good things, Cat.*

The good things were Hawkwinds, my new friends, and Mr. Morgan and his delicate, shell-like ears. Also Geoffrey and Dad and Iz. I dutifully wrote my mother about all of these, and about Mrs. Bonneville and her list of rules because I knew she'd get a kick out of that. My mother has a really good sense of humor.

I didn't mean to complain, really I didn't. I knew she needed to concentrate on her mission at the space station. But who else could I talk to? Iz had her hands full with Geoffrey and her job, and besides, she was living in her own little "Sisters are forever friends" world. It would be too awkward trying to explain to her what a twerp her daughter was, anyway. I knew I should probably talk to my father, but he'd been away the last couple of days collecting data on the spring Chinook salmon run in the Columbia River Gorge.

By Thursday night my spirits were as soggy as the weather. The diorama had disappeared, but Olivia and I were still barely on speaking terms. After dinner Iz shooed us upstairs to do our homework. Which we did, sort of. Olivia was talking to Piper on her cell phone, and I was using Iz's laptop to IM with A.J. With my earbuds in to block out my stepsister's annoying voice, I could almost pretend I was back in Houston. This was what A.J. and I did every night—worked on our homework while we instant-messaged each other.

I have a bad case of Olivia-itis, I wrote.

Poor you, he wrote back, adding a frowny face.

Need cure. Can u help?

No known remedy. Will ask NASA to arrange imme-diate airlift.

I had to laugh at that. A.J. always managed to cheer me up. Iz poked her head in the door just then and saw me smiling. "I'm so glad to see you two getting along," she said. "One big happy family."

Olivia waggled her fingers at her sweetly. The second Iz left, though, she looked over at me and pretended to stick them down her throat. I stuck out my tongue at her and turned my attention back to the computer screen. A few seconds later I jumped when Olivia let out a loud squeal at something Piper had said. I pulled out one of my earbuds. "Could you maybe keep it down a little? I'm working on pre-algebra and it's hard."

"I'm working on pre-algebra and it's *haaard*," she mimicked in a high voice.

I sighed and stuck the earbud back in. A.J. was right. There was no known cure for Olivia Haggerty.

CHAPTER 4

On Friday morning Olivia sabotaged our bathroom schedule, hogging it until five minutes before the bus came. Usually Dad monitors the schedule closely, since she has a habit of doing this, but he'd left before dawn for Klamath Lake. Every spring he drives down to help out with the annual count of the migrating waterfowl, then stops in Ashland to visit my grandparents. Olivia was taking full advantage of his absence, and Iz was distracted with Geoffrey, who had developed a bad case of spaghetti leg.

Spaghetti leg is what Iz calls it when Geoffrey goes all limp and doesn't want to do something. For some reason he'd decided that he didn't want to go to preschool this morning, so he was on strike, lying flat on his back on the rug in his bedroom. Iz couldn't get him dressed because he wasn't cooperating. I could tell that her patience was wearing thin. My stepmother is not a morning person.

"She's an artist," my dad always says. "Lots of artists are night owls."

My father, on the other hand, is an early bird. Which is appropriate, given his choice of career.

"Olivia! Hurry up in there!" Iz shouted, trying to stuff my little brother's legs into his pants. "Give me a hand, would you, Cat? I'll deal with your sister."

Stepsister, I thought automatically, but didn't say aloud, of course.

I crossed over to them. "C'mon, G-Man," I encouraged. "Preschool is fun."

He shook his head, clutching his blanket. He's had the thing since he was a baby, and if he were my kid, I'd make him throw it away. It's totally disgusting. Once upon a time it was a down comforter, but it had long since lost its feathers and its original color. Now it just hung there like a limp, dingy, bluish gray rag. Plus, it *smelled.*

"All aboard for fun!" I called, trying again. I pretended to be a train and raced around the room on my knees, following the pattern on his carpet. Geoffrey likes it when I do that. It's one of those Traffic Tyme rugs that they sell in all the kids' furniture stores. My dad calls it "little-boy heaven"—it's got traffic lanes and parking spots and stop signs and stuff like that.

Geoffrey pulled his finger out of his mouth and smiled at me.

"Gotcha!" I said, pulling him upright. I wrestled him into his clothes, then gave him a piggyback ride down the hall to where Iz was standing outside the bathroom.

"Olivia!" she called again, rattling the door handle.

"Almost done!" my stepsister called back.

Iz took Geoffrey from me. "Thanks, sweetheart."

"No problem."

"Did I take too long?" Olivia asked as she finally emerged, her eyes wide in feigned innocence.

I pushed past her without a word and closed the door behind me, glancing at the clock on the wall. There was no time for a shower, and Iz had already told me she couldn't drive me because she had to go right from dropping Geoffrey off at preschool to a photo shoot.

I had to settle for washing my face and brushing my teeth and swiping a brush through my hair. I looked at myself in the mirror and sighed. It wasn't much of an improvement. The left side of my hair was still full of snarls and sticking out where I'd slept on it.

To get even, I took Olivia's toothbrush and dunked it in the toilet. Served her right.

The day went from bad to worse. Every time I got anywhere near Olivia at school, she wrinkled her nose and sniffed suspiciously. Pretty soon she had Piper and their friends doing it too. I knew I didn't smell—I might not have showered but I'd remembered to put on deodorant, at least—but still, it was starting to give me a complex.

And then, at lunch, I was sitting at the band table talking to my friends when I heard a tapping noise behind me. I turned around to see Olivia and Piper and the Hawk Creek Tappers heading toward me across the cafeteria.

Tappety-tappety-tappety-tappety-tappety-tappety-SNIFF! *Tappety-tappety-tappety-tappety-tappety-tappety*-SNIFF! The cafeteria fell silent as they danced their way around our table. On every seventh beat they'd pause, lean toward me, and inhale—then simultaneously hold their noses.

"What's going on?" asked Rajit, mystified.

Boys can be really dense sometimes.

Rani shot me a sympathetic glance. "Ignore them," she whispered.

How could I? Anger welled up in me and I stood up, ready to have it out with Olivia, but just then the Tappers swung into a big Broadway finish. My stepsister and her friends ended their number down on one knee in a semi-circle around me, one hand flung into the air and one hand pointing toward me as Olivia shouted, "Heeeeeeeeeere's . . . CATBOX!"

I stood there, frozen, as the cafeteria exploded with laughter.

The day couldn't end fast enough after that.

"Cat?" said Iz when I walked in the front door after school with a face like thunder. "What are you doing home so early? I thought you had Hawkwinds practice."

I didn't answer, just ran upstairs. I didn't stop until I got to the attic. It was the only place in the house I could think of where I could go to be alone, and right now I didn't want to talk to anyone ever again.

It was cold up there, and I was grateful for the fleece lining on my rain jacket. Zipping it all the way to the top, I looked around the dimly lit space, spotted an old trunk in the far corner, and dragged it over to the window that overlooked the front yard. I slumped down on it and gave in to the tears that had threatened to overflow on the long bus ride home. *Catbox.* Olivia's new nickname for me had gone around school like wildfire. I'd never felt so humiliated in my entire life. The snickering, the whispers—people sidling up to me in the halls and sniffing me. I'd never live it down.

There was no way I was going back.

I stared down at the silver ring on my finger. The aqua-marines shone softly in the late-afternoon light that slanted through the window. *What a joke,* I thought bitterly. The words seemed to mock me. They should really read STEP-SISTERS ARE NEVER FRIENDS.

Angrily, I fished my cell phone out of my backpack and punched in my father's number. My call went right to his voice mail, as I knew it would.

"Dad?" I said, my voice cracking. "I need to talk to you as soon as possible. Please call me."

He wouldn't, though. Not before Sunday night. He'd warned us when he left that he'd be out of cell phone range all weekend.

I heard footsteps on the stairs, then a soft knock on the attic door. "Cat?"

It was Iz.

"Go away," I said, not caring if I sounded surly.

The door opened a crack. "Honey? What's wrong?"

I shook my head miserably. I didn't want to talk about it.

My stepmother crossed the dusty room and sat down on the trunk beside me. I could hear the sound of the TV downstairs, where Geoffrey was watching *Robo Rooster,* his favorite cartoon. Olivia was still at school. She'd stayed to practice for the talent show, then the Hawk Creek Tappers were all supposed to go to Piper Philbin's for a sleepover. I could only imagine how they were congratulating themselves on their little triumph.

Iz didn't say a word; she just put her arm around my shoulders and waited. Some people have a gift for kindness.

My stepmother was one of those people, and before long my defenses crumbled.

"What's wrong?" she asked again.

"Everything!" I wailed, pouring out the whole story. I didn't leave anything out, not even my own part in escalating things with the sabotaged diorama.

"Oh my," said Iz faintly when I was done. She wrapped her arms around me and pulled me close. "I'm so sorry, Cat. I should have been more tuned in to what was going on between you two. I've been distracted with work, and I guess I just wanted so much for things to be perfect that I didn't see the warning signs." She released me and stood up. Her face was grim. "I have to be downtown at a gallery opening in half an hour. I can't get out of it; I'm introducing the guest of honor. But as soon as things wind down, I'll go pick up Olivia. No sleepover for her tonight. The two of us will be having a long talk, I can promise you that."

She hesitated, and bit her lip. "Are you still okay with baby-sitting Geoffrey for me? I could call someone else if you're not feeling up to it."

I shook my head. "I'll be fine," I told her, wiping my nose on my sleeve.

Iz looked relieved. "I've ordered a pizza for you two. There's money on the table in the front hall."

I nodded.

"And Cat?"

I looked at her.

"We'll straighten this out, I promise."

I didn't hold out much hope for that. But it was good to have Iz in my court, and I was feeling a little better by the time she left.

After dinner Geoffrey and I watched a *Robo Rooster* DVD, then I promised to read him a bedtime story if he didn't hassle me about taking a bath. He'd gotten over his earlier bout of spaghetti leg, fortunately, and he hopped happily into the tub, and from there into his jammies.

"Do you want to choose a book?" I asked, and he nodded.

Dragging his limp rag of a blanket, he scuffed over to his bookshelf, careful to follow the traffic lanes on his rug. He picked out a book, then clambered up onto the bed and snuggled down next to me with a contented sigh, spreading his smelly blanket over both of us. I leaned down and kissed the top of his head. It's fun having a little brother.

Technically, I'm an only child. I was in first grade when my parents split up and Dad moved back to Oregon. My mother has never remarried—she says she's married to her job for now—but Dad met Iz a year after the divorce, and they got married and had Geoffrey a year later.

"It's a case of yours, mine, and ours," Dad always says when people ask him which kids belong to which parents.

I think maybe there are a few too many last names floating around, though. Dad and Geoffrey and I are Starrs. Olivia is a Haggerty, of course, because of her father. Iz didn't want Olivia to feel left out, so she went with Haggerty-Starr. Mom doesn't have a hyphen, but her professional name has always been Fiona MacLeod Starr, and she kept it after the divorce. She says this way people know that the two of us are related, plus what better name could there be for an astronaut than Starr? It's all a bit much.

Geoffrey may only be my half brother, but his looks are all Starr. He has straight light brown hair and greenish blue eyes, just like Dad and me. Olivia, on the other hand, looks a lot like her mother, with the same curly blond hair and brown eyes.

"Cat," said Geoffrey, taking his finger out of his mouth. "Cat, Cat, Cat, Cat, Cat." He loves my name.

And I love him. Geoffrey is one of the best things about being here in Oregon.

After we finished reading, I tucked him into bed and we said good night to all the zoo animals on his wall mural. Then I sang him the lullaby that my mother always used to sing to me when I was little:

> *"Bed is too small for my tired head,*
> *Give me a hill soft with trees.*
> *Tuck a cloud up under my chin,*
> *Lord, blow the moon out, please!"*

Geoffrey and I blew in each other's faces when I finished, and Geoffrey giggled. He gave me an angelic smile and whispered "Cat" again, then plugged his finger back into his mouth and closed his eyes.

"Good night, G-Man," I whispered, kissing his cheek. Checking to be sure his night-light was on, I left the room. He was already snoring by the time I closed his door.

Geoffrey's snoring is a big joke in our family. Iz says that all the breath he saves by not talking during the day comes out at night. It's hard to believe that such a little kid can make such a loud sound. We have to take earplugs with us whenever we all go camping.

I went downstairs, looking forward to having the house to

myself. I planned to read a little, practice my bassoon a little, and maybe IM with A.J.

My peaceful evening was short lived, though.

A few minutes later, I heard the car door slam. Then the front door flew open and Olivia stormed in.

"Thanks for tattling, *Catbox*," she snarled.

"Olivia!" said Iz, who was right on her heels.

My stepsister ignored her and stomped upstairs.

Iz sighed deeply. "Sorry about that," she said to me, then followed Olivia to her room. I heard the door close and then the sound of muffled voices—Iz's low-pitched murmur playing a steady counterpoint to Olivia's indignant staccato tones. Like a cello and a piccolo, maybe.

After a while I heard the door open again as Olivia went down the hall to the bathroom. Iz came back downstairs. She was holding something in her hand, and I spotted a telltale flash of silver as she tucked it into the pocket of her skirt—it was Olivia's sister ring.

"I'm knackered," she said wearily. "I think the message finally got through to Olivia, though. She's going to bed, and I guess I will too. Don't stay up too late, okay?"

"I won't."

I waited, listening for a while to the duet between Geoffrey's rhythmic snores upstairs and the steady ticking of the grandfather clock in the front hall downstairs. I wanted to be sure Olivia was asleep before I went up to our room.

She wasn't, though. She was lying in wait for me, still furious.

"You ruined everything!" she whispered as I climbed into bed. "I wish you'd never come to Portland!"

The flame of anger I'd felt earlier today in the cafeteria rekindled. "I wish I'd never come too!" I whispered back hotly.

"Why don't you just leave, then?"

"I would if I could!"

"I hate you!"

"I hate you back!" Seething, I flung one last retort at her. "And by the way, I dunked your toothbrush in the toilet."

Olivia let out a howl of rage. "You stupid, rotten . . . *Catbox!*" she sputtered, hurling her pillow at me.

"Girls!" Iz flung our door open and flipped on the light. "What in heaven's name is going on in here?"

Bursting into tears, I grabbed my quilt and pillow and fled downstairs to the living room. I was blowing my nose when my stepmother came down to check on me a few minutes later.

"I'm sleeping down here," I told her stiffly.

She smoothed my hair back from my face. "I guess that's okay," she said, then added with a sigh, "I wish your dad were here."

I did too. But he wasn't, and my mother was a million miles away. Okay, not really a million—more like 220, straight up—but it might as well have been a million. It sure felt like it. My fingers found their way to the gold charm on the necklace she'd left for me. HOLD FAST, it said. To what?

Iz gave me a kiss and tucked the quilt around me, then went back upstairs to bed.

I lay there until the house was quiet again—well, as quiet as it could be with my little brother's elephantine snores—then slipped my cell phone from the pocket of my pajamas, where I'd placed it earlier. It was time to put my emergency plan into action.

Desperate times call for desperate measures, I texted to A.J.

What's up? he texted back.

The reign of terror continues, I wrote, quickly hitting the highlights of the day's events.

Ouch! he replied. **Catbox? Really?**

Uh-huh.

So you're going to do it?

Yeah, I told him.

Good luck, he texted back. **Let me know what happens.**

I stared at my phone. My mother had given me an emergency number before she left, but she'd also pounded into me the importance of not using it unless I absolutely, positively had to.

This qualified as an emergency, didn't it? How was I supposed to show my face at school after this?

I got up from my makeshift bed and crept into my dad's study. After closing the door, I sat down in the leather chair at his desk and dialed the number my mother had given me.

"This is Mission Control," said a voice a few seconds later.

"Uh," I replied, feeling really, really stupid all of a sudden. For some reason I had it in my head that my mother had given me the direct line to the International Space Station. But of course there was no such thing. What was I thinking? I was talking to NASA in Houston. "This is Catriona Starr," I finally managed to stammer. "I'd, uh, like to speak to my mother, sir."

There was a long, long pause on the other end.

"Catriona Starr, did you say?"

"Yessir."

"You're Fiona MacLeod Starr's daughter?"

"Yessir."

Another long pause.

"That's a long-distance call, young lady." The operator paused again, then laughed.

Just my luck. A comedian. "Yessir," I replied. "But I *really* need to talk to her."

"Okay, honey, let me see what I can do," he said, finally taking pity on me. "This may take a bit, so hang on."

I sat there, swiveling idly back and forth in my dad's chair and playing with the chain of my necklace. A minute or two later the phone line got all crackly and hollow-sounding. "Cat?"

It was my mother.

"Mom!" A wave of relief washed over me at the sound of her voice. I hadn't realized how much I missed her.

"Is everything okay? Nobody's hurt or anything, are they?" She sounded sleepy. I'd checked the map of the world this morning, the one Dad had put up on the bulletin board over the breakfast table—we'd been using a little American flag pushpin to track the space station's progress—but for the life of me I couldn't remember where she was right now. Probably over Outer Mongolia or something. Obviously, I'd woken her up.

"No," I assured her, then blurted out the whole humiliating story about the Hawk Creek Tappers and their "Catbox" number in the cafeteria, ending with all the reasons that I needed to go home, right now.

"Have you talked to your dad?" she asked when I was finished.

"I can't!" I told her. "I tried, but he's at Klamath Lake this weekend, counting grebes or something. He won't be home until Sunday night."

"What about Iz?"

I explained how Iz was trying to help but that it wasn't working. "I can't do it, Mom!" I said, my voice rising. "I can't take another minute of Olivia!"

My mother's sigh was barely audible above the static. "Right. Well, sweetheart, there's not a whole lot I can do about it from up here. Do you think you can hang in there just a little while longer?"

I know it's not fair to cry on the phone to your mother when she's in outer space and can't just hop on a bus or a plane and come home. Really, I do. But I couldn't help it.

"Oh, honey," she said, sighing again when she heard my sobs. "I really, really wish I could be there right now. But I can't; I have a job to do up here. An important job."

"I know," I managed to whisper.

"And you have an important job to do too, remember?"

I nodded. "I'm your support system. Team Starr."

That's what my mom calls us. She says no way could she do her job without me.

"That's right, and I need you to hang in there for me and stay strong." She was quiet for a minute, and I pictured her sailing through the silent darkness, winging past the stars. "Maybe there is something I can do," she said finally.

"Really?" Hope bloomed in me as I wondered what she had in mind. Dropping something on Olivia from orbit, maybe?

"I can't promise anything, but I'll try, okay?"

"Okay."

She told me that she loved me, and I told her I loved her back, and we hung up. As I turned my cell phone off for the night, I realized I'd forgotten to ask her about the necklace.

Nothing happened on Saturday except Olivia and I both got a long lecture from Iz, who managed to forge a frosty truce between us. I slept back in my own bed that night, ignoring Olivia's silent treatment. By Sunday morning I started to worry that maybe my mother had forgotten. As we turned onto our street coming home from church, though, I spotted her solution sitting in the driveway. Its Arizona license plate read "ABYCNU."

Uh-oh, I thought. I knew that RV.

My mother had called Great-Aunt Abyssinia.

CHAPTER 5

The door to the RV flew open, and a large figure in a bright orange rain poncho emerged.

"Catriona!" cried Great-Aunt Abyssinia, launching herself down the steps and swooping me up in a bear hug. She smelled like roses and something else—vinegar, maybe, or curry. It was a pungent combination, and my eyes started to water.

"And you must be Olivia," she said, putting me down and pouncing on my startled stepsister.

Olivia stared up at her, openmouthed. Olivia is tall, but even she had to tilt her head back, because Great-Aunt Abyssinia is *really* tall, like Julia Child or one of the Harlem Globetrotters.

"Let's go inside out of the rain," said Iz, unbuckling Geoffrey from his car seat.

Once indoors, Great-Aunt Aby shook herself like a big wet dog, sending water flying everywhere, then removed her poncho and handed it to my stepmother. Iz took it from her, looking a little bewildered, but then, my great-aunt tends to have that effect on people.

"You're looking lovely as always, Isabelle," said Great-Aunt Aby.

"Thank you," said Iz, trying not to stare at my great-aunt's hair, which was short and spiky and dyed traffic-cone orange, the same shade as her poncho. "You're looking lovely yourself."

Great-Aunt Abyssinia grinned. "You know what they say, 'A laugh a day keeps the wrinkles away.'"

Behind me, Olivia snorted. Great-Aunt Aby had plenty of wrinkles. She might not be road-map-wrinkles-and-chin-hair old, but still, she was *old*. She wasn't deaf, though, and I was pretty sure she'd heard Olivia even if she didn't say anything. She just gave her a sidelong glance and then turned to my little brother.

"This young man can't be Geoffrey!" she exclaimed, lifting her glasses from their resting place on her shelflike chest and peering down at him. He was hanging back behind Iz, clutching his blanket shyly, but he removed his finger from his mouth long enough to reply, "With a G!" as he always did when someone said his name.

"So I've heard," said Great-Aunt Aby, nodding solemnly.

Geoffrey pointed at the chain attached to her glasses.

"You like this, do you?" My great-aunt lifted it over her head and handed it to him. Looking over his shoulder, I saw that the chain's links were actually rhinestone cactuses. It was just the sort of bizarre thing Great-Aunt Aby loved to wear.

"Found it at a thrift store in Arizona," she told us as

Geoffrey's chubby little fingers traced the sparkling stones. "Though why anybody'd want to part with a treasure like this is beyond me." She shook her head regretfully, then took it back from him and slipped it over her head once again, settling the glasses onto her large nose.

Olivia's gape had turned into a smirk. I could practically see the wheels in her head turning and could only imagine the mileage she'd get out of my weird great-aunt at school. If I ever went back, that was.

Great-Aunt Abyssinia swiveled her head sharply in my stepsister's direction. Her eyes glinted behind her glasses. "'The cat who ate the canary' is not always an attractive look," she told her. "You'd do well to remember the rest of the tale, my dear—the part we rarely hear these days. Puss came to a sad end when he choked on the feathers."

Olivia blinked. I was pretty sure I understood what my great-aunt was getting at, but she tended to talk in circles. It took some getting used to.

"Well then," said Iz brightly, "would you like to join us for lunch, Abyssinia? We're just having chili and corn bread, but there's plenty, and it's all homemade."

"Sounds divine," Great-Aunt Aby replied. She patted the pockets of her sweater and frowned. "Now, where did I put that? Oh yes, here it is." She pulled a small plastic bag out of the pocket of the ratty sweatpants she was wearing. We all peered at the brownish powder in it. "Add a pinch of this," she told my stepmother. "It'll give the chili a little snap. It's my secret ingredient—works on diaper rash, too." She gave a slight nod in Geoffrey's direction.

Iz's mouth fell open. My little brother wasn't quite out of

diapers yet. He still wore them at night. But how could my great-aunt have known that?

"How . . . interesting," said Iz, taking the bag from her.

"Isn't it?" Great-Aunt Abyssinia replied, beaming. "The world is so full of interesting things. And I have seen many of them."

Over lunch she proceeded to tell us about a number she'd seen recently, ending with her Christmas trip to the Grand Canyon.

"Everyone should spend time in the canyon in winter," she enthused. "Best time of year—hardly any tourists, and all that snow frosting everything! It's pretty as a picture."

Olivia yawned.

Great-Aunt Abyssinia's eyes glinted behind her glasses again.

I took a bite of corn bread and watched her surreptitiously. Except for the new hair color, she looked exactly the same as the last time I'd seen her, when my mother and I vacationed with her at Mount Rushmore. My great-aunt has a large, Mount Rushmore–worthy nose planted firmly in the middle of a big moon of a face, eyes that can twinkle or blaze depending on her mood, and prominent front teeth that shoot forward slightly, as if maybe they're trying to escape from between her lips. Over her sweatpants she was wearing a baggy green sweater with two denim pockets sewn onto it. I figured Great-Aunt Aby had sewn them on herself, because they were lopsided. Like me, my great-aunt doesn't have much patience for crafts.

The sweater itself was probably another thrift-store find. Great-Aunt Aby loves thrift stores and flea markets and yard sales. "Junking," as she calls it, is one of her hobbies. You can barely move in her RV for all the knickknacks and souvenirs she's collected.

Across the table I noticed Olivia sizing her up too. Her gaze lingered on the crooked pockets, and I sighed. I'd be hearing about them, too, no doubt.

Great-Aunt Aby caught my eye, and her lips quirked up at the corners. I smiled back sheepishly. I had the feeling that she knew exactly what I was thinking. She winked at me. It was a great big wink because her glasses were the kind that magnify your eyes. They made her look like a lemur or a bush baby.

After lunch we went into the living room for tea and cookies. Geoffrey seemed to have overcome his shyness, and once Great-Aunt Aby had lowered herself onto the sofa—kind of like a hippo sinking into a water hole—he climbed up into her enormous lap. Popping his index finger back into his mouth, he leaned back against her with a sigh of contentment.

"Would you care for a piece of shortbread, young man?" asked my great-aunt, offering him one from her plate.

Geoffrey shook his head. My little brother is probably the only kid in the entire world who doesn't like sweets. Iz unwrapped a cheese stick and handed it to him instead, and he swapped it for his finger.

"I hope you can stay and visit for a few days," my stepmother said politely.

Great-Aunt Aby shook her head, sending shortbread crumbs flying. "No can do, I'm afraid, Ms. Iz. I just got a hankering to pop in and say howdy to Catriona here." She gave me another big wink. "I'm a road warrior—footloose and fancy-free. Us rolling stones gotta keep moving on, so I'll be hitting the road bright and early tomorrow. California is calling, and I'd like to visit the redwoods again. They're particularly beautiful in the spring."

"Well, I'm glad you're staying long enough to see Tim, at least," Iz replied. "I know he'd be sorry to miss you. He should be home this evening." She glanced out the window, then turned to me. "It's stopped raining, Cat. Why don't you take your great-aunt for a walk?"

"Splendid idea!" boomed Great-Aunt Abyssinia.

I thought so too. I was dying to find out what my mother had told her, and why the heck she'd even called her in the first place, but it wasn't something I could ask in front of Iz and Olivia.

Great-Aunt Abyssinia turned to my stepsister. "Olivia, would you care to join us?"

My heart sank. So much for alone time with Great-Aunt Aby.

"I'd love to, Mrs. . . . uh, I mean—" Olivia hesitated.

"Just call me Aby."

"I'd love to, Mrs. Aby, but I have to finish my math homework."

I gaped at her, astonished. Since when did Olivia give two hoots about math?

"Ah," said Great-Aunt Aby. "Well then, Catriona, it looks like it's just you and me." Setting down her teacup, she stretched her large legs out in front of her and gave Geoffrey a nudge. He launched himself down them like she was a slide at the playground, landing on the floor with a thump and a giggle.

"And you, young man, could use a nap," said Iz.

My great-aunt and I put our raincoats on just in case—Oregon is as famous for its short-lived sun breaks as it is for its rain—and headed out the front door.

"There's nothing quite like the smell of rain-washed earth, is there?" Great-Aunt Aby asked, inhaling with deep satisfaction.

It wasn't a question that really needed an answer, but I nodded anyway. As we made our way past the Dixons' house, I spotted Connor and his older brother, Aidan, playing basketball in the driveway. The two of them stopped and stared at us as we passed by, and I could feel my face turn bright red. It was hard not to feel embarrassed walking down the street with someone like Great-Aunt Abyssinia. She was impossible to miss, what with the orange poncho and matching hair. Plus, she was so, well, big. Not fat, really, just tall and solid. It was kind of like having an elephant on a leash or something.

"Afternoon, boys!" she boomed, waving at them. They waved feebly back.

We walked just past the entrance to our dead-end street, then turned onto the muddy path that led into Forest Park.

"Good thing I wore my hiking boots," said my great-aunt.

I had to smile at that. My great-aunt always wears hiking boots. Last time I was in her RV, I'd counted seventeen pairs of them.

"Eighteen," she said absently, poking at one of the shrubs we passed. "Ah, eighteen rhododendron buds, I mean. They'll be blooming before you know it. Dogwood, too."

We continued on, with her taking note of all the trees and plants we passed. It was almost like going for a hike with my father. I'd had no idea that my great-aunt knew so much about the outdoors, but then again, it made sense, what with her obsession with the national parks and everything. We emerged into a clearing, and she paused to catch her breath, then turned to me, abruptly changing the subject.

"So what's all the fuss about, Catriona? I must say, when I spoke with your mother last night, I was expecting a life-and-death situation. It looks to me like you have it pretty good here in Portland."

"It's not all that bad," I admitted grudgingly. "Except for Olivia."

Great-Aunt Abyssinia gave me a shrewd look. "A bit of a pill, isn't she?"

I looked up at her, surprised. Most grown-ups think Olivia is perfect. That halo of blond curls fools them every time.

"It does, does it?" said Great-Aunt Aby.

I started. Had I spoken that last thought aloud?

Great-Aunt Aby inspected some moss on the side of a nearby tree.

"Why don't you tell me what's going on between you two," she said, and listened quietly as I told her everything that had happened over the past week. She chuckled at my description of how I'd sabotaged the diorama and dunked Olivia's toothbrush in the toilet, and scowled when I got to the "Catbox" tap dance.

"Little weasel," she muttered.

Encouraged by this reaction, I told her about the stuff that had happened when we were younger, too, like the time back in third grade when Olivia cut off my bangs while I was sleeping. "She swore up and down that she'd had nothing to do with it, and that I had been sleepwalking and had cut them myself."

Great-Aunt Aby's big teeth peeked out from between her lips, took a look around, then vanished as she squelched a smile. "She did, did she? And did your father and Iz believe her?"

I wrapped my arms around myself. The sun had disappeared behind the clouds again, and the wind was picking up. "I think maybe Dad thought it sounded fishy, but he didn't say anything. I know they really want us to get along, so sometimes they kind of ignore things, you know? But it's not fair!"

"Not everything in life is fair, Catriona," Great-Aunt Aby replied. "However, sometimes it's possible to stack the deck a little in one's favor."

"Really?" I replied cautiously. I wasn't sure if this was an offer to help or not. I hoped she wasn't going to pull another plastic bag out of her pocket. Stepsister-B-Gone that doubled as antiperspirant or flea powder or something.

"I understand that Olivia doesn't have the most generous of spirits, but it seems to me that what you two need is to find some common ground."

I snorted.

"Surely there's something you two share that you can build on?"

I shook my head. This conversation had taken a disappointing turn. I'd been hoping for something with a little more oomph, not just a piece of lame advice. Like maybe an offer to spirit Olivia away in the RV. That would serve her right. See how she liked living on pickled eggs and seaweed.

Great-Aunt Abyssinia smiled, her eyes glinting behind her glasses again. "You have a delicious sense of humor, Catriona. You're very like your mother was at your age—and like the Catriona for whom you were named."

I looked at her in surprise. "You knew my great-great-grandmother?" Exactly how old was Great-Aunt Aby, anyway?

"Very," she replied, then coughed. "I mean, of course I did. I mean—oh, never mind." She cocked her head sharply, suddenly alert. "Your father's heading home early," she announced. "We'd better go back."

My mouth dropped open. How could she possibly know that? Ignoring me, Great-Aunt Aby turned abruptly and charged back down the Wildwood Trail. I had no choice but to follow her, my head spinning from all the strange twists and turns of our conversation.

"Such a lovely little cottage," my great-aunt said as we emerged onto our street again. "And such a lovely family."

"Except for Olivia," I muttered under my breath.

Great-Aunt Abyssinia gave me a fleeting smile that told me she'd heard what I'd just said. She might be old, but she had ears like a hawk.

"Would you like to come in for a minute?" she asked, gesturing at her RV. "Archibald would love to see you again."

I nodded. "Sure."

Archibald stretched and hopped down from his perch on the sofa when we came in. He's the best thing about Great-Aunt Abyssinia's RV. He's huge, twenty pounds at least, which could be why Great-Aunt Aby picked him. "Big woman like me needs a big cat," I remember her telling me back at Mount Rushmore.

"Hey, Archie," I said, scratching him under his chin. "Remember me?"

He twined himself around my legs and blinked up at me, his bright green eyes glowing like traffic lights against his coal black fur. When you talk to my great-aunt's cat, he cocks his head to one side like a dog. You could swear he understands every word you say.

"Have a seat," said Great-Aunt Aby. "Help yourself to anything you'd like in the fridge."

Fat chance, I thought, but I checked anyway, more out of curiosity than anything else. Sure enough, there were half a dozen bottles of Great-Aunt Aby's favorite breakfast beverage, the green stuff my mother and I had dubbed SuperGloop, along with a half-eaten burrito, two lemons, some prickly pear yogurt (I didn't know it came in that flavor), the ever-present pickled eggs, and what looked like leftover fish sticks but which I was pretty sure had never been anywhere near the ocean. Surprisingly, there was also a can of root beer. I reached for it and sat down at the table.

"Now, where the dickens did I put that rascal?" muttered Great-Aunt Aby, stooping down in front of the bookshelves that lined the short hallway leading to the back of the RV, and her bedroom.

I looked around curiously. Everything seemed pretty much the same as the last time I was here. Same knickknacks; same clutter. The wall of souvenir plates had expanded—I spotted one with a picture of Old Ironsides and another of the Alamo—and I was pretty sure she'd added another shelf over the dining table for her growing collection of fairy-tale snow globes. I would have remembered the Little Red Riding Hood one for sure.

And the books! Another of my great-aunt's hobbies is collecting secondhand books, and there were piles of them everywhere, including on the table in front of me. I picked up the one on top, a dusty old volume with PACIFIC NORTH-WEST FLORA AND FAUNA printed on the cover.

"Great-Aunt Aby, can I use your phone for a sec?" I asked, suddenly remembering I'd promised to call Rani about our science homework. "I left my cell in the house."

"Sorry, honey, I don't have one," she replied, distracted.

"How about your computer, then?" I could send Rani an e-mail or an IM that way.

She shook her head regretfully. "No computer, either, I'm afraid. And no VCR, DVD, or GPS. No alphabet soup of any kind—well, except for TV. I love the Food Network. Other than that, though, I'm off the grid."

Great-Aunt Aby watched cooking shows? This was surprising news. You sure wouldn't know it by the contents of her fridge. Then something else occurred to me. "But I thought you said you talked to my mom last night."

"Did I?" She straightened, blinking owlishly at me. "Oh—pay phone. Yep, that's it. Pay phone." She turned back to the bookshelf and ran her fingers across the spines. "Perrault, Grimm, Andersen—it's got to be here somewhere."

I sipped my root beer, puzzled. A pay phone? Did they even exist anymore? And how would my mother have known which one to call, anyway? Before I could ask, though, my great-aunt gave a cry of triumph.

"Aha!" She plucked a tome off the shelf and blew on it. Dust flew everywhere, and Archibald sneezed. The book's green leather cover was shabby and worn; the gold lettering on its spine faded. I couldn't make out the title. Great-Aunt Aby leafed through the pages.

"No, no, not that one," she murmured, scowling. "Nasty side effects." She flipped a few more pages, then paused again. "This could work." She tapped a large finger against the side of her equally large nose. "Hmmm. Perhaps not, though. Those scales were most unpleasant."

What on earth was she talking about?

I opened my mouth to ask, but just then Archibald leaped up onto the fabric-covered bench beside me and started kneading my leg.

"Ouch, Archie! Quit it!" Distracted, I carefully detached his claws from my jeans and placed his paws on the bench instead.

"Now, this one," continued my great-aunt, "this might just do the trick. Yes indeed, folks, I think we have a winner."

"Winner of what?" I asked her.

She snapped the book shut, sending up another puff of dust. Beside me, Archibald sneezed again. "None of your beeswax," Great-Aunt Abyssinia replied loftily. "Let's go say hello to your father."

CHAPTER 6

Monday morning I was the first one up, which was unusual. Most days I'm awakened by the sound of my father rattling around in the kitchen or by the smell of his coffee. The two of us are early birds, but he's a *really* early bird. He's always first in the shower, then me, then Olivia. Except when Olivia decides to sneak in ahead of me and hog it.

Today, though, the house was completely silent. Well, except for what sounded like a flock of geese coming in for a landing behind Geoffrey's door but which was only his snoring, of course.

I figured my father must have been wiped out from the field expedition and all that driving yesterday, to sleep in past six. The two of us had had a long talk last night after dinner, and he'd managed to convince me to go back to school.

"I'm not saying it was okay for Olivia to call you that name, because it wasn't, but you don't need to do a belly flop into the puddle of self-pity because of it," he'd said, using one of his favorite expressions. "Suck it up, Kit-Cat. 'Sticks and stones,' remember? We Starrs are made of strong stuff. Your ancestors came across the Oregon Trail in a covered wagon!"

I gave him a crooked smile. That's another of my dad's favorites, one he loves to trot out whenever he feels I need encouragement.

"Plus," he continued, "the Hawkwinds need you. You can't bail on them the day before the talent show."

He had a point.

I squinted at the clock by my bed, yawning. I had enough time to eat breakfast first, before it was my turn in the bathroom. Putting on my robe and slippers, I started to tiptoe out of the room, pausing by Olivia's bed. She was sound asleep on her back with her mouth wide open. I fought the temptation to do something, like maybe drop a dirty sock in it. Dad had read us both the riot act last night, though, and made us promise to shape up. So I left her where she was and crept quietly out of the room.

On my way downstairs I glanced through the stained-glass window on the landing. Great-Aunt Aby's RV was gone, just as she had said it would be. For a fleeting second I found myself wishing I could have gone with her. But maybe now that Dad was home things would be different. Besides, I was starting to look forward to the talent show. Great-Aunt Aby had asked me to play my bassoon for her, and she'd praised my Bach piece to the skies.

She hadn't asked Olivia to tap-dance, I'd noticed.

I was just sitting down at the kitchen counter with a bowl of cereal when my little brother appeared, clutching his smelly blanket.

"Hey, G-Man, how about some breakfast?" I asked.

Something plopped into my bowl, sloshing milk onto the counter. Geoffrey's eyes widened. He pulled his index finger from his mouth, which was shaped in an O of surprise, and pointed at my breakfast. "Cat?" he whispered.

I glanced down and nearly fell off my stool. An equally surprised-looking toad was crouched in my cereal, staring back at me.

"Whoa!" I cried in astonishment.

Plop. Another toad joined the first one. The two of them splashed frantically in the bowl, trying to escape. Geoffrey stared at them, then at me. His face got that worried look it always does when he's about to cry. Or barf.

No way, I thought. Absolutely no way had I just made that happen! It would be completely crazy to think that those toads had anything to do with me. And just to prove it, I said my brother's name aloud.

"With a G," he added automatically as toad number three tumbled into the bowl.

I shrieked, only the sound came out as a croak, along with another toad, which missed my cereal and skittered across the counter, then fell to the floor at Geoffrey's feet. My little brother backed away and started to cry. With panic rising in me, I jumped down from my seat, grabbed him by the hand, and dragged him into the living room. I didn't want him to wake anyone—especially not Olivia. I had to figure out what was going on first.

"Shhh, G-Man, it's okay!" I said, setting him on the sofa.

Geoffrey's sobs escalated to wails as another toad plunked down beside him. I scooped it up and stuffed it into my bathrobe pocket, looking around for something to distract him with. I grabbed the remote and turned on the TV. Fortunately, *Robo Rooster* was on. The wails subsided as he eyed the screen, toads temporarily forgotten. After waiting until his finger had crept back into its usual place, I ran upstairs, my heart racing and my hand clamped firmly over my mouth, just in case.

I went directly to the attic. It was the only place I could think of to hide. I needed to be alone while I figured out what was going on. There had to be a logical explanation. This was a trick or a coincidence or something. Spring was probably toad season here in Oregon and everybody had just forgotten to tell me. Maybe they'd crawled into the house through the dryer vent.

The attic was just as dim and dusty and cold as it had been the other day when I was up here. Wrapping my bathrobe tightly around me, I moved closer to the trunk by the front window and took a deep breath.

"Hello," I said softly to the empty room. A toad sprang to the floor.

I sank down on the trunk, fighting the urge to cry. This was no illusion, then, no trick. It was *me.* I nudged the creature with the toe of my slipper and watched it hop off into the shadows. It was definitely an amphibian of the order Anura, from the Greek *an* ("without") plus *oura* ("tail"). I wasn't a wildlife biologist's daughter for nothing. I knew a real live toad when I saw one.

I drew a shaky breath. It still made absolutely no sense. Middle schoolers didn't just spontaneously start spewing toads. How could this be happening? How could that creature have come from me? My mouth still tasted of breakfast cereal, not toad. Not that I knew what toad tasted like.

I must be dreaming, I thought. Yes, of course, that had to be it! This was just a nightmare. A weird, vivid nightmare involving my little brother, breakfast cereal, and toads. It was that chili I had yesterday for lunch, or maybe Great-Aunt Abyssinia's root beer. All I needed to do was wake up.

I hopped down off the trunk and jogged to the other window and back, then did some jumping jacks as I tried to jolt myself out of the nightmare.

"Hey! Keep it down up there!" my father shouted, his muffled voice rising through the floorboards.

"Sorry!" I called back, releasing yet another toad.

As impossible as it seemed, this wasn't a dream, it was really happening. I moved across the attic, as far from Dad and Iz's bedroom below as possible. I wanted to try an experiment.

"Good morning," I whispered: one toad. "Good morning," I sang: two toads. Ditto for humming. I made a mental note to myself to avoid music. Except for whistling. Whistling didn't produce toads, for some reason.

Pretty much everything else did, however, and three minutes later the attic was carpeted with them. It didn't matter how loud or soft I said anything, whether I sang or spoke, or what language I chose to speak in—French (*"Bonjour!"*), German (*"Guten Morgen!"*), Spanish (*"Buenos días!"*), or Swahili (*"Jambo!"*)—every time I opened my mouth and made a noise, a toad appeared.

I watched unhappily as they hopped, scrabbled, and skittered off across the floor. There were twenty-seven by my count, most of them looking as dazed as I felt.

What the heck was I going to do? I knew I should probably go downstairs and talk to my father and Iz, but what exactly was I supposed to tell them? That I'd suddenly turned into a freak show?

Should I call my mother again? A toad infestation of this magnitude absolutely, positively qualified as an emergency. She might even leave the space station and come back to Earth for something like this. This was a hopeful thought. I decided it was worth a try, and began picking my way across the toad minefield toward the attic door. Then I stopped in my tracks.

Olivia.

What if my stepsister found out? "Catbox" would seem like a compliment compared to what she'd come up with if she caught me spouting toads. I couldn't risk it.

There was only one solution.

I couldn't tell anyone.

Not yet.

I had to keep this whole thing a secret until I figured out what was happening and until things got back to normal again.

What if they don't go back to normal? whispered a little voice in my head. *What if you're stuck like this forever?*

Tears welled up again at this appalling thought, and this time I couldn't hold them back. Fortunately, it turned out that crying didn't cause toads, nor did snuffling. What it did cause, unfortunately, was sympathetic croaking. The toads I had already produced, including the one still stuffed into my bathrobe pocket, interpreted my sounds as some sort of amphibian song or distress signal, and they began to chorus back to me from all corners of the attic.

A toad's croak is not like the *ribbit* sound a frog makes. It's more like a creaky hinge. A single toad isn't all that loud, but twenty-seven of them croaking in unison is enough to wake the dead.

"WHAT IS GOING ON UP THERE?" my father yelled, and this time I heard his footsteps pounding up the attic stairs.

I picked up the hem of my bathrobe and flapped it frantically at the toads in an attempt to scatter them under the eaves. My father couldn't know about this. Not yet.

"Nothing!" I called back, adding yet another to the amphibian population. *Twenty-eight,* I thought, counting automatically. "I'm just—uh—practicing my bassoon. For the talent show." *Twenty-nine and thirty.*

"For crying out loud, Cat, it's six thirty in the morning! Put that thing away!" The door started to open, then halted as a bloodcurdling scream echoed down the second-floor hallway.

"Mom!" screeched Olivia. "Help me!"

I heard my father's footsteps pounding back down the attic stairs. I crossed swiftly to the door, opened it, and listened.

"What's happening to me?" I heard my stepsister wail.

Was Olivia afflicted with toads too? It would certainly level the playing field if she was. I could tell Dad and Iz, for one thing. I tiptoed downstairs to see.

My father was standing in the doorway to the room I shared with my stepsister. Geoffrey was beside him, clutching his blanket. It takes a lot to pry my little brother away from his favorite cartoon, but I guess hearing his sister holler like she was being skinned alive did the trick. I drew closer, craning for a better view.

Iz was sitting on the edge of Olivia's bed, surrounded by flowers. Piles of flowers. I spotted bachelor's buttons and buttercups, marigolds and daisies and rosebuds. My stepsister saw me peeking over Geoffrey's shoulder and frowned.

"What are you staring at?" she snapped. As she spoke, a cluster of thistles fell from her lips, along with something else, something that winked and flashed in the early-morning light. My stepmother plucked it from the bedspread and held it up.

"Tim," she said, her face full of wonder. "This looks like a diamond!"

My mouth dropped open. "No way!" I whispered.

Geoffrey whipped around just in time to see my latest toad make its escape. "Cat!" he shrieked, then leaned over and barfed.

I turned and fled back upstairs to the attic.

CHAPTER 7

Between cleaning up my little brother and all the excitement over Olivia, nobody noticed my absence.

I closed the attic door quietly behind me and leaned against it, stunned. How could this be happening? How could I be stuck spouting toads, while Olivia was showered in flowers and diamonds?

It wasn't *fair*!

I desperately wanted to talk to my mother. Calling her was out of the question, though—for one thing, my cell phone was downstairs. For another, even if NASA didn't mind connecting another call from me to the space station, the house would be overrun with toads by the time I finished trying to explain all the weird stuff that was happening.

An e-mail would be better. But all the computers were downstairs too, and no way was I going back down there again. Not just yet.

For now I was on my own.

I chewed my lip, trying to imagine what my mother would say if I could talk to her. *Pull up your socks,* probably. That's her all-purpose advice for curing the droops, as she calls it whenever I get moody or worried or sad.

But how? My socks, unfortunately, were full of toads. I knew I had to do something, but what?

I need a game plan, I thought, glancing around the toad-strewn attic. First things first, I decided. Time to get rid of the evidence. I crossed to the trunk and opened it. It was jammed with ancient camping equipment; Jurassic-era stuff that must have been my dad's back when he was a Boy Scout. Sifting through the moldering heap, I pulled out a decrepit duffel bag. It would have to do. I spotted a tattered butterfly net and pulled it out, then gave the air a tentative swipe. I had a sudden urge to laugh. *Just call me Cat Starr, Toad Huntress.*

Toads aren't easy to catch, even in the best of circumstances. In a dimly lit attic, when you're trying not to attract attention, it's nearly impossible. The little suckers spotted me coming a mile away. Every time I sneaked up on one and brought the net down, it would somehow manage to skitter out of reach. Finally I got down on my hands and knees and waited, motionless, until one of them unwisely hopped into range.

"Gotcha!" I said triumphantly, and scooped it up, along with number thirty-one as it sprang from my lips. I was getting better at this.

Ten minutes later I was breathless, crabby, and covered with dust. So much for getting better at this. I'd corralled exactly three toads in the duffel bag, in addition to my

"Gotcha" one. That left twenty-seven more to go.

I needed a new game plan.

I went back to the trunk and rifled through it again. A length of frayed rope—useless. A decaying tent and a bag of tent stakes—nope. At the very bottom was a mildewed old tarp, though, which gave me an idea. I dragged it out into the middle of the floor and spread it out, then went to get something in the far corner that I'd glimpsed when I was up here the other day—a broom. It was missing half its straws, but it might just do the trick for the idea that was beginning to form in my head.

It was time for a little street hockey, toad huntress–style.

I kicked off my slippers. This was a game that called for stealth mode. No point attracting any attention from downstairs. Eventually my family would miss me and come looking, but I hoped to clear out the toads before they did.

Holding the broom out in front of me like a hockey stick, I jogged around the attic counterclockwise, sweeping every amphibian I encountered toward the tarp in the center of the room. The toads fled in panic before me, croaking madly. So much for stealth mode. If I didn't wind this game up quickly, the entire neighborhood would be up here to see what was going on.

Once I had a decent number of them cornered on the tarp, I leaned down and grabbed an edge, folding it over like a taco. A lumpy, toad-filled taco. Then I grabbed another edge and folded it in half again. Picking it up and holding it tightly to keep its occupants from escaping, I carried the tarp to the waiting duffel bag. My method wasn't pretty, but it did the trick. Mostly. A few toads managed to hop out as I made the transfer, so I spread the tarp out again and made another pass around the room. This time I was pretty sure I'd gotten them all.

I sat down next to the duffel bag, panting. Toad huntress was not a job I'd want on a regular basis. After I caught my breath, I unzipped the duffel gingerly and counted the wriggling bodies. *Thirty*.

I was one toad short!

A flicker of movement in the far corner alerted me to the lone straggler, which was busy wedging itself under the eaves behind some insulation. I decided to leave it for now and move on.

A duffel bag stuffed with thirty panicked toads is not exactly invisible—or inaudible. No way was I going to be able to get it downstairs without being seen or heard. Recalling the length of rope I'd seen in the trunk, I crossed the room and grabbed it, then headed for the window above Geoffrey's room, which overlooked the backyard.

I unlocked it and tried to ease it open. It didn't budge. I pushed harder; no luck. No matter how much I wrestled and tugged, the window was completely stuck. Finally, after one last all-out effort, it lurched upward. But the accompanying screech of wood on wood froze me in my tracks. Several seconds ticked by, but there was no response from downstairs. Apparently, Dad and Iz were still preoccupied with Olivia.

Wincing at each creak and groan, I inched the window up until it was open wide enough for the duffel to pass through. I tied one end of the rope to the squirming bag's handles, then lowered it carefully toward the ground, watching as it came to rest on the back deck. Satisfied, I tossed the rope out after it. I'd have to hope that no one spotted it before I managed to get downstairs.

After forcing the window shut again, I crossed to the attic door. I opened it a crack and waited, listening to the low murmur of worried voices from the floor below. Good; they were still busy. I crept down the attic stairs, pausing again at the end of the hall to make sure no one had heard me, then tiptoed past the open door, hoping no one would notice.

They didn't.

I continued on down to the kitchen, steering clear of the living room, where Geoffrey was once again glued to the TV. There was no sign of the breakfast toads; they must have gone into hiding. I'd have to track them down later. Slipping out the back door onto the deck, I bent down to grab the duffel.

"Hey, Cat!"

I spun around to see Connor Dixon waving at me from his backyard. He was taking advantage of a lull in the drizzle to walk Peanut, his family's dachshund. I blushed, acutely aware of how stupid I must look in my bunny jammies and dust-covered robe. I might not have a crush on Connor the way Olivia and Piper did, but still, who wanted to get caught looking like this, let alone holding a bag full of indignant toads?

I maneuvered the duffel behind me and waved back as casually as I could.

"Better hurry if you're going to catch the bus," he called.

No way was I opening my mouth to reply. The stupid bunny jammies were bad enough. Toads would be a disaster. I made a face and pointed at my throat, then mimed coughing.

"Too bad. Well, hope you're feeling better in time for the

talent show tomorrow night. I heard you guys practicing last week—you sounded really good."

I gave him a thumbs-up. He tugged on Peanut's leash and the two of them headed inside. "See ya in band!" he called, shutting the door behind him.

Connor Dixon played the saxophone. Technically, the saxophone is a woodwind like the bassoon, since they're both reed instruments, but unlike the bassoon, the saxophone is one of the cool instruments, like the trumpet or the drums. Those are the instruments of choice for the popular boys. The only one lower than the bassoon on the bandie food chain is the tuba.

I stepped off the deck. My slippers sank into the wet ground. Squelching my way across the soggy grass, I headed for the enormous rhododendron bush at the far edge of my dad's property, the one Geoffrey loves to play under. Last summer I'd helped him build a fort inside it.

Ducking under the branches, I felt myself relax for the first time all morning. I was finally safe—out of sight and sound of anyone in our house or the Dixons'.

I squatted down and unzipped the duffel bag. "Hi, guys," I said, adding a new toad to the ranks. I turned the bag upside down and watched as they scrambled to freedom. As I stood up again, my bathrobe wiggled. I'd forgotten about the one still in my pocket. I scooped it out and set it down, and it hopped off after the others.

That took care of the first action item on my to-do list. Next up, I needed to get ahold of my mother, or A.J., or both. One of them would know what to do. I squelched my way back toward the house.

"Where have you been?" my father asked as I came in, startling me. He lifted an eyebrow at my muddy slippers.

Thinking fast, I grabbed a pad of paper from the counter by the phone, along with the pen beside it. *Needed a little fresh air,* I wrote. *Not feeling too well.*

His brow furrowed in concern. "Really? What's the matter, Kit-Cat?"

I gestured at my neck and grimaced, then scribbled again. *Sore throat. I think I have laryngitis.*

He patted my shoulder. "Maybe you should go back to bed. I have to call the school anyway—your sister's staying home too."

As I turned to go, a toad hopped out from behind the refrigerator.

"Oh, for heaven's sake," said my dad in disgust. "Geoffrey!"

I scooted upstairs, feeling like a traitor. One good thing about having a little brother is that you can blame all sorts of things on him, including stray toads.

Olivia wasn't in our room. I heard the shower running and hoped she'd save me some hot water, as I was covered with attic dust. I could only imagine what my hair looked like. I fished my cell phone out of my backpack and was just turning it on to text A.J. when Iz came in.

"Sorry, sweetie, but we're a cell-phone-free zone this morning," she told me, plucking it from my hand. "Your dad says you're not feeling well." She pressed the palm of her other hand against my forehead. "Hmmm. You do feel a little warm." She inspected me, her forehead crinkling with concern. "What's with all this dust?"

I shrugged, swatted at the streaks on my bathrobe, and she

sighed. "Never mind. You can shower later. Under the covers with you. I think it's just as well that both you girls stay home from school anyway, given everything that's happened around here."

My father came in, trailing Geoffrey. "G-Man's been collecting pets again," he informed my stepmother. "Toads this time. I found two of them under the refrigerator."

"Cat," said Geoffrey, pulling his finger out of his mouth and pointing it at me.

I sucked in my breath. Busted! Fortunately, however, my father completely misinterpreted him.

"Sorry, buddy. I know you want a cat, but the answer is still no. And no toads, either."

My little brother desperately wants a pet. He points to every kitten and puppy he sees, but he can't have one because Iz is allergic.

My stepsister breezed in just then, her hair wrapped in a towel. "What's going on?" she asked. "Why's everyone crammed in my room?"

Our room, I wanted to say, but didn't, of course. My lips were firmly sealed for the time being.

Iz bent down and plucked another diamond from the drift of daisy petals that fluttered to my stepsister's feet. "Just collecting cell phones," she told her, staring at the gem. "Your stepfather and I have discussed it, and we think it's best to keep this, uh, development under our hats for the moment."

"Mo-om!" protested Olivia, clutching her cell phone to her chest. My stepsister's cell phone is her life. "What's the big deal?"

Iz pointed to the pile of snapdragons that her protest had produced. "That's the big deal," she said. "We don't need word of this getting out to anyone. Not until we figure out a solution. Understood?"

Olivia heaved a dramatic sigh, and a dandelion puff arced from her mouth to the floor. Then she nodded reluctantly.

"Good," said Iz, prying her cell phone away. "I'm going to go call the school." She and my father left with Geoffrey, shutting our bedroom door behind them.

Olivia flopped down on her bed. "You're quiet this morning," she said, showering her pillow with what looked like columbine.

I shrugged, and she looked at me with sudden suspicion. "Hey, you're not, you know"—she pointed to her mouth—"like me, are you?"

I almost laughed. *Like you? As if!* Instead I shook my head, then clutched my throat and grimaced. I would have ventured a cough, but I was worried that it might result in a toad.

"You think *you* have a sore throat!" Olivia sighed dramatically again, catching another dandelion puff in her cupped hands. "You should try dealing with this." She gestured at the flowers that were piling up on her bedspread.

You are so clueless, I thought bitterly. Turning my back on her, I reached into my backpack and pulled out a book.

Somehow I managed to make it through the rest of the morning without speaking. Everyone was so wrapped up in my stepsister that it wasn't all that difficult. Between phone calls to Portland's big research hospital, in hopes of finding a specialist who might be able to cure Olivia, my father and Iz kept coming in to check and see if maybe her affliction was only temporary and had worn off. No such luck, of course. Only Geoffrey kept a wary eye on me. He didn't say anything else, though, and I hoped that after a while he'd think this morning was just a weird dream.

Olivia was thrilled to be the center of attention and kept up a steady stream of chatter, squealing whenever she produced another diamond. By lunchtime she had quite a collection. Iz slipped out toward the middle of the afternoon and drove downtown to a jewelry store to have them checked out. She returned home looking thunderstruck.

"They're real," she said to my father. "Every one of them."

My father smiled weakly. "Well, I guess we can be grateful your college education is now paid for," he told Olivia.

She gave me a smug look, as if maybe she'd planned the whole thing. My stepsister's predicament didn't seem to be disturbing her all that much, and I fought the urge to blurt out a toad and scare the socks off her. Miss Prissy Pants hated anything to do with the outdoors, especially insects and creepy-crawlies. When we were little she used to cry just at the sight of an earthworm on the sidewalk after a rainstorm, and I could only imagine what she'd do if I unleashed an amphibian or two.

My father and Iz called a family meeting after dinner.

"We've been talking, Olivia, and we don't think we should let you go back to school tomorrow," my stepmother began.

"Mo-om!" she protested amid a gust of poppies. "Why not? It's not like I'm sick or something. It's boring being stuck in my room with nobody for company."

"You've got Cat," her mother corrected her.

"She doesn't count."

"Olivia!"

"Well, she doesn't," Olivia retorted, spitting out a small shard of ice. Or what looked like ice. It was another diamond, of course.

My stepmother took it from her and tucked it into the black velvet drawstring bag she'd been using to hold the other gems. She sighed. "The thing is, this—whatever it is of yours—is bound to attract a lot of attention, and that's not necessarily a good thing."

Olivia lifted a shoulder. "What if I promise not to talk? I can pretend to have laryngitis too, just like Cat."

"Cat is not pretending!" said Iz, coming stoutly to my defense. I dropped my gaze, feeling guilty. I don't like to deceive anyone, especially not my stepmother. But what other choice did I have?

All of a sudden a stricken look crossed Olivia's face. "What about the talent show?" she cried. "You've got to at least let me go back to school for the talent show tomorrow night!"

"We'll have to wait and see what the doctor says," her mother told her. "We've managed to track down someone who may be able to help you."

Good luck with that, I thought grimly.

"And this week is Field Trip Friday, too!" my stepsister wailed, gushing out an enormous hydrangea blossom. "We're supposed to go to the zoo!"

Geoffrey did his little happy-feet dance. The zoo is my little brother's favorite place, and Iz had promised to bring him along when she chaperoned.

"Like I said, we'll have to wait and see," Iz repeated.

My father turned to me. "How about you, Cat? You seem to be feeling better."

I nodded, then wrote: *Yeah, but I still can't talk.*

"Hmm," said my dad. "I'm going to see if Dr. Douglass can fit you in after we finish with Olivia tomorrow. But I don't see any reason you can't go back to school meanwhile. As long as you promise you won't breathe a word of what's happened here today, okay?"

I held up three fingers of my right hand in the Scout's honor salute. Telling anyone anything about what had happened was the furthest thing from my mind. My lips were sealed. Possibly permanently, at this rate.

He smiled. "Good. I'll write a note explaining your situation, then."

"Lucky," murmured Olivia, shooting me a spiteful glance. She coughed, then spit a bright green coneflower into her hand. I knew it was a coneflower because I'd helped Iz plant some in the garden last summer. We'd bought them at the nursery together. I remembered that they had a funny name. But what was it?

Echinacea purpurea. Green Envy, that's what.

I stared at the flower in my stepsister's hand. Was it just a coincidence, or was Olivia's floral output linked to her mood? And speaking of coincidences, how weird was it that we'd both just happened to come down with this strange whatever-it-was at the very same time? I mulled this over as I got ready for bed.

I thought about tomorrow, too, and wondered if I could really make it through an entire day of school without a single toad slipup. Mrs. Bonneville didn't take any guff, and

I doubted she'd take any toads, either. They might not be on her list of rules, but spitting was, and somehow I was pretty sure she wouldn't be thrilled if I started spitting them in class. And there was the talent show, too!

I was going to have to stay on my toes.

CHAPTER 8

"Cat still got your tongue, Cat?" said Olivia as she pranced downstairs to breakfast the next morning. She was all smiles, of course. It's easy to be all smiles when you're popping out priceless gems and petals instead of wart-encrusted amphibians. I shrugged and nodded as she held something out to her mother.

Iz took it and added it to the drawstring bag matter-of-factly, but I noticed that my father looked a little freaked out. He'd probably been hoping that a good night's sleep would cure Olivia.

It hadn't, and it hadn't cured me, either. I knew that for a fact because I'd been up early again, out under the rhododendron bush talking to myself. Myself and I were in agreement—we still seemed to be a bottomless source of toads.

Iz tucked Olivia's priceless crop into the messenger bag she used as a purse and a camera case. "Eat quick, honey," she told my stepsister. "Our appointment's in forty-five minutes." She turned to me, and I noticed the shadows under her eyes. Iz obviously hadn't slept much. "I expect we'll be a while, but we should be home in plenty of time to get you to Dr. Douglass's office after school."

I nodded, and she looked at me closely. "You'll be okay getting yourself to the bus, right?"

I do it all the time at home in Houston, I wrote on the notepad I carried with me everywhere now.

"We'll drop Geoffrey off at preschool on our way this morning," she continued a few minutes later as she helped my little brother on with his raincoat. "He's going to go home afterward with one of his friends, so you won't have to worry about him." She gave me a hug. "You're sure you're okay?"

I nodded again, but inside I didn't feel all that okay. I was dreading facing the whole "Catbox" thing again, plus what if, despite my best efforts, I had another toad episode at school? Who could I call for help? My father and stepmother would be at the specialist with Olivia, and they'd confiscated our cell phones.

For the first time since the toads appeared, I was tempted to say something. *What about me?* I wanted to holler. *I need a specialist too!* I didn't open my mouth, though. For one thing, Iz and Dad had enough on their minds without worrying about me, and for another, no way did I want Olivia to find out about the toads. I would never live it down.

The house was oddly quiet after they all left. I was used to being on my own—sometimes my mother had to be at the Johnson Space Center at the crack of dawn, and she often worked long hours—but it was different here than back home. The Houston high-rise where I lived with my mother was always full of other people. The D'Angelos were just a quick elevator ride away. Here in Portland, my dad's house was on a stub of a dead-end street nestled in the woods, with only the Dixons for company. Plus, the bungalow was older and creakier than our condo back home, and I found it a little creepy when it was empty like this. To distract myself, I finished my breakfast in front of the TV, then went upstairs to get dressed.

A few minutes later I heard Connor Dixon calling good-bye to his mother and looked out the bedroom window to see him heading down his driveway. I glanced at the clock and gave a squeak of alarm. Snatching the web-footed creature my squeak had produced from off my bedspread, I pelted downstairs and grabbed my raincoat and backpack. I slammed the front door behind me, tossed the toad over the porch railing into the bushes below, then vaulted down the steps and ran toward the bus stop at the end of our street. Connor waved when he saw me.

"Hey," he said.

I jerked my chin in response.

"Where's your bassoon?"

I looked at him, aghast. I'd run right out of the house without it! This toad thing really had me rattled. I turned and started back up the street, but Connor grabbed my sleeve.

"Too late," he said, pointing to the bus that was now rounding the corner. "Don't worry, it's not that big a deal. I forgot my sax once, and Mr. Morgan was really nice about it."

Of course he was, I thought. Mr. Morgan was probably happy for any excuse to spare his delicate, shell-like ears. Connor played the saxophone about as well as I played basketball.

I just gave him a regretful smile in response, as if to say, *Oh, well.* Connor was right—Mr. Morgan was nice, and he would probably let me off the hook as far as band went, but the Hawkwinds had planned a final run-through during lunch for the talent show tonight. The bus wheezed to a stop in front of me, and I mounted the steps glumly. My friends were going to be disappointed.

When Mrs. Bonneville took attendance, I held up my hand and waved.

My teacher frowned. "I thought I made myself clear, Cat. Mrs. Bonneville prefers her students to speak up and say 'Present.'"

Well, this one won't be speaking up anytime soon, I thought, handing her the note from my dad.

"Ah," said Mrs. Bonneville, scanning it. "Laryngitis. I see." She narrowed her eyes at me, and for a minute I was sure she could tell I was faking. Then she shrugged and said, "All right, then."

I sucked it up just like my dad told me and ignored the scattering of "Catbox" comments as best I could, and I managed to make it through homeroom, social studies, math, and band without spilling a single toad. As predicted, Mr. Morgan was very nice about me forgetting my bassoon.

"Just lend us your ears today, Cat," he said, waggling his own at me, "and your moral support. As for tonight, I'm sure we have nothing to worry about, given that you're such an experienced musician."

Lunch was a little tricky, and I almost slipped up twice, but the notebook-and-pen routine worked pretty well. As

I'd suspected, Rani and Juliet and Rajit were disappointed that I wasn't able to practice the Bach piece with them one more time, but I dutifully sat through the final run-through anyway.

After lunch Rani and I headed off to PE. Only one more class after that, and I was home free! Without Olivia around to hassle me, I found myself beginning to relax a little about halfway through the basketball game. For once, I didn't totally stink, and I even made a basket.

Then Piper Philbin ruined everything.

"Pass the ball, Catbox!" she shouted to me from half-court.

"Ladies!" scolded Ms. Suarez. "Watch the trash talk!"

I gaped at her. I hadn't said a word! Why was she blaming me, too?

Piper smirked and beckoned for the ball. I passed it to her, all right—hard. She grunted as she caught it and spun away, scowling. I moved down the court, saw an opening under the basket, and slipped through when Taylor Brown, who was supposed to be guarding me, looked the other way.

I was wide open.

I motioned wildly to Piper to pass the ball back. She ignored me and faked past Taylor instead. I could tell she had no intention of giving me the chance to score; she wanted to make the basket herself. I moved toward her, hoping to force her hand. Instead she drove for the net, giving me a sharp jab with her elbow as she dribbled past. I went flying into the sidelines, where I stumbled and fell to my knees with an "Oof."

A toad promptly sprang onto the court.

I froze. Behind me, a cheer went up, and for one awful

second I thought I was in for a repeat of Friday's "Catbox" uproar. Nobody was paying the least bit of attention to me, though. They were cheering for Piper.

I grabbed the toad and stuffed it under my jersey, then scrambled to my feet.

"Everything okay, Cat?" asked Ms. Suarez.

I hesitated for a fraction of a second, then shook my head. Faking a limp, I headed for the locker room. It was the only thing I could think of to do.

"Cat!" she called.

I ignored her and kept walking.

Ms. Suarez blew her whistle, but I still kept walking. I could hear her trotting after me as I ducked through the door. *Croak.*

I had to get rid of the evidence, fast. I opened the first locker I saw and flung the toad inside, then slammed it shut and sprinted across the room. By the time Ms. Suarez poked her head in the door, I was sitting on a bench rubbing my leg.

"What's the matter?" she called. "Are you okay?"

I winced and pointed to my knee, which was conveniently still red from where I'd fallen on it.

She glanced back over her shoulder, checking on the rest of the class, then jogged over and inspected it quickly. "You'll be all right," she told me. "Stop by the nurse and get some ice afterward, if you want. Class is almost over anyway."

Ms. Suarez returned to the gym, and a few moments later the bell rang. *Uh-oh,* I thought, as my PE classmates flooded through the doors. I stood up quickly and limped over to my locker, then busied myself getting changed.

Thirty seconds later there was a loud shriek from the far

side of the room. I turned around to see Piper Philbin cata-pult onto the bench, where she hopped up and down in a panic, pointing at the floor.

I'd accidentally put the toad in Piper's locker.

"Calm down, calm down," said Ms. Suarez, crossing to join her. "What's the big deal?"

"What's the big deal? It's a *FROG*!" screamed Piper.

Fleabrain, I thought scornfully. Didn't she know the differ-ence between a frog and a toad?

Croak. The creature sprang across the aisle, and the room erupted in terrified squeals as my classmates stampeded for the door.

"Girls!" called our gym teacher crossly, blocking their path. "For heaven's sake, it's not Sasquatch." Grabbing a towel, she threw it over the toad and picked it up. "Sit down and put your head between your knees," she ordered Piper, who was still hysterical. "Try and breathe normally. I'll be back in a sec."

As she carried the toad outside, Piper looked up. "Who put that thing in my locker?" she demanded. She scanned the room, her gaze settling on me.

Wiping my face clean of expression, I held out my hands and shrugged, as if to say, *Who, me?*

"I don't know how you did it, but nice work," whispered Rani as we headed down the hall to science class.

I ducked my head to hide my smile. Maybe there was an upside to this whole toad thing. It wasn't every day that someone like me could give someone like Piper Fleabrain a taste of her own medicine. I felt more cheerful than I had since this whole mess started.

I was also more worried than ever. I'd come close to blowing it back there on the basketball court. Nothing but sheer dumb luck had saved me. If I had been spotted by anyone—especially Piper—well, it was bad enough that I was the laughingstock of the school, thanks to the Hawk Creek Tappers and their stupid stunt in the lunchroom. If someone saw me spouting toads, I could only imagine the uproar. The school would probably expel me, for one thing. I was pretty sure toads were considered some sort of health hazard. Even if they didn't kick me out, though, I'd have no friends. Nada. Zilch. I doubted even the Hawkwinds could handle toads. The chaos in the locker room had just proven that. Toads are scary. People are afraid of them—especially girls.

By the time I finally got home, I had a bad case of the droops. I needed to talk to someone. I'd promised not to use the phone or computer, but I was feeling desperate. I went directly into my father's office and turned on his computer, then sent A.J. an instant message.

Please be there, I thought as long seconds ticked by. Finally the cursor blinked.

What's up? he messaged back.

I need your help. Typing as fast as I could, I poured out the entire story. Everything. From the first toad that plopped into my cereal bowl yesterday morning to Olivia's flowers and gems.

When I was done, the screen stayed blank for a long time. So long that I thought maybe there'd been some sort of computer failure. And then—

No way.

Yes way, I replied.

**Gotta see it to believe it. Does your dad's computer
have a webcam?**

Yeah.

We quickly set up a video chat. We do this all the time at
home, too, even though the D'Angelos' condo is only two
floors away. A minute later A.J.'s face appeared on-screen. I'd
never been so relieved to see anybody in my entire life.

"You're kidding, right?" he said, grinning his familiar gap-
toothed grin at me. "This is some sort of a joke."

I shook my head.

"C'mon, Cat. Toads? Stuff like that doesn't really happen."

I gave a snort of nervous laughter. Out popped a toad. A.J.
stared at it in disbelief.

"Freaky, right?" I replied, producing another one.

His mouth dropped open. "You are seriously creeping me
out."

"I'm not doing it on purpose," I snapped back. "It's not
like I can control it or anything. It just . . . happens."

A trio of toads leaped from my lips to the keyboard as I
said this. I glanced down at them ruefully.

"Oh. My. Gosh," said A.J. "What are you going to do?"

"That's why I'm talking to *you*, dork!" I replied. "You're
the genius—find me a cure." I picked up the wastebasket
from beside the desk as I said this and started sweeping for
toads.

A.J. is supersmart. He had an internship at NASA last
summer, working with his dad in the computer department.
I, on the other hand, went to band camp and watched old sci-
fi movies. At least while I was in Houston.

"Right. I'll just google 'spontaneous toad eruptions,'" A.J.

said sarcastically. I shot him a look and he sighed. "Let me do some research. I'll see what I can find out. But, Cat?"

"Yeah?"

"You've got to tell your mom."

After we signed off, I checked my e-mail. There were two from my mother, one wanting to know how the visit with Great-Aunt Aby went, and another asking how Hawkwinds was going.

I'll be cheering you on from afar tonight at the talent show! Break a leg! Or a reed, or whatever. You know what I mean. I love you!

A.J. was right. I probably should tell my mother what was going on.

If I did, though, the first thing she'd do was tell my dad and Iz, and then Olivia would find out, and she'd tell Piper Philbin, and the whole school would know in a heartbeat. It wasn't difficult to imagine how Olivia's Reign of Terror would expand after that. I'd be begging for the good old days of "Catbox," that's for sure. Not only would Olivia invent some new, more horrible nickname for me, she'd probably rat me out to the Health Department and personally spearhead the campaign to get me expelled from school. And then the media would get ahold of the story, and I'd be hounded out of Portland and most likely the whole state. Maybe even the country. I'd have to go live in the woods, like Sasquatch. Life would not be worth living if Olivia found out.

So I still couldn't tell my mom. Not just yet.

CHAPTER 9

"There's nothing physically wrong with her," said Dr. Douglass later that afternoon, tapping her pencil thoughtfully against the chart on her clipboard.

My dad and Iz were sitting across from me in the examination room. I was perched on the padded table, decked out in one of those embarrassing paper robes that crinkle every time you move.

"But she hasn't spoken a word for two whole days!" Iz protested.

Dr. Douglass nodded. "I understand," she replied. "May I speak to you two in private for a moment?" She turned to me. "We'll be right back, Cat. You can get dressed if you'd like."

If I'd like? *Crinkle.* I slid off the table the second they left the room and made a beeline for my clothes.

A moment later the door opened and a nurse popped her head in. *Crinkle.* I jumped back, clutching the paper robe to my chest and wishing I weren't standing there in my underpants.

"Oh, excuse me, honey," she said. "I just came in for your chart."

I pointed wordlessly to the table where Dr. Douglass had left it. The nurse took it and left the room again, not quite shutting the door behind her. The murmur of voices from the office on the other side drew me like a magnet.

"It's nothing to be overly worried about at this point," I heard Dr. Douglass say. "Let's keep a close eye on her, though. She's exhibiting symptoms consistent with those of a selective mute. It could be related to any number of things—separation from her mother, perhaps, who is, after all, in outer space. That would certainly make me anxious, if I were twelve."

"I suppose you have a point," my father replied.

"Or it could be related to Olivia's, shall we say, *unusual* condition," Dr. Douglass continued. "That, too, must be a bit traumatic."

"More than a bit," said Iz glumly. "For all of us, in fact."

"How did your appointment at the research hospital go?" Dr. Douglass asked.

"They'd never seen anything like it before," Iz told her. "They wanted to keep Olivia there for a few days to run some tests—"

"But Iz didn't like the way the staff were eyeing her, uh, output," my father added. "So we brought her home."

"Well, what did you expect me to think after that lab assistant slipped a diamond into his pocket?" Iz replied indignantly. "I don't think he would have given it back if I hadn't said anything."

"I'm sure it was just an oversight," replied my father.

My stepmother snorted. "Timothy Starr, you can be so naive sometimes!"

I couldn't help wondering what the specialists at the research hospital would make of me. Somehow I couldn't picture anybody wanting to pocket my toads.

"Look on the bright side," said Dr. Douglass. "At least you know you'll be able to pay for Olivia's treatment."

My father laughed uneasily.

I pondered Iz's point as I pulled on my jeans and T-shirt. It hadn't occurred to me that other people might try and take advantage of Olivia's weird talent, but what Iz was saying made a lot of sense.

"I just thought maybe a few people were a little more interested in the gems than they were in Olivia," my stepmother continued, sounding defensive.

"It's only natural that you want to protect her until this all gets sorted out," Dr. Douglass said soothingly. "If Olivia were my child, I'd have brought her home too. As for Cat, I recommend that you continue to treat her as you always have, and give her lots of reassurance. She's a normal, healthy young lady who simply has a lot going on in her life at the moment."

You have no idea, I thought. Selective mute! I could show Dr. Douglass in two seconds flat just how mute I was, but I didn't think toads would be very welcome in her office.

"If the condition persists, I'll give you a referral to a therapist," Dr. Douglass continued, "but my guess is she'll be right as rain in a few days."

"And the talent show?" asked my father.

I held my breath. I really didn't want to let the Hawkwinds down.

"I don't see any reason she can't participate. Olivia, either, although I would stress the importance of not broadcasting her current situation."

"So we'll be sending two mutes onstage tonight?" said Iz. "I'm not so sure about that."

"How about I write a note excusing them both from speaking?" Dr. Douglass offered. "Given the unusual circumstances, I don't mind stretching the truth a bit." I heard her scribbling. "There you go—Olivia and Cat are now officially afflicted with a rare form of laryngitis."

I heard the three of them getting up from their chairs and raced back across the room. I hopped up onto the examination table and pasted an innocent look on my face just as Dr. Douglass entered the room.

She gave me a big smile. "So, young lady, I understand you're scheduled to play a little Bach tonight?"

I nodded.

"I wish I could be there to hear it. What's the piece you're playing?"

I took my notebook and pen from my rain jacket pocket. *The Fugue in G Minor,* I wrote.

Dr. Douglass's eyebrows shot up. "Ambitious for a middle school quartet."

Iz put her arm around my shoulders. "My stepdaughter plays with the Houston Youth Symphony," she said proudly, giving me a squeeze.

I almost told them everything right then and there. Almost.

The ride home was quiet. Dad and Iz both seemed lost in

thought, and I was determined not to give in to the temptation to spill the beans. Toads. Whatever. It didn't matter how
nice my stepmother was—my stepsister wasn't, and that was
the problem.

We stopped to pick up a pizza for dinner. Nobody was
in the mood to cook. Back at the house we found Geoffrey
all by himself in the living room, happily building a LEGO
castle. At first I thought he was humming something by
Mozart—the Twelve Variations—then realized it was the
tune to "Twinkle, Twinkle, Little Star."

"Where's your sister?" Iz asked, glancing around. Olivia
was supposed to be babysitting. She'd obviously been there,
because the rug was strewn with flowers. Plus, a line of diamonds glittered at us from atop my little brother's fortress
walls.

Geoffrey pulled his finger out of his mouth and pointed
upstairs. Iz marched over to the foot of the stairwell. Dad and
I were right behind her. A laugh rang out, and then we heard
Olivia squeal, "No way, Piper! You really said that to him?"

My stepsister was on the phone.

Iz drew herself up into the full mad-mom pose, hands on
hips and mouth in a thin, flat line. My mother uses the exact
same one when she's ticked off at me. They must teach it at
mom school.

"Olivia Jean Haggerty!" she hollered.

"Um, I'll get dinner on the table," said my father, backing
away with the pizza boxes and disappearing into the kitchen.
It was no fun being around when Iz got mad.

"Yes, Mom?" Olivia called back, her voice dripping sweet-
ness and light and who knew what else.

"Come down here this minute, young lady!"

My stepsister appeared at the top of the stairs.

Busted, I thought, suppressing a grin. It might be stupid and childish, but I still get a kick out of it when she gets in trouble.

Iz held out her hand. Olivia slumped down the stairs and handed over her cell phone.

"Where did you get this?"

"Your dresser drawer," Olivia replied in a low voice.

"You *promised!*" Iz said grimly, looking hurt and disappointed.

As usual my stepsister tried to weasel out of it. "I know I did, Mom, but I had to check with Piper about my math homework."

Right. As if the two of them had ever discussed math in their entire lives.

Olivia's brown eyes filled with tears. "You can't expect me not to have any friends at all just because of this," she said, pointing to the bouquet of wilted-looking lupine that now lay on the floor at her feet.

"What I expect is for you to keep your word when you give it," Iz replied.

I felt a flicker of guilt. I'd broken my promise too.

My stepmother sighed. "I don't think you understand the gravity of the situation, Olivia. We need to keep this *completely quiet* until we find a remedy for you."

"I am keeping it quiet! The only person I've told is Piper."

I almost laughed out loud. Piper Philbin is the biggest blabbermouth at Hawk Creek Middle School. If she knew Olivia's secret, all of Portland would know it within the hour.

Iz shook her head. "What's done is done," she said. "I

guess I'll have to call Piper's mother. Help me clean up this mess first."

The three of us started gathering flowers off the rug. Geoffrey protested as my stepmother stripped his LEGO castle of its glittering ornaments.

"Sweetie, your castle is beautiful," Iz told him, "but these twinkle stars belong to Olivia. Why don't you and Cat go help Daddy set the table? One of the pizzas is Hawaiian— your favorite."

My little brother brightened at this, but his was the only smiling face at the table. Dinner was nearly as silent as the car ride home had been. Olivia picked at her pizza, scowling, obviously still peeved about the loss of her cell phone.

"Dr. Douglass cleared you girls for the talent show tonight," my father told her, and she perked up at this.

"Hold on, Tim," said Iz. "After what Olivia pulled this afternoon, I'm not sure she deserves to participate."

Olivia's face fell.

Serves you right, I thought. *Blabbermouth.* My conscience prickled again as I thought about my video chat with A.J., but I pushed the guilty feeling away. That was different.

"I say we let her attend on one condition, and one condition only," my father replied. He passed Dr. Douglass's note across the table to her. "Absolutely no talking! To anyone, understand? Until we tell you otherwise, Olivia, you and Cat are in the same boat."

Great, I thought. *All aboard the USS Laryngitis.*

Olivia shot me a look. One that clearly said, *I don't want to be in any boat with you, anyplace, anytime, ever.*

She pushed back from the table and stood up. "I'm going

upstairs to get my costume on," she said icily, littering the table with milk-white snowdrops.

As I watched her leave the room, I started to worry. Dr. Douglass might have cleared us for takeoff, but Houston, we definitely had a problem. My stepsister was ready for the talent show, but was the talent show ready for her?

CHAPTER 10

Backstage at Hawk Creek Middle School swarmed with activity.

Using my bassoon case as a wedge, I inched my way through the knots of excited students. Olivia was right behind me, dressed in a sequin-spangled sailor costume.

How appropriate for the USS Laryngitis, I thought bitterly.

My stepsister spotted Piper and peeled off toward her. Half a dozen other tap dancers in identical costumes joined them, and a minute later the sound of their shoes tapping on the wooden floor rose above the hubbub of the crowd as the Hawk Creek Tappers began warming up.

I passed two magicians, a flock of ballerinas, a comedy act (at least, I assumed it was a comedy act, since it consisted of three football players in helmets, pink leotards, and matching tutus), a baton twirler, a juggler, and a skinny kid with two fluffy little dogs on leashes and a big sign that said STUPID PET TRICKS R US.

Finally I made it to where my friends were standing.

"There you are," said Rajit. "We were starting to get worried about you."

Rani held out a copy of the program. "We're on right after your stepsister and her friends," she told me. "We'll be closing the show."

"That's because they're saving the best for last," Juliet said with a smile.

I looked around, wishing there were someplace we could go to warm up. With all the excitement at home this evening, I hadn't even had time to tune my instrument.

"People!" said Mrs. Bonneville, lifting her voice to be heard above the buzz of excitement backstage. "Listen up! Is everyone in their assigned places?" She marched down the checklist on her clipboard, calling out the acts and checking them off when someone replied. I felt sorry for anyone who didn't answer "Present." Mrs. Bonneville didn't take any guff even from kids who weren't her students.

"Five minutes to showtime!" she said when she was done. "Mrs. Bonneville suggests you visit the girls' and boys' rooms now, because there won't be time later."

"Good idea," said Rani. "I'm getting nervous, how about you?"

I nodded vigorously. I always get nervous before concerts.

Juliet joined us, and the three of us left our instrument cases with Rajit, then headed out the stage's exit door and down the hallway. There was a line inside the bathroom. I spotted Olivia at the sink, adjusting her sailor hat. Piper was standing next to her, clutching a fistful of pink tulips. I caught her eye in the mirror and she gave a start, then elbowed Olivia and nodded in my direction.

Olivia turned around and I scowled at her. *I know exactly what you're up to,* I thought, with a significant glance at the flowers. My stepsister hadn't been at school five minutes and she'd already broken her promise to Dad and Iz.

My first instinct was to go and find them and tell on her. I knew it wouldn't work, though. By the time I tracked them down and wrote out an explanation, the flowers would be long gone.

Olivia gave me the stink eye, then flounced out. A few minutes later, when Rani and Juliet and I emerged back into the hallway, she was waiting for me, along with the rest of the Hawk Creek Tappers.

My stepsister pinched her nose with her fingers.

"Catbox!" cried Piper, right on cue.

Their friends laughed and held their noses too, backing away from me as if they smelled something horrible. Dissolving into giggles, they tapped away down the hall toward the backstage door.

I had no choice but to stand there in silence, stifling the urge to tell Olivia off in front of everyone. I couldn't, of course. I couldn't say a word. I might as well have been wearing a gag. Hot tears of rage welled up in my eyes.

"Don't pay any attention to them, Cat," said Rani, with a glance at my burning face. "Sometimes they still call me Curry Head Kumar. Especially if there aren't any teachers around."

We made our way back to where Rajit was waiting for us, careful to keep our distance from my stepsister and her friends. Olivia thought she was so smart, getting all her friends to gang up on me like that. It would serve her right if

I did tell my father and Iz about the tulips in the bathroom.

But there wasn't time now. The curtain was going up.

The first act was the baton twirler. As she went onstage, I stood in the wings, watching Olivia. My stepsister made me so mad I could just spit. Suddenly I realized that I could do better than spit. I could *toad*.

Emboldened, I considered the idea. Maybe it was time to unleash the weapon that would allow me to even up the score. Maybe it was time for a little guerrilla toad-fare. I was Cat Starr, Toad Huntress, after all.

Olivia had no idea who she was dealing with.

I bided my time as act after act went out onstage. Some of them, like the juggler and the kid with the fluffy dogs, were awful. The juggler dropped everything he flung into the air, and the dogs wouldn't do anything except sit, and kept scratching themselves and wandering off the stage. The audience thought this was funny, but the skinny kid was practically in tears by the time he was finished. A few of the other acts were pretty good, though, especially the football players in the tutus. They'd worked up a ballet routine, and they were really funny.

Finally it was time for the Hawk Creek Tappers. I crept forward as my stepsister and her friends ran onstage and took their places, concealing myself in the folds of the heavy velvet curtain. As their music started, I bent down, pretending to tie my shoe as I quietly whispered, "Olivia stinks."

Out popped a toad. I caught it and held its squirming body to my chest. Good thing I'm not squeamish. Then I did the same thing two more times, figuring a trio of toads was enough to do the trick.

By this time the dance routine was well under way. I placed the toads on the floor and lifted the hem of the curtain. The toads blinked in the spotlights. I gave them each a nudge with my foot, and as they hopped off toward the line of dancers, I casually walked back to rejoin my friends.

A minute later I heard squeals and shrieks from the stage, followed by laughter from the audience. The dancing stopped abruptly, replaced by the rat-a-tat-tat of a dozen pairs of tap shoes as the Hawk Creek Tappers scattered.

Take that, Miss Prissy Pants, I thought smugly. You don't mess with the Stealth Toader.

Everyone waiting backstage crowded forward to see what was going on. When they spotted the toads and the shrieking girls, they started laughing too.

My homeroom teacher clutched her clipboard to her chest and sent in the football players, still in their tutus, for toad control, causing another wave of laughter to sweep through the audience.

"Oh man, that was hilarious!" said Rajit after everything finally calmed down.

People were still giggling as he and Rani and Juliet and I took our seats. We set our music on our stands, and Rajit took out his electronic tuner. Flute, check. Clarinet, check. Oboe, check. Then it was my turn. I closed my eyes as I always did when I tuned up, shutting out the world and listening intently for the pitch. As I played the note and adjusted my bassoon to match it, I heard a gasp from the audience, then a giggle. When I opened my eyes to see what was so funny, though, the only thing I saw was Rajit's nod, signaling us to begin.

The audience stilled as the first haunting notes of the fugue echoed across the stage. I sat back, counting the measures and waiting for my cue. The bassoon was the last voice to join in. Finally it was my turn. As soon as I lifted my instrument to my mouth and began to play, though, the giggles started again. I frowned, concentrating on the music. The snickers grew into guffaws, then belly laughs.

The fugue limped to a finish, drowned out by howls of delight from the audience.

My friends were looking at me strangely.

"Cat!" whispered Juliet, pointing urgently at my feet.

I looked down at the floor and gasped. I was surrounded by a sea of toads. They could only have come from one place—me. I played a tentative note, just to check, and sure enough, a toad popped out the end of my bassoon.

My face went scarlet. No wonder everyone was laughing! Only Mr. Morgan looked unhappy. He was standing in the wings with his face buried in his hands.

"How was that for a grand finale?" cried Mr. Randolph, our principal, bounding up the steps onto the stage and facing the delighted audience. He shook his head and chuckled. "What a showstopper! I don't know how you kids did it—or what you're planning to do with all these, uh, frogs, are they? I'm sure the Biology Department can find a use for them. At any rate, congratulations!"

He beckoned to Mrs. Bonneville, who minced carefully across the stage to join him. She let out a squeak as one of the toads sprang onto her shoe, which set the audience off again.

"If you'd all care to join us in the cafeteria," she said stiffly, flicking it off, "we'll be serving refreshments in just a few minutes." She turned to head for the stairs, and as she passed me and my fellow Hawkwinds, she whispered, "Mrs. Bonneville expects you to clean this mess up!"

The tutu-wearing football players came back onstage as the auditorium started clearing out. While they gleefully herded toads, my friends and I packed up our instruments. Rani, Rajit, and Juliet were strangely quiet. None of them would meet my gaze.

I was so embarrassed I didn't know what to say—not that I could say anything. I had no intention of opening my mouth ever again.

"Thanks a lot, Cat," said Rani bitterly, as she stood up to go. "That toad in the locker room was funny, but this? I thought you were my friend. I don't know how you did it, or why, but way to ruin everything for us."

"Yeah, some practical joke," her brother added.

I gaped at them. They thought I'd deliberately sabotaged the quartet! I started to explain but caught myself just in time. I gave Rani a beseeching look. She ignored it and turned her back on me. Before I could reach for my pen and paper, Juliet and Rajit turned away too. My heart sank as the three of them stalked off.

Feeling worse by the minute, I went to look for my father and Iz. All I wanted to do right now was go home.

"You!" shrieked Olivia as I stepped through the door into the cafeteria. "I just know it was you who put those toads onstage and wrecked our dance number. You . . . you—*Catbox,* you!"

The crowd fell away like Moses parting the Red Sea, leaving me and my stepsister facing each other amid a drift of bright red roses, complete with angry-looking thorns. Olivia's hands were on her hips, and she was spoiling for a fight. *Fine,* I thought. The heck with the consequences—it was time to let her have it.

Before I could open my mouth and launch a toad at her, though, Iz broke through the perimeter of the crowd and swooped in, reaching for my stepsister.

"Olivia," she warned.

My stepsister backed away. "You had no right to mess us up like that!" she hollered at me over her mother's shoulder.

The crowd gasped as they watched the scarlet blossoms arc from her lips. Olivia made no move to try and catch them; she just let them tumble to the floor. It was almost as if she wanted everyone to see.

"That's enough!" said her mother sternly. "Hush, now. We'll straighten this out at home."

"I will NOT hush! I *hate* Cat!" Olivia stormed.

The baton twirler's little brother dived for her feet. "Look, Mommy!" he piped, holding up a gemstone. The diamond glittered like a comet under the cafeteria's fluorescent lights.

A hush fell over the crowd. Iz grabbed Olivia and hustled her out the door. My father snatched Geoffrey up and followed. Clutching my bassoon case to my chest, I ran after them.

CHAPTER 11

The phone was ringing as we walked in the front door.

"Do you want to tell us what's going on?" my father asked me sternly, ignoring it.

I took a deep breath. I hadn't said a single word in the car on the way home, but obviously it was time to spill the beans. And the toads.

"There's something I haven't told you," I said.

A fat toad plopped onto the living-room rug. Olivia recoiled, screaming. Iz turned pale. My dad sank onto the sofa.

"Oh my," he said weakly.

"Frog!" cried Geoffrey, pulling his finger out of his mouth and pointing at it.

We all turned and stared at him. It was the first new word he'd said in six months.

"Actually, it's a toad," I told him, popping out another one. Somewhere between yesterday morning and now, my little brother had gotten over his fear of amphibians, and of me, because he grabbed his LEGO bucket and chased after the pair of them, yodeling with delight.

My father turned to me. "Honey, why didn't you tell us?"

I lifted a shoulder. Wasn't it obvious? Olivia was dripping diamonds, and I was stuck dribbling toads—why would I want to tell anyone? "I really want to talk to my mom," I mumbled.

"Of course you do," said Iz. "And I'm going to call Dr. Douglass right away."

"I don't think there's a cure for spontaneous toad eruptions," I told her miserably, erupting once again.

"Spontaneous what?" asked my dad, eyeing the creatures at my feet.

"Toad eruptions. That's what A.J. calls, uh . . ." My voice trailed off, although the toads didn't.

"Busted!" said Olivia triumphantly. An orange dahlia blazed from her lips like fireworks on the Fourth of July.

The stern look returned to my father's face. "You told *A.J.* about this?"

Squirming inside, I nodded. Much as I hated to admit it, I'd done exactly what my stepsister did—broke my promise. "Sorry," I replied, avoiding his disappointed gaze. "But Olivia did it again too! I caught her talking to Piper in the girls' bathroom right before the talent show."

"Liar!" screeched Olivia, turning scarlet. What looked like a piece of broken glass flew from her mouth and clinked to the floor. Iz bent down automatically to pick it up. She gasped as she saw the size of the pear-shaped diamond.

"Call Rani and Juliet if you don't believe me," I retorted.

"They saw the tulips too. We caught her in the act!"

Our little brother was having a field day by this time, racing around the living room scooping toads into his LEGO bucket. At least someone was having fun.

"Great," said my father, sighing deeply. "Just great. I can't believe you girls went back on your word! I'm ashamed of you both."

I hung my head again. Across the room Olivia had the grace to do the same.

"There's nothing to be done for it now," said Iz crisply. "It would seem the cat is out of the bag." She glanced down at the gem she was holding, then over at Geoffrey's bucket. "Make that diamonds—and toads." She looked at my father. "Tim, we have a problem here. A big problem. After what happened tonight, there's no way the girls can go back to school. Not until we find a cure."

He nodded. "Yeah, I know."

Olivia and I stared at each other in horror. Did that mean we were stuck here in the house together indefinitely?

"I really, really want to talk to my mom," I said.

Iz nodded. "Let's see, it's nearly nine here, which means she's somewhere over, hang on, let me check." She dashed into the kitchen to consult the map on the wall, then reappeared. "Somewhere over Iceland, I'd estimate. Which means it's the middle of the night on the space station."

"Can I wake her up?" I pleaded. "Please?"

My father shook his head. "You've waited this long, you can wait until morning to talk to her," he told me. "Send her an e-mail instead. Tell her everything, Cat. That way she'll be up to speed when you call her tomorrow."

I nodded and headed into his study, closing the door behind me. My fingers hovered over the keyboard as I thought about how to explain what had happened.

Dear Mom, I began finally. *Something really strange has happened to me. . . .*

When I finished, I pressed send. I had no idea what my mother would make of my e-mail. Would she think I was crazy? Or that it was some elaborate joke? It sure sounded like one. This was the stuff of supermarket tabloid headlines: STEPSISTERS IN PORTLAND, OREGON, SPOUT DIAMONDS AND TOADS WHEN THEY SPEAK!

The rest of my family was in the living room exactly where I'd left them. Geoffrey had managed to capture all the toads and was crooning to them as they battered against the lid of the LEGO bucket, struggling to escape. It seemed my little brother finally had some pets. My father and Iz were talking quietly together while Olivia watched TV.

I slumped onto the sofa beside her. All of a sudden there was a knock at the front door.

"Who could that be at this hour?" asked Iz.

My father crossed to the front hall and opened the door. There was a blinding flash, and a microphone was thrust into his face.

"Is this the house where the diamond girl lives?" asked a woman. Her face looked familiar, but I couldn't quite place it.

"Oh my goodness," whispered Iz next to me. I turned, and glancing over her shoulder, I saw the same woman on our TV screen. Now I knew where I'd seen her before—she was a television reporter.

Olivia was staring at the screen, mesmerized. Alongside

the reporter, my father's surprised face looked back at us. We were watching him on live TV. *They were outside our house filming this.*

Iz leaped to her feet. "For heaven's sake, shut the door, Tim!"

We heard the sentence in stereo as the TV news cameras picked it up and broadcast it back to us.

Olivia's mouth dropped open.

The reporter spotted her and craned her neck for a better view. "Is that her?" she asked, sounding excited. "Is that the diamond girl?"

"No comment," my father said, and slammed the door in her face.

CHAPTER 12

The four of us huddled on the sofa, staring at the TV screen. Geoffrey was oblivious, of course, focused only on his bucket of toads, but the rest of us couldn't tear ourselves away. The TV crew had caught everything that had just happened and was now filming the reporter as she stood on our front doorstep.

"Stay tuned for more of this breaking story," she announced solemnly. "Up next: an eyewitness report from tonight's astounding incident at Hawk Creek Middle School. Was it really a diamond or wasn't it?"

"I can't believe this is happening!" moaned Iz. "This is exactly what I've been worried about."

"Do you think I'll get to be on TV?" asked Olivia hopefully.

I turned and stared at her. My stepsister was actually *enjoying* this! I knew she liked being the center of attention, but this was different. Didn't she know what this could mean, not only for her, but for our entire family? Hadn't she seen what happened to celebrities who were hounded to pieces by the paparazzi?

Worse than that, though, when people got wind of the valuable stuff Olivia was producing, there was bound to be trouble. Had she already forgotten the lab assistant at the hospital who'd tried to pocket one of her diamonds?

I shook my head in disgust. This was all just a game to her—like one of her stupid Barbie dioramas. "Photo Shoot Barbie," maybe, or "Magazine Cover Barbie." With Olivia as the star, of course, posing for the camera. She was completely clueless!

The phone in my dad's office started to ring. So did the cell phone in Iz's messenger bag on the table in the hall, and so did the one in the pocket of my dad's pants. He pulled it out and glanced at it. "Seattle number," he said, frowning. "More reporters, probably. The wire service must have picked up the story."

Iz ran around the bottom floor of our house, turning off the lights and closing all the curtains and shades. Once the living room was dark, she peeked out through a crack in one of the blinds.

"The news van is still parked at the foot of the driveway!" she fretted. "They're not going away."

"They'll get bored soon enough," my father assured her. "Especially when all they get from us is 'No comment.'"

But the news media wasn't ready to let up, and the phones rang off the hook the whole time Olivia and Geoffrey and I were getting ready for bed. Finally my dad called the police to complain, then unplugged the phones and shut off all the cell phones too.

By the time the ten o'clock news came on, the story had gone national. The stone that the little kid had picked up in the cafeteria had been verified as a diamond, and Olivia was a sensation, her school picture plastered over all the channels.

"I hate that picture," she grumbled as a narcissus fell from her lips to the living-room coffee table. "My hair is awful. I look stupid."

"That's because you are stupid," I told her as she scooched down the sofa away from me—and the inevitable toads. I moved closer, just to spite her. "Don't you get it? This is not a good thing, Olivia. Somebody's going to want those diamonds, just like that guy at the hospital. They're going to come for you."

"That's enough of that," Iz said sternly, swatting at the toads with an afghan. "Time for bed."

But I noticed she made sure to lock all the windows and doors before following us upstairs.

There was another uproar, though, when Olivia flat-out refused to share a bedroom with me.

"Be reasonable, sweetheart," said Iz. She looked exhausted; it had been a very long day.

"What if Cat talks in her sleep?" Olivia protested amid a fretful flurry of forsythia. "I hate toads!"

"It's not like I'm doing it on purpose!" I retorted, but I couldn't help smirking as the resulting toad hopped down from my bed and over to her side of the room.

Olivia shrieked and flung one of her pillows at it and the other at me. "I hate you!"

"I hate you, too!" I shouted back.

"Girls!" said Iz. Our fight had woken Geoffrey, who trailed

into our room rubbing his eyes. He lit up when he saw the toad-covered floor.

"Frog!" he shouted happily, chasing after them.

"Tim!" called Iz. "Some help in here, please?"

While my dad put the toads outside and Geoffrey back to bed, Iz tried to calm Olivia down. It wasn't any use. The end result was that I slept on a sleeping bag in my little brother's room, which was fine with me. I was as glad to be away from Olivia for the night as she was to be away from me. And as for Geoffrey's snoring, well, that's what earplugs were for, right?

CHAPTER 13

I woke up the next morning feeling cold and soggy. The window was wide open and it was pouring rain outside. My sleeping bag was soaked.

It was my own fault that I'd gotten wet; I'd opened the window last night to get some fresh air before crawling into my sleeping bag. Geoffrey's room can turn into a smelly little bear den sometimes, what with the snoring and the diaper and the blanket and all.

I wriggled free and splashed across the rain-spattered floor, shivering as I shut the window. I stood there for a moment, watching Connor Dixon—he was huddled on his back lawn under an umbrella, waiting for Peanut to hurry up and go—then turned around, frowning. The room was oddly quiet.

"Geoffrey?" I said, popping out my earplugs and a toad. There was no response. Picking up the toad, I squinted at the clock across the room on his bedside table. It was 5:30 a.m.—way early for my little brother to be up. Like Iz, he isn't a

morning person, and *Robo Rooster* didn't start for a while yet.
Still, he must have gotten up for some reason, as the covers
on the bed were thrown back. He was probably downstairs,
waiting in front of the TV.

I figured I'd go downstairs and check on him, then check
to see if my mother had e-mailed me back. I pulled on my
robe and slippers—dry, fortunately, since I'd thrown them on
the armchair over by the bookcase, away from the window—
then went downstairs, pausing on the landing to peer out
the stained-glass window. A sheriff's car was parked in our
driveway, and the single news van from last night had grown
to an entire fleet. The whole street, in fact, was clogged with
reporters and cameras.

I glanced down at the creature that was struggling in my
hand. This news story was not going away, any more than my
toads were.

I needed to talk to my mother.

The smell of coffee and bacon wafted up from the kitchen,
where my early-bird dad was rattling around making breakfast. Geoffrey was probably in there with him; bacon is his
favorite food, and the aroma would have drawn him like a
magnet. My stomach rumbled; I was hungry too. I wanted to
check my e-mail first, though, so I crossed the front hall to
my father's study, closing the door behind me.

My mother had gotten my message. Her reply was short
and sweet:

> *Look for the envelope inside the lining of your suitcase,*
> *and call me after you read the letter it contains.*

I sat there staring at the computer screen for a moment,
surprised and intrigued by her response. Then I tiptoed back

upstairs to find that Olivia had locked our bedroom door. This was nothing new—she used to do it all the time when we were little. Fortunately, being a 1912 bungalow, Dad and Iz's Northwest Honeymoon Cottage has the original doors, with the original old-fashioned keyholes under the handles. I'd squirreled away a spare key years ago, when my stepsister had tried this trick before. I crept down the hall to the bathroom and lifted a loose corner of wallpaper in the bottom cupboard, behind where Iz stored the toilet paper.

Yep, the key was still there.

Unlocking the door as quietly as I could, I slipped into our bedroom, squelched the urge to pop a toad under my still-sleeping stepsister's covers, and knelt on the floor by my bed. I slid my suitcase from underneath it, pulled out the clothes still piled inside, and started prodding at the lining.

Top? Nothing. Sides? Nothing there, either, nor on the bottom. Hmmm. Had I understood my mother's instruction correctly? My fingers worked across the surface of the bottom lining again and stumbled over an almost-imperceptible thickness. That had to be it. I tugged at a small zipper tucked beneath a pleat in the lining and slid my fingers inside. They closed on an envelope.

Pulling it out, I sat back on my heels and looked at it. There were words emblazoned in bright red marker across the front:

OPEN ONLY IN CASE OF EMERGENCY!

This whole thing was getting more bizarre by the moment. But if anything qualified as an emergency, this did.

I stuffed my clothes into the suitcase again and shoved it back under my bed, then left the room, shutting the door quietly behind me. I relocked it and returned the spare key to its hiding place, then started downstairs. When I reached the landing, I hesitated. I wasn't ready for anyone else to know about the envelope yet. My instincts told me the contents were important, and I wanted to be alone when I read whatever was inside.

There was only one place to go: the attic. I spun around and ran back up the steps, then on to the door at the far end of the hall. By the time I reached the top of the attic stairs, my heart was pounding like crazy. What could possibly be in this envelope that had caused my mother to hide it so carefully?

I crossed to the trunk by the front window, tugging it slightly to one side so as not to be seen by the reporters below. I peeked out at the street to check on them; they were still there, of course. People were starting to emerge from their cars and vans, yawning and stretching. It would stink to work for a magazine or newspaper that made you sleep in your car outside someone's house, hoping to snag a story.

I sat down and slid my fingernail under the envelope's flap. Then I took out the letter and began to read:

Dear Cat,

If you're reading this, then something odd has happened in your life.

You can say that again, I thought, and continued:

There's something I've been meaning to tell you, but my assignment came up so quickly that I

*didn't get the chance. I'd planned to talk to
you about it during our special birthday trip.
Normally, the way it works in our family is that
this information is passed along to the eldest
daughter when she turns 12. I decided it would
be okay to wait until my return, but if you're
reading this now, that's probably not the case,
and I miscalculated. There's no way to prepare
you for this, so I'll just say it bluntly: Great-Aunt
Abyssinia isn't really your great-aunt.*

My forehead wrinkled. What did Great-Aunt Aby have to
do with any of this?

She's your fairy godmother.

My mouth dropped open. "No way," I whispered, heedless of the toad that popped out. It squatted next to me, blinking in surprise.

*She was mine when I was your age, and my
mother's before me, and her mother's before her.
In fact, Abyssinia has been with our family
for several centuries now. She's a most faithful
servant, but she does get in a muddle sometimes.
And occasionally more than a muddle, sometimes
a downright mess. I hope you're not in the middle
of a muddly mess, sweetheart, but if you're
reading this, you probably are, so you need to*

*find Abyssinia right away and see if she can set
things to rights again.*

All my love,

Mom

I stared at the letter. Great-Aunt Abyssinia was a *fairy god-mother*? And more specifically, *my* fairy godmother?

Yeah, right.

It was a joke, obviously. I laughed out loud at the absurdity of the idea. Then I looked at the toad that had just plunked down on the trunk beside the other one, and my laughter faded.

The toads were just as absurd, and they were real. Could my mother be telling me the truth?

No way. Fairy godmothers didn't exist. And even if they did, they belonged to princesses in fairy tales, not to girls like me.

I stood up and jammed the letter and envelope into the pocket of my bathrobe. I didn't care what time it was on the space station, my mother and I needed to talk. She had some major explaining to do.

I sped back downstairs into my father's study and fished around in the bottom drawer of his desk, where I'd seen Iz stash our cell phones last night. The second I had a dial tone, I punched in the same emergency number I'd called last week.

My mother must have left word with the operator at NASA to expect a call from me, because this time they put me straight through without any chitchat.

"Cat?" My mother's voice was all echoey and distant, like she was at the bottom of a deep well.

"Mom!" I burst out. "What's going on? Is this true?"

There was a long pause.

"Toads, huh?" she said finally.

"Everywhere!" I replied miserably, looking at the trio that stared back at me from my father's desk.

"Well, I suppose it could have been worse."

"What do you mean, 'it could have been worse'?" I demanded, fighting back angry tears. "And what do you mean about Great-Aunt Abyssinia being my—"

"Your FG?" my mother quickly said. "Let's just use that for now, shall we? Never know who may be listening." Her deep sigh drifted to me from deep space. "Honestly, Cat, I planned to tell you the minute I came home. I realize now that I should have stuck to the usual schedule."

"You mean my birthday?"

"Uh-huh."

I was quiet for a few seconds, thinking back to the birthday party the D'Angelos had thrown for me the day after my mother blasted off. There'd been no mention of a fairy godmother. Just a trip to Splashworld and a cake. Well, that and a pile of presents, including the iPod from Dad and Iz and the necklace from my mother. "So this is for real, then?"

"'Fraid so."

"Does Dad know?"

"Not really. I mean, he knows there's something a little odd about Abyssinia. But has her actual, uh, title ever crossed my lips when we discussed her? No."

There was so much I wanted to ask! "But why . . . I mean who . . . what . . . ," I stammered as I tried to frame my questions. I sighed. "Did you get toads the first time too?"

She laughed. "Oh no, it was much worse than that. Let's just say that I had a close encounter of the feathered kind."

"What? Seriously?"

"Yep. All over."

I tried to imagine my mother covered in feathers. It was a bit of a stretch.

"I was a late bloomer," she went on to explain. "I was always fretting about my looks. Great-Aunt Aby was trying to teach me a lesson about patience and about not being obsessed with my outward appearance—you know, 'Beauty is as beauty does' and all that. Our family's FG is all about building character, boosting self-reliance, and that sort of thing."

I frowned. What the heck was my mother talking about?

"At any rate," she continued, "she muddled things up."

"No kidding," I said. "So this muddling-things-up stuff— wait a minute, are you telling me I have a defective fai—FG?"

"I don't know if I'd go so far as to call Abyssinia *defective*," my mother replied. "She always means well. Occupationally challenged, perhaps."

I laughed bitterly, then jumped, startled, as a toad fell onto my lap. It was just my luck to get stuck with an "occupationally challenged" fairy godmother.

"Abyssinia's heart is in the right place, Cat," my mother went on. "She's just trying to teach you a life lesson, darling."

"I thought it was an FG's job to, you know, wave a wand or something and make all your dreams come true."

My mother laughed again. "Sorry, honey, it may work that way in the movies, but not for the MacLeods."

"Great," I said morosely. "And speaking of our family, who exactly are we? And how come we get an FG?"

My mother's voice dropped to a whisper. "That part really will have to wait, sweetheart. We'll have plenty of time to chat when I get back to Houston."

I needed answers now, not three months from now. "Can you at least tell me what kind of a life lesson involves toads?"

"Well, what did you and Great-Aunt Aby discuss that day she came to visit?"

I shrugged, trying to remember. "Olivia, mostly, I guess."

"Ah. And how is your stepsister, anyway?"

"A whole lot happier with what happened to her than I am with what happened to me," I said bitterly. "But you should see our front yard! It's like a zoo out there—the street is crawling with reporters and camera crews!"

"I see," she said. "This is escalating quickly. There's really only one thing to do, and that's to find Great-Aunt Aby right away."

"How the heck am I supposed to do that?" I protested, swatting at the toads that by now threatened to overrun not only my father's desk, but also the chair and the floor. I'd have to bring Geoffrey and his LEGO bucket in here for cleanup duty. "She doesn't have a cell phone, and she's on the loose in some national park someplace."

"Hang on a sec, I can help with that," my mother replied.

Seconds ticked by. I heard the thump of feet on the floor above me. Iz must be awake.

"Okay," said my mother, returning to the phone. "She's in the redwoods."

"How the heck do you know that?"

"Um, the FGPS. It's the you-know-who positioning system. I have the transceiver up here with me—I was planning to give it to you on our mystery trip, along with the necklace."

"You're tracking Great-Aunt Aby by *satellite*?"

My mother laughed. "It's the only way to keep tabs on a free spirit like Abyssinia."

"Is that how you got through to her before? To send her to see me, I mean?"

"Uh-huh. It's a kind of combination GPS tracker and walkie-talkie."

"Can't you just call her again, then, or whatever it is you do—why do I have to go find her?"

My mother sighed. "I tried. The reception doesn't always work well when the RV's in remote places."

Like national parks? I thought. Great. Not helpful, considering that was where Great-Aunt Aby spent half her time.

"But it may be that I'm just getting a weak signal because of the space station's position," she continued. "You should be able to find her eventually."

"How? You've got the transceiver! Fat lot of good it's going to do me up there."

My mother hesitated, then dropped her voice to a whisper. "I've thought about that, and there might be a way to patch you through from Earth. The only thing is, we'd have to, uh, go around certain protocols—"

"You mean you don't want NASA to find out we're linking their satellite to it."

"Uh, exactly."

"Let me call A.J. and see what he can do."

"Good idea." My mother knows A.J. almost as well as I do, and certainly well enough to know that if anybody could get her scheme to work, he could. "Just remember, you don't need to tell him everything. The FG part, I mean. Tell him you need to find your great-aunt and that your mother installed a tracking device on her RV, just in case. Because she's elderly."

"You think he'll buy that?"

"Why not? It's logical. Well, sort of. Listen, Cat, *do not* tell him—or anyone else, for that matter—about Great-Aunt Abyssinia's true identity. You've got to trust me on this. If you do, people will think the cheese slid off your cracker."

She had a point.

I promised, and she promised to e-mail me all the technical information that A.J. would need, and we hung up. I sat by the computer until her e-mail came through, then forwarded it to A.J., along with the explanation my mother had suggested as to why I needed the satellite link.

And then I went back upstairs to get dressed and discovered there were worse things than toads.

Far, far worse.

CHAPTER 14

I spotted it the minute I walked through the door of my little brother's room, looking for my sneakers. How could I have missed it before?

A sheet of paper was pinned to his pillow. I crossed the room and leaned down for a closer look.

"Dad!" I screamed, launching a toad halfway across the room.

The terror in my voice brought him up the stairs at a run. Iz was right behind him. Shaking, I pointed to the note.

A single sentence had been written in big block letters with one of Geoffrey's crayons:

**YOU GET YOUR BOY BACK WHEN WE
GET THE DIAMOND GIRL!**

The color drained from my stepmother's face.

Olivia came in just then, blinking sleepily. "What's going on?"

"Geoffrey has been kidnapped, that's what!" I shouted, spraying the room with toads. "It's all your fault—you should have kept your mouth shut at the talent show!"

"You were the one sleeping in here with him!" she shouted back, spattering me with a hail of thistles. "You should have stopped them!"

"I had my earplugs in!" I protested, then sat down on the edge of Geoffrey's bed, stricken. Olivia was right. It didn't matter, I still should have heard the intruders.

"I'm going downstairs to tell the police," Iz said, and bolted from the room.

"They must have come through the window," I told my father. "I left it open last night. It gets stinky in here sometimes, you know?" My voice cracked as I picked up my little brother's blanket, which the kidnappers had left behind. I gulped back a sob, almost choking on a toad in the process.

"It's not your fault, Cat," he said tersely, crossing the room in two strides. "Yours either, Olivia."

I joined him at the window and we both leaned out. There was no trace of my little brother, or anyone else for that matter. Had the kidnappers parachuted in? How had they managed to avoid the media circus out front?

"Forest Park," my dad muttered, casting an eye at the thick tangle of undergrowth that bordered our property. There was no path through it, but an ambitious bushwhacker could make his or her way to our backyard from the main trail at the end of our street.

"They wouldn't have wanted to be seen, obviously," he added. "They just went for the first open window. But why take Geoffrey if they were after—"

"Me?" said Olivia.

My father and I pulled our heads back in and turned to see tears streaming down my stepsister's cheeks. My dad was at her side in an instant.

"Honey, it's going to be all right," he said gently.

Olivia shook her head vehemently, shredding the camellia petals that emerged with her words. "No," she said. "Cat's right—it's my fault. I locked my door last night. To keep her out. They would have taken me otherwise. But they took Geoffrey instead."

If there's a single good thing about Olivia, it's the fact that, deep down, she loves our little brother as much as I do.

My father pulled her close. "We're going to find him," he said. "You'll see. Let's go downstairs to your mother, okay?"

Iz was just coming back inside. "The sheriff is radioing for backup," she told us. "He said they'll be here in a couple of minutes."

"Good," said my father, putting his arms around her. Iz began to cry.

"What about Great-Aunt Aby?" I blurted out, sending a toad soaring onto the countertop. It had suddenly occurred to me that if my mother was right, and my great-aunt could fix spontaneous toad eruptions, she could probably help us find Geoffrey too.

Iz looked up, wiping her eyes.

"What about her?" my father replied, puzzled.

"I, uh, just thought maybe she could, you know, help. . . ." My words trailed off as a dejected-looking toad joined its neighbor on the countertop. I realize how crazy this must sound, especially since no one but me knew that Great-Aunt Aby was my fairy godmother.

My dad and Iz exchanged a glance. One that meant, *I think the cheese has slid off Cat's cracker.*

Before anyone could say anything, though, Olivia started to wail.

"I want Geoffrey!" she sobbed. "I didn't mean for this to happen!"

As my father and Iz rushed to comfort her, I edged my way out of the room and slipped my cell phone out of my pocket.

Any luck with the link to the space station? I texted to A.J.

Slight delay, he texted back. **Sun spots. Orbital position. Too complicated to explain.**

Hurry, please.

I'm trying! What's going on up there in Portland, anyway? You guys are all over the news.

I tapped furiously on the keypad, telling him about Geoffrey's disappearance.

Whaaaaaaaaa? No way!

Yes way. Please hurry. I really need to find Great-Aunt Aby.

If A.J. sensed a connection between my urgency and the media flap about the diamonds, he didn't question it, and I was just as glad that he didn't. A.J. D'Angelo was my best friend in the whole world, and it was going to be really hard not to confide in him about my great-aunt. But in my heart I knew that my mother was right—the less anyone else knew about the whole fairy godmother thing, the better.

A couple of minutes later the sheriff knocked on the front door. Iz had managed to calm Olivia down in the meantime, and she and my father paused on their way to answer it.

"Cat, honey, let's keep the toads on the down low for now, okay?" said Iz. "Olivia's, um, condition may be public knowledge at this point, unfortunately, but yours isn't, and we need to keep it that way, understand?"

I nodded and mimed zipping my lips.

The sheriff was quickly joined by a squad car from the Portland police, and within the hour our house was swarming with men and women in uniform. Once they heard what had happened, the police brought in the FBI.

"We're always called in on kidnappings," one of the agents explained to my dad and Iz. "And since this is a rather high-profile case"—he glanced over at Olivia, then continued—"we wanted to make sure no, uh, stone was left unturned."

"We appreciate that," said my father.

"I've put in a call to our forensics team," the agent continued. "They'll need to examine the house, the grounds outside, and the ransom note. May I see the note, Mr. Starr?"

My father passed it to him, and the agent read it somberly, then handed it to his female colleague. "Diamond Girl, eh?" he said, looking at Olivia again. "I guess that's what the media is calling you, right?"

Olivia nodded. For the first time since this began, though, she didn't look too happy about it. Geoffrey's disappearance had really shaken her.

The two FBI agents stood there expectantly. So did a trio of policemen. Iz glanced over at Olivia and nodded to her.

My stepsister leaned forward and looked at the closest

agent's badge. "It's nice to meet you, Agent Salgado," she said. "I'm Olivia Haggerty." Fragrant white lilies of the valley tumbled from her lips, along with twin diamonds. They lay on the living-room rug for a moment, twinkling like stars.

With a pang I thought of Geoffrey's LEGO castle. He'd been so thrilled with it!

Iz bent down, picked up the diamonds, and handed one to Agent Salgado, a tall African-American man with glasses and a soft voice, and another to Agent Reynolds, his female colleague. They both had kind faces, and just having them here made me feel a little better already.

"Wow," said Agent Salgado weakly.

Agent Reynolds was speechless.

"Do you understand now what we're dealing with?" my father asked them.

"Not really," replied Agent Salgado, looking dazed. He tapped out a few notes on his computer tablet. Agent Reynolds and the trio of police officers just stared at Olivia, stunned.

Iz finally broke the silence. "How can we best help you get our son back?"

A few minutes later I found myself upstairs in Geoffrey's bedroom.

"Did you happen to notice what time it was when you got up?" asked Agent Reynolds, her pen poised over her notepad.

I scribbled the answer on my own notepad: *5:30 a.m.*

She looked surprised, and I patted my throat and winced. I was getting good at this. "Laryngitis, huh?" she asked.

I nodded.

Agent Salgado pulled his head back in the window. "Looks

to me like there are some holes in the ground below," he reported. "Let's go check."

They all trooped outside in the pouring rain, then came back into the kitchen a few minutes later to report that they'd found a ladder under the back deck, and twin holes in the flower bed directly under Geoffrey's window.

Agent Reynolds wiped the mud from her shoes. She looked like a drowned rat. "The intruders definitely used the ladder to gain access to your son's bedroom," she told Iz and Dad, glancing across the table to where my stepsister was sitting. "We found traces of wet mud on the carpet runner in the hall outside Olivia's bedroom as well. Looks like they may have tried your daughter's door first."

Olivia's face flushed, and she looked like she was going to burst into tears again. She was right, then. They had taken Geoffrey because they couldn't get to her.

"There are footprints across the lawn leading toward the woods," Agent Salgado added. "It's going to be difficult to lift any decent prints in this downpour, but the forensics team should be here any minute to give it a try. We've got search and rescue dogs on the way too." He patted my stepmother's shoulder. "We'll follow up on every lead, ma'am. I know this is difficult, but there's no reason to believe we won't get your son back."

Iz nodded. "Thank you," she said softly.

"We'll be setting up a phone trace too. The kidnappers will likely contact you soon to make arrangements for a handoff."

"You're not going to give me away, are you, Mom?" Olivia asked anxiously.

Fair trade, I thought. I'd swap my stepsister for Geoffrey any day of the week.

"Of course not, darling," Iz reassured her.

At lunchtime the FBI had Chinese food brought in for everyone. Not that we were hungry. I could barely swallow, and it wasn't because of toads.

Afterward, I slipped up to the attic again to text A.J.

Any luck?

Just got it up and running. Found ur great-aunt. She's at Redwood National Park. What next?

Not sure, I told him. Will call when I figure it out.

I made sure my cell phone was silenced—the last thing I wanted was for Dad or Iz to discover that I'd swiped it back—then tucked it into my pocket and went slowly downstairs. How on earth was I supposed to get to the redwoods? Weren't they in California or something?

Cat Starr, Toad Huntress, was fresh out of ideas.

CHAPTER 15

The day dragged on with no word yet from the kidnappers.

Police officers and federal agents came and went as they set up a command station and tested the equipment they'd be using to trace all incoming calls. They were trying to keep the kidnapping under wraps, but the reporters were getting restless, what with all the activity. Finally Agent Salgado went outside and made a vague statement, telling them that due to the sensitive nature of the events of the last twenty-four hours, his office had been called in to offer assistance.

"I think that will buy us some time," he said to my father and stepmother when he came back inside. "They'll assume I was talking about Diam—uh, Olivia. No need for them to know about your son yet."

Iz nodded. She looked drained and pale. "Thank you," she said, and then sent me and Olivia upstairs to our room for the afternoon to shield us from prying eyes. People weren't snooping, really, but they couldn't help themselves; they were curious about Diamond Girl.

We were supposed to be doing our homework, but I'd left my backpack in the kitchen and didn't feel like going down to get it. I doubted we'd be returning to school anytime soon anyway—maybe never—unless I could somehow figure out a way to get to Great-Aunt Aby.

Across the room Olivia took out her glue gun, flipped on the radio, and started another diorama. I needed something to take my mind off everything too. My gaze wandered over to my bassoon case, which had been sitting at the foot of my bed ever since Tuesday night's fiasco. Practicing it was out of the question, and at this rate I might have to kiss my dream of playing with a symphony orchestra good-bye too. No one was likely to hire a toad-spouting bassoonist. Not unless some composer out there got busy writing the Amphibian Concerto.

I stuck my earbuds in and cranked up the Bach, then lost myself in a book.

Olivia slipped out a little while later to use the bathroom, which we now had to share not only with our whole family, but also half the Portland police force plus the FBI. I waited until she was safely down the hall, then sneaked over to her bed to take a look at her latest creation. Call it morbid fascination on my part, but I had to see what she'd come up with this time, now that she knew about the toads.

My stepsister surprised me for once. The Skipper-who-was-me was nowhere in sight. Instead, Olivia had made an exact replica of Geoffrey's room.

Well, sort of. Geoffrey's room if it were suddenly

transformed into Ali Baba's cave, maybe, or transplanted to Broadway.

The furniture was all there—his bed and the armchair in the corner and his bookcase, too, complete with little titles written on the construction paper books. She'd re-created the zoo mural, and there was even a LEGO castle in the middle of the floor. But in Olivia's version of Geoffrey's room everything sparkled. The walls sparkled; the ceiling sparkled; the windows and doors sparkled; the eyes of the zoo animals in the mural sparkled. There were diamonds glued to everything. It was dazzling.

While I was plugged into my iPod reading, she must have been talking up a storm or singing along to the radio or something to have produced so many gems. I frowned. But where were the flowers? There should be flowers around here too somewhere. I glanced around to see what she'd done with them and spotted a lumpy-looking pillowcase by the bed. Sure enough, she'd stuffed them inside.

Turning back to the diorama, I traced the stones on the diorama's floor. She'd even re-created Geoffrey's Traffic Tyme carpet. Something was different, though. Looking closer, I saw that she'd tweaked the design. Instead of multiple lanes there was just one. It looked kind of like an arrow. In fact, it *was* an arrow. A long, shimmering arrow that ran from the tiny open window—the one the kidnappers had climbed through—to Geoffrey's door, which was open, and pointed down the hall to Olivia's door, which was also open. On her door she'd posted a big sign: DIAMOND GIRL THIS WAY!

I sat back on my heels, stunned. I wasn't sure what to think. She'd been truly, genuinely upset this morning. Was

Olivia trying to make things right? Was this diorama her way of saying she was sorry?

Not wanting to get caught spying, I headed back to my side of the room. By the time my stepsister came through the door, I appeared to be deeply engrossed in my book. I pretended to jump when she poked me in the leg, and pulled out an earbud as I lifted my eyebrows questioningly.

She pointed urgently toward the stairs. "I think they just got a call from the kidnappers!" she whispered, showering me with morning glories. Blue. Her favorite color. I took this as a hopeful sign.

I jumped up and followed her out of the room. The two of us crept downstairs to the landing and huddled behind Iz's messenger bag, which was hanging over the banister. From there we had a clear view across the front hall to where my dad was seated at the dining-room table. A knot of FBI agents and police officers were clustered around him. He had the phone on speaker.

"We'll make the exchange at the zoo," said a gravelly voice. "Friday morning, nine o'clock sharp. Bring her to the penguin exhibit."

Olivia elbowed me in the ribs. Friday was the day of our school field trip.

"Don't bring anyone else with you," the gravelly voice continued. "If I get so much as a whiff of a police uniform, the deal is off."

Agent Salgado made a stretching motion with his hands, like he was pulling on a rubber band. He was telling my father to try and keep the conversation going. I figured they must be trying to trace the call.

"Hang on a minute!" protested my dad. "I'm not just going to hand my daughter over to you!"

Stepdaughter, I thought automatically.

"How do I know you even have my son?" he continued. "And how do I know you're going to keep your word?"

The kidnapper gave a short bark of laughter. "What's this world coming to? Doesn't anybody trust anybody anymore? Hey, Geoffrey!"

From somewhere in the background came an answering, "With a G!"

Beside me, Olivia sucked her breath in sharply. Our little brother's voice sounded very small and very far away. Downstairs in the dining room I saw my father reach over and squeeze Iz's hand. "Okay," he said. "Okay. We'll be there."

"Good."

There was a click and the line went dead. The kidnapper had hung up.

Agent Reynolds took off her headphones and shook her head. "Sorry, Mr. Starr. We couldn't quite pin down the location."

"I don't like the idea of using my daughter as bait," said Iz.

"She won't be," Agent Salgado assured her. "We just want to lead the kidnapper to believe that you're willing to make the switch."

Agent Reynolds tapped her notebook thoughtfully. "Why the zoo? Why Friday?"

"I don't know if this has anything to do with it, but that's Field Trip Friday," said Iz. "Half the schools in Portland will be there."

Agent Salgado gave a low whistle. "I think you hit the nail

on the head, ma'am. Smart move on their part. If the place is crawling with kids, it makes our job all the more difficult. Not that we aren't up to it," he added hastily.

"The problem is, we can't alter the schedule and cancel the field trips, or they'll smell a rat," said Agent Reynolds, and her partner nodded.

"I understand," said Iz.

"Please don't worry," Agent Reynolds continued gently. "We'll have agents in place all over, no matter how many people are there. You won't be able to move in that penguin exhibit without bumping into one of ours. I can promise you that your daughter will never for a moment be in harm's way."

Olivia stood up abruptly. I watched her walk back up the stairs, wondering how I'd feel if I were in her shoes. Not so great, I guessed.

The afternoon wore on. The rain, which had stopped sometime before lunch, started up again. Olivia had discarded her diorama and lay on her bed, staring listlessly at the ceiling. I wandered over to our bedroom window, almost feeling sorry for the reporters outside. They looked pretty miserable huddled in their cars and under their umbrellas. Not too sorry, though. They were the ones who'd fueled this whole fire, after all.

As the last shreds of daylight faded, I heard another knock at the front door, and I tiptoed down to the landing again. Olivia bestirred herself to get up and follow me.

"For heaven's sake, now who?" said Iz, sounding irritated.

"I'll get it, Mrs. Starr," said Agent Salgado, crossing to the front door. He opened it a crack and peered out into the gathering darkness. Someone passed him a business card. He looked at it, then turned toward my stepmother. "We'd better let him in," he said. There was a funny expression on his face.

"Tim!" Iz called anxiously, and my father came out of the dining room, where he'd been talking with the FBI agents. He crossed the front hall to join her. I could have reached down and touched his hair, which was starting to thin on top.

The FBI agent opened the door, and a scrawny, nondescript man in glasses and a dark raincoat hurried inside. Agent Salgado closed the door again as an explosion of blinding flashes erupted from the news cameras at the bottom of the driveway.

"What can we do for you, Mr. . . . ?" said Iz.

"Dalton. Dr. Seymour Dalton. Special envoy of the United States government." The man was soft spoken, and there was a twang in his voice that I didn't think was Texas but was probably not too far away. Arkansas, maybe, or Oklahoma.

Wordlessly, Agent Salgado passed the man's business card to my father and Iz. They were standing directly beneath us, and I peered down, just able to make out the address. It was a post office box in Nevada, and below Dr. Dalton's name were printed the words "Senior Scientist, Biological Research Division, Area 51."

"Area Fifty-one?" My father's voice shot up an octave. "You have got to be kidding me. What is this, some kind of cruel joke?" He marched over to the front door. Opening it wide and ignoring the excited buzz from the news media, he jerked his thumb toward the government envoy. "You. Outside. Now."

"Mr. Starr," said Dr. Dalton. "I don't think you understand."

"You might want to hear him out," said Agent Salgado quietly, exchanging a glance with Agent Reynolds.

My father sighed and shut the door. "Fine. What exactly is it that you want?"

"We're very interested in your daughter," said the scientist. His eyes flicked up to where Olivia was kneeling beside me on the landing. Uh-oh, we'd been spotted. "I'm authorized to take her with me back to Nevada."

"What?" screeched Iz. "Absolutely not! Tim, tell him."

My father nodded. "My wife is right. There is absolutely no way we're going to agree to that."

"I'm afraid this isn't a voluntary removal," said Dr. Dalton. I could see the sweat beads forming on his forehead.

"What do you mean it isn't voluntary?" My dad's eyes narrowed.

"What I mean is that the government has the legal right to remove your daughter, although I'd rather have your permission, of course."

"Nonsense," said my father. "I'm calling my lawyer."

Dr. Dalton snapped open his briefcase and pulled out a thick document. "You do that, Mr. Starr," he said, handing it to him. "Be sure that your lawyer looks this over. He or she will want to pay close attention to page three hundred twelve, article seventy-six. The one about obstructing an authorized federal envoy."

My father didn't even bother to look at it, he just threw it down on the hall table. "I don't care what you or any piece of paper says, my daughter isn't going anywhere with you."

Stepdaughter, I thought again.

Agent Salgado picked up the document and turned to a

page at the back, then gave a deep sigh. "I'm afraid he's right, Mr. Starr. Dr. Dalton does have the authority to take Olivia into custody."

"Over my dead body," said my father flatly.

"I'm sure that won't be necessary," said the government scientist with an uneasy chuckle. "I promise you she won't come to any harm, and we'll have her back to you safely in a matter of months."

"Months!" wailed Olivia, suddenly leaping to her feet. "Mom! Don't make me go!"

A handful of zinnias quivered over the banister to the floor of the front hall. Dr. Dalton bent down and scooped them up.

My stepsister looked genuinely frightened, and I couldn't help feeling sorry for her.

At least until she opened her mouth again.

"What about Cat?" she said spitefully. A diamond tumbled from her lips to the hall floor as she pushed the messenger bag aside, exposing my hiding place.

"Olivia!" said Iz, shocked.

The government scientist's eyes lit up at the sight of the bright gem. He bent over to pick it up, then pulled out a jeweler's loupe and examined it more closely. "Of course you can bring your cat," he said absently.

"Not *my* cat—*Cat*!" Olivia said in disgust.

"That's enough!" Iz said sternly, shaking her head in warning.

Dr. Dalton looked up at Olivia and blinked. "Who's Cat?"

My stepsister pointed to me.

The government agent's unblinking gaze shifted in my

direction. "Why would we want to bring her, too?" he asked as I shrank back.

"Because she—" Olivia began.

"Olivia Jean!" thundered her mother in a tone that meant business.

Olivia hesitated, then mumbled, "Nothing. Never mind."

Dr. Dalton stared up at me, his glasses reflecting the light of the front hall chandelier. A ripple of fear shuddered through me. No way was I going anywhere with him, ever.

It was time to take matters into my own hands.

Reaching into Iz's messenger bag, I felt around for the velvet drawstring pouch that contained Olivia's accumulated gems. My fingers closed on it just as Dr. Dalton started up the stairs.

"Oh, no you don't," said my father, moving to block him. Iz ran to join the barricade.

I stood up and gave a sharp whistle. All eyes in the house turned toward me as I opened the drawstring, then leaned over the bannister and emptied the pouch.

The diamonds fell in a bright stream, tumbling and glint-ing in the light of the hallway lamp like a dazzling waterfall. I caught a glimpse of Olivia's silver "Sisters are forever friends" ring among them.

Pandemonium struck. Every FBI agent and police officer present fell to his or her knees, scrambling frantically for the glittering stones, just as I knew they would.

Dr. Dalton turned away from the staircase and joined them. My father and Iz watched, stunned.

Time to go!

I grabbed Olivia by the hand and dragged her down the

rest of the stairs and into the kitchen. My backpack was still on the bench where I'd left it when I got home from school yesterday. I slung it over my shoulder, slipped my father's rain poncho from its hook by the back door, and fled with my stepsister into the darkness.

CHAPTER 16

"What do you think you're doing?" whispered Olivia furiously as she struggled to tug her hand out of my grasp. "It's pouring rain out here!"

I gripped her more tightly as I dragged her across the lawn. My stepsister might be bigger than me, but I was more determined. "Trying to save your life, you moron," I whispered back, ducking under the rhododendron. "Do you want to end up in some zoo exhibit?"

"What are you talking about?" She glared at me as we squatted in the shrub's branches.

I pulled the poncho over us, hoping it would help conceal us from the searchers who I knew would soon appear. "Area Fifty-one, that's what!"

My stepsister looked at me blankly.

"Are you telling me you've never heard of it?" I said in astonishment, ejecting toads right and left. "Don't you ever watch science fiction movies? It's where the government keeps aliens and UFOs and stuff. That's why Dad was so worked up."

Olivia snorted. "Yeah, right. There are no such things as UFOs."

I pointed silently at the ground in front of us, which was covered with diamonds, toads, and enough flowers to open a florist shop. "There's no such thing as this, either," I reminded her.

Olivia flapped an edge of the poncho at the toads to scatter them. She snorted again, but it was an uncertain kind of snort.

"Fine then, don't believe me." I jerked my chin toward the back door, which had just flown open. "Go on, go ahead back inside. I'm sure Dr. Dalton will be delighted to see you."

Olivia fell silent. The lights by the back door came on, and we watched as the government scientist strode onto the deck. My father and Iz and the two FBI agents were right behind him.

"They can't have gone far," said Dr. Dalton, scanning the yard. Fortunately, the pool of light by the deck didn't reach as far as the rhododendron bush where we were hiding. "We have to find them!"

"Don't make a sound," I whispered to Olivia as another pair of toads fell from my lips. "Not unless you want to spend the rest of your life as a biology experiment."

She hesitated, then nodded.

Agent Salgado stepped out onto the lawn. "We're going to need a flashlight," he told his colleague, peering into the darkness.

"There's one in the car," Agent Reynolds replied, and holding her raincoat over her head, she cut around the corner of the house toward the driveway.

Agent Salgado and Dr. Dalton started across the grass. I could hear their shoes squishing into the lawn. I looked over at Olivia and pressed my finger against my lips.

"Awful lot of footprints out here," grumbled the government scientist as Agent Reynolds reappeared with two flashlights.

"That's because an awful lot of people have been working this case," she snapped. "Kidnappers, police, our team, and as if that wasn't enough, now you." Agent Reynolds seemed to hold the same low opinion of Area 51 as my father did. She handed a flashlight to Dr. Dalton. He pointed it across the yard toward the Dixons' house.

"It's hard to see what's what," he complained.

Thank goodness, I thought.

Iz watched from the deck as the FBI agents and Dr. Dalton fanned out across the yard. My father trailed behind the government scientist. As they moved closer toward the rhododendron, Olivia squeezed her eyes shut. I held my breath as Dr. Dalton came to a stop right in front of us. I could have reached out and touched his shoe.

Croak.

I stiffened.

"What was that?" cried Dr. Dalton, swinging his flashlight wildly. "Did you hear something?"

"This is Oregon," my father replied, sounding disgusted. "We have frogs."

If anyone knows the difference between a frog and a toad, it's my father. He was sending us a message—he knew we were here!

"Oh, right," said the government scientist, with another forced chuckle. "All this water. I forgot."

"I'm going back inside," Iz called from the deck. "Someone needs to stay by the phone in case the kidnappers call again."

"We'll be right there, honey," my father called back.

Agent Salgado squelched over to join him. "Mr. Starr, do you have any idea which direction the girls may have headed?"

"Not really," my father replied, walking slowly away from the bush where we were hiding. I couldn't be sure, but I thought he was leading them away from our hiding spot. "They both know the Wildwood Trail fairly well. I'd start there."

He was sending us another message! We had to stay away from obvious places like Forest Park and the Wildwood Trail.

"Good idea," the FBI agent said. "I'll organize a grid search. They can't have gotten too far."

He jogged back across the lawn to the house. My dad and Dr. Dalton followed at a slower pace in his wake. I waited until the door had closed behind them, then turned to Olivia. "We're going to need some help," I whispered, brushing away the inevitable toad. I pulled my cell phone out of my pocket.

"No fair!" said Olivia when she spotted it. "I want to call Piper."

"Absolutely not," I said, powering it off. "Besides, I can't use it now anyway. The first thing the FBI will do is track our cell phones."

"How do you know this stuff?"

"I watch a lot of TV."

Olivia regarded me. "Why are you doing this?" she whispered. "You don't even like me."

"True," I replied evenly. "But I do like Geoffrey, and if

you disappear to some zoo cage in Nevada, we may lose our chance at getting him back."

My stepsister fell silent again. "Do you have a plan?" she asked finally.

"No, I'm making this up as I go along. In music it's called improvising." I grabbed Olivia's hand again. "Come on, we've got to keep moving. They'll be back in a minute."

We crawled cautiously out from under the rhododendron, taking care not to step on any toads. Keeping to the shadows, we made our way over to the Dixons' backyard.

"Stay here," I told Olivia, shoving her under their deck. "I'll be back in a sec." I grabbed a pebble and flung it up at Connor's window. At least, I assumed it was Connor's, since I could hear saxophone scales coming from it. If he kept practicing like that, he might eventually produce something worth listening to.

There was no response.

I flung another one.

Still nothing.

C'mon, Connor! I willed him to hear me as I threw one more. This time a face appeared, frowning. He looked out, then opened the window and stuck his head through, looking around suspiciously.

"Hey!" I whispered, making sure to stay out of range of the back porch light. I didn't want the toads to alarm him.

"Who is it?" he demanded.

"Shhhh!" I replied. "It's Cat and Olivia. We're in trouble and we need your help."

"Trying to evade those stupid reporters? Man, what a pain!"

"Something like that."

"Hang on," he said. "I'll be down in a minute."

I fished my stepsister out of her hiding place. "You're going to have to do the talking," I told her. "Unless he's been living under a rock for the past twenty-four hours, he already knows about the flowers and stuff, but the toads might freak him out."

"They freak me out," she retorted.

"Shut up."

"You shut up!"

I sighed. This was getting us nowhere.

"Oh, all right," Olivia said. "What should I say to him?"

"That he's the man of your dreams and you want to marry him."

"Cat!"

"Sorry—couldn't resist. Tell him about Area Fifty-one—he's a guy, he'll know exactly what it is and why you don't want to go there. Tell him we need to use his cell phone and that we need a place to hide."

"Don't you think this will be one of the first places they'll search?"

She had a good point. "Yeah, so we're not going to hide here for long. I have an idea, but I need to make a phone call first."

Olivia's forehead wrinkled. "I still don't get it," she said. "Where are we going to go? This is the *FBI* we're talking about, Cat. They're gonna find us."

"Maybe," I admitted. "But there's no point making it easy for them." I didn't add that if we could find Great-Aunt Abyssinia first, the rest of this might all go away.

The back door opened and Connor appeared. I gave Olivia a shove. "Be convincing," I told her.

She was. Two minutes later we were holed up in the Dixons' basement.

"You've gotta be really quiet," Connor told us, pointing to the ceiling. "My parents are right upstairs watching TV, and I'm supposed to be up in my room practicing my saxophone and doing homework. If they find out about this, I'll be grounded until I'm thirty."

I nodded vigorously, then mimed talking on the phone.

"Oh yeah, right." He fished his cell phone out of his pocket and handed it to my stepsister.

"Thanks, Connor," Olivia said. She'd barely taken her eyes off him since we came inside. Not that he noticed. He was too fixated on the flowers and sparkling stones that fell from her lips every time she spoke to notice the sappy expression on her face.

Olivia picked up a diamond and handed it to him. "We really, really appreciate your help," she said, showering him with more petals.

"No problem," Connor replied, brushing them away. He turned the gem over, examining it. "Is this thing real?"

Olivia nodded proudly.

"Cool." Connor shoved it in his pocket. "I'm going to leave you guys down here for a few minutes. If my parents don't hear saxophone music soon, they'll get suspicious."

He sneaked upstairs, closing the cellar door behind him. I grabbed the phone away from Olivia and walked over to the laundry area. She trailed behind me as I punched in A.J.'s number. He picked up on the first ring.

"I'm so glad you're there!" I said in relief, the words tumbling out of me. So did a couple of toads, which I scooped up and stuffed in the laundry hamper. "I'm in trouble and I need your help."

I put him on speaker so Olivia could hear, and explained as quickly as I could about our escape from Dr. Dalton. She kept chiming in too, and the laundry hamper was nearly full of flowers and toads by the time we were done. Olivia was getting good at snagging the gems, though, which she tucked into the pocket of her jeans.

"I knew it!" A.J. crowed. "I knew there really was an Area Fifty-one!"

I sighed. "That's not the point."

"Okay, okay, I know. But still, Cat—*Area Fifty-one!*"

"A.J.!"

"Sorry." He was quiet for a few seconds, thinking. "The first thing you need to do is find a safe hiding place until I figure out how to get you down to the redwoods."

"Huh?" said Olivia. "Why are we going to the redwoods?"

I ignored her. "What do you have in mind?" I said to my friend.

"Someplace the feds won't think of looking," he replied. "They're gonna be all over the Dixons' house any time now, once the search dogs arrive, so you've got to get out of there."

"I know," I said glumly. "But where can we go?"

"Not a public place—half the city will be looking for you, and with Olivia's face plastered all over the news, you'll be way too easy to spot. Are there any other friends you trust?"

"Piper Philbin," said Olivia.

"Not Piper Philbin," I replied.

"Oooookay," said A.J., sensing this was a bit of a sore point for us. "Any other ideas?"

We thought for a bit.

"Maybe Rani and Rajit," I said finally.

Olivia rolled her eyes. "The dork twins?"

"They're not twins, and they're not dorks," I retorted. "They're talented musicians, and they're my friends."

"Dorks," Olivia muttered, picking petals off her lips. I threw a toad at her and she yelped. "Knock it off!"

"You knock it off!"

"You and your stupid toads!"

"Hey," said A.J. "Don't you think maybe you'd better concentrate on the mission here?"

Olivia and I glared at each other.

"Truce?" I said finally, bending over the hamper. A toad plopped in right on cue. Olivia eyed it with disgust, then nodded grudgingly.

"By the way," said A.J., "you haven't really explained why you're so desperate to find your great-aunt. What's she got to do with all this?"

"You're looking for Great-Aunt Aby?" said Olivia, surprised. "Why?"

This was so not the time to bring up the whole fairy godmother thing. I whooshed out my breath—along with another toad. "Guys," I told them, "you're just going to have to trust me on this one."

CHAPTER 17

"Ouch! You're on my hair!" whispered Olivia, elbowing me sharply.

"Quit it!" I elbowed her back.

"Shut up! You're making toads!"

"You shut up!" I whispered.

"Get those things away from me!" she said between clenched teeth. "I mean it, Cat."

The truce was over.

I fumbled around in the darkness for the escaped toads, then stuffed them into the pillowcase I'd brought with me from Connor's laundry room for just that purpose. Olivia and I were wedged into the trunk of Connor's older brother's car, covered with a blanket. The blanket was itchy and smelled like Peanut, their dog, and there was barely room for one of us under it, let alone both of us plus Connor's saxophone case.

So far I was less than thrilled with Connor's Woodwinds

to the Rescue plan. Not that I'd been able to come up with anything better.

"How else are you going to get over to the Kumars'?" he'd asked, when Olivia explained our predicament. "You can't walk, you can't take a cab—and the bus? No way. All of Portland is looking for you two."

Aidan Dixon's girlfriend lived a few doors down from Rani and Rajit, and since he went over to her house most evenings to hang out anyway, it was easy enough for Connor to concoct a reason to need a ride.

"I'll tell my parents I'm thinking about auditioning for Hawkwinds," he said. "They'll be thrilled—my mom's been bugging me about it. I'll just tell her that the Kumars offered to practice with me."

Getting Rani and Rajit on board wasn't easy at first. Connor really had to lean on them hard to get them to agree to see me. They were still pretty ticked off about the talent show.

"She says if you just let her come over, she can explain," he told them when he called, reading the note I'd prepared. "She promises."

My friends softened when Connor told them about Geoffrey, and by the time he got around to Olivia and Area 51, Rani especially was her old self again. She asked him to put me on the line.

"Cat, are you sure you're not missing a golden opportunity here?" she asked. "Olivia would look pretty good in a cage."

I almost laughed at that. But I wasn't quite ready to reveal my secret.

Afterward, Connor sneaked Olivia and me into the garage, then helped us hide in the trunk of his brother's car. The plan was for us to stay there until Aidan went into his girlfriend's house, then Connor would let us out.

I felt bad about leaving the laundry hamper full of toads in his basement, but I'd explain soon enough and Connor could probably get to them before his mother did. Mrs. Dixon is really nice, and the last thing I wanted was to give her heart failure or something.

Now we were bumping and swerving our away up to Council Crest, where the Kumars lived. I started to feel a little queasy, which reminded me of Geoffrey. I missed him so much, even if he was a little Barf Bucket.

"Is a saxophone really a woodwind?" Olivia whispered into the total darkness of the trunk, her words carrying the sweet scent of hyacinth.

It seemed like a random question, but I knew the way my stepsister's mind worked. She was thinking about Connor and trying to figure out why one of the popular jocks like him would want to team up with band kids like me and Rani and Rajit. To Olivia, even though Connor played the saxophone, he wasn't really a band kid. He was too cool for that.

"Yup," I told her, spitting the toad that accompanied the word into the pillowcase. "It's the only one that's made of brass, though."

"Ohhh," she replied, as if to say, *Well then, that explains it.*

The car swerved again and I was thrown against her. She shoved me away, and I was just getting ready to shove her back when we came to a stop. We both froze as the engine cut off. Connor's plan was about to be put to the test.

A couple of minutes later the trunk opened and he grinned down at us. "Come on," he said. "They're waiting for us inside."

I left the pillowcase full of toads in the car—sorry, Aidan!—and followed Connor across the street, to where Rajit was holding the side door open.

"In here," he said. "Quickly."

We followed him inside and downstairs. His sister and Juliet Rodriguez were waiting for us in the rec room. "Hope you don't mind," said Rani apologetically. "She was working on a social studies project with me when you called."

I shook my head. Having Juliet here wasn't going to make what I had to do any easier, though.

"So what's going on, Cat?" asked Rajit as everyone sat down on the big L-shaped sofa. "You and Olivia are all over the news. There's a huge reward for your return."

"There's something you don't know about me yet," I told them miserably.

Juliet let out a small yip of surprise and Rani blanched as a pair of toads sprang from my mouth to the coffee table.

"Whoa," said Rajit. "That explains a lot about the talent show."

"Cool," Connor said, staring at me in fascination. I blushed. He really was pretty cute, what with those deep blue eyes and that shaggy blond hair. If a person paid attention to that sort of thing.

Of course his reaction made Olivia jealous, and she spent the next couple of minutes talking nonstop, trying to produce as many diamonds as she could.

I picked up four of them and held them out to my friends. "Help yourselves," I told them. "There's more where these came from. Olivia's like a gum ball machine. We can double or triple any reward out there."

Warily eyeing the toads that proliferated with my speech, they each selected a gem.

"So is this thing real?" asked Rajit.

I shrugged. "Why else do you think they want to take her to Area Fifty-one?"

"Is that cool or what?" crowed Connor, who I was beginning to think was a little dim.

"No, it's not cool," I snapped. "Would you want to spend the rest of your life in some lab in the desert, being poked and prodded by scientists?"

Olivia shuddered.

"Uh, no, I guess not," he admitted.

"All right, then."

"We'd better do something about the toads," said Rani, glancing around the rec room. "They're kind of getting out of control." She darted over to a cupboard on the far wall and returned a minute later with an armful of trash bags.

"So how did this happen?" asked Rajit, taking one from her and using it to trap my latest offerings. "The toads, I mean. Well, that and Olivia, too."

I shrugged. "I have no idea," I replied, grabbing a bag and opening it up just in time. I held it under my chin as I talked. "We both just woke up on Monday morning like this. And by the way, I had no idea that it would happen when I played my bassoon, too. Honest. I didn't mean to wreck the talent show."

"Oh, yes you did," said Olivia, spitting something into her hand. Two daffodils and another diamond.

I smirked at her. "Well, your part in it, yes. My part in it, no."

"Catbox," she muttered.

"You deserved it."

"C'mon, you two," said Juliet.

"So what's the plan?" asked Rajit.

"Hang on a sec, I'm going to call my friend A.J.," I told him, pulling Connor's cell phone from my pocket. "He's in on this too." Thirty seconds later I had A.J. on speakerphone.

"This is Mission Control," he intoned in a fake announcer voice.

"Shut up, A.J. You're on speakerphone. I'm here with a bunch of band friends."

"Oh," he said sheepishly, his voice bouncing back to its normal tone. "Hi, band friends!"

"Hi, A.J.!" they chorused back.

"They want to know what the plan is," I told him.

"Do they know about the, uh—"

"Toads?" I asked, bending over the trash bag again. "Yup. And I told them—well, some of them—that Olivia and I have to find my great-aunt and that she's at Redwood National Park."

Rani and Rajit and Juliet looked surprised to hear this.

"I'll explain later," I whispered to them, then continued, "She's still there, right?"

"Hasn't moved an inch," said A.J.

"How does he know that?" asked Juliet.

"We're tracking her on GPS," I replied, stretching the truth. I didn't want to get into the whole NASA connection just yet.

"I still don't get it," said Olivia. "Why are you so obsessed with finding your great-aunt?"

"You just have to trust me," I told her again.

She shook her head. "Nope. I'm not going anywhere with you until you explain what's going on."

I sighed out a toad. "The thing is, Great-Aunt Aby might be able to help us with all this."

"With all what?" asked Rani.

My friends were all looking at me expectantly.

"The toads," I said, gesturing toward the trash bag in front of me. "The diamonds. Geoffrey. Everything."

Olivia laughed. "You're kidding, right? *Your* great-aunt Aby, the crazy, orange-haired giantess—"

"She is not a giantess!"

"I saw her," said Connor. "She kind of is."

I sighed again, scooping up the inevitable toad before it had even hit the coffee table. I knew that I'd promised my mother I wouldn't say anything, but what else was I supposed to do? How else would anyone believe me?

"Here's the thing," I said. "She's not exactly my great-aunt."

"So who is she, then?" asked A.J.

"She's, uh, well—actually, she's my fairy godmother."

The room went dead silent, except for a furious *croak* from the bag I was holding.

"That's it," said Olivia, standing up and brushing off the petals that had accumulated on the legs of her jeans. "I'm going home."

"Olivia!" I protested. "You can't! What about Dr. Dalton?"

"I'd rather deal with him than with a lunatic!" She snorted. "Fairy godmother? Do you think I'm stupid?"

Yes, I thought, but wisely held my tongue. This wasn't the time to pick another fight. "Hold on a sec," I pleaded.

"I know it sounds insane, but will you just think about it for a minute? Is it any crazier than what's happened to us these past few days? I mean, look at us!"

The trash bag I was holding bulged with amphibians. Olivia was ankle-deep in flowers. Connor and Juliet were on their knees picking gems out of the pile. Rani and Rajit were scampering around the room as they tried to collect the toads still on the loose. The Kumars would probably be finding reminders of my visit for weeks to come.

I was suddenly struck by how ridiculous the whole situation was. I started to laugh. Once I started, I couldn't stop, and pretty soon I was howling. I hadn't laughed in days, and it felt good. No, it felt *great*. But laughing wasn't such a smart idea. Each burst produced not just one toad, but a gush of them.

"Cat! Stop!" shrieked Rani, rushing to position her trash bag under the amphibian waterfall. Watching her frantic efforts made me laugh even harder. I laughed so hard that tears sprang to my eyes.

"Please, Cat!" begged Juliet.

I pressed my hands to my mouth, but I couldn't help it, I couldn't hold it—or the toads—in.

Finally Olivia reached across the coffee table and slapped me. Hard.

I stared at her, stunned.

"Sorry," she said, not looking sorry at all.

"I want this to stop," I whispered shakily. "I want to be normal again, and I want Geoffrey back, and my mother said Great-Aunt Aby can help."

"Fine," my stepsister snapped. "Have it your way. We'll go find this stupid fai—this great-aunt of yours."

"Can you give us a hand with the toads first?" asked Rajit. "If my parents come home and see this, they're going to, uh—"

"Croak?" offered Rani, suppressing a slightly hysterical giggle.

I grinned.

"Don't you start again," warned Olivia.

I shook my head vigorously and began to help with the toad roundup. A few minutes later we had things back under control, and the Kumars' rec room was pretty much back to normal.

"Here's what we're going to do," A.J. announced over the cell phone speaker. I could hear him tapping away at his computer keyboard. "It's nine p.m. You have exactly thirty-six hours until the handoff at the zoo. There's a bus leaving Portland for Grants Pass tomorrow morning at six thirty a.m. It makes a few stops and gets in around two. You'll have to hang out there for an hour or so, and then you'll catch another bus to Crescent City, which is the closest town to the national park."

"How are we going to get tickets?" I asked. "Won't the police have our pictures posted everywhere?"

"I've already bought them for you," he said smugly. "I'll e-mail them in a minute, and you can just print them out. That way you don't need to worry about any nosy ticket agents."

"Wait a minute," said Rani. "How do you even know there's going to be a hand-off at the zoo? Word of this is bound to get out, and if there's some big manhunt for you two, it will be all over the news, and if the kidnappers think Olivia is missing, why would they show up?"

She had a point. *Time to improvise,* I thought. I took out my pad of paper and scribbled a note to my father. "Do you have an envelope?" I asked Rani. She nodded and ran out of the room, returning with one a minute later. I stuck the note inside, sealed it, and wrote FOR TIMOTHY STARR in big letters on the front, then handed it to Connor. "See if you can get this in our mailbox without anyone seeing you."

He frowned. "With all those reporters and police crawling all over the place? Good luck."

"Dude, I'm counting on you."

"I'll do my best."

Rajit printed out our bus tickets. Olivia stared at hers, chewing her lip. "Won't they be on the lookout for two girls traveling together, though?"

"I know how we can get around that," said Connor. "They're looking for two kids, not five of them. What if Rajit and Rani and I go with you as far as the bus station? We can all carry instruments and say that it's a band trip, or that we're going to a woodwind ensemble competition or something."

"I don't play an instrument," Olivia pointed out.

"And I can't go home for my bassoon," I added.

"You can use my old flute case," Rani told me.

"And you can borrow my clarinet, Olivia," Juliet offered. "I'll leave it here with you when I go home tonight."

I looked over at Connor. "How are you going to get back here tomorrow morning?"

"No problem," he said. "I can get a ride from my brother."

"At six in the morning?"

"I'll tell him we have Hawkwinds practice and bribe him with my allowance."

"Just don't try and bribe him with a diamond," I warned. "You'll give us away." I turned back to his cell phone, and A.J. "So what are we supposed to do once we get to Crescent City?"

"I haven't totally figured that out yet," my friend replied. "There's a shuttle bus into the park, but the schedule is kind of sporadic. You might have to rent bikes or something."

I looked over at my stepsister. Miss Prissy Pants wasn't really the athletic type. "Great," I muttered, catching what came with it in midair.

Cat Starr, Toad Huntress, had gotten pretty quick on the draw.

CHAPTER 18

Olivia and I spent an uncomfortable night on the floor under the Kumars' pool table. Rani and Rajit draped it with a bed-spread so that their parents wouldn't spot us in case they came downstairs. I hardly slept a wink, expecting to be dis-covered any minute. There were so many things that could go wrong with this harebrained scheme, and so many rea-sons that the FBI might find us before we were able to catch the bus to Grants Pass.

Plus, now I had something new to worry about. What if Connor couldn't figure out a way to get the note to my father? In it I'd told him that Olivia and I were okay, and that some-how he had to make sure the kidnappers showed up at the rendezvous on Friday because we had a plan. Which wasn't exactly true. The plan part, I mean. I was still improvising.

I didn't mention anything about Great-Aunt Abyssinia or Redwood National Park. That would need a whole lot more than just a scribbled note to explain, anyway.

I must have fallen asleep, though, because the next thing I knew, Rani was shaking me awake.

"What?" I said groggily. A toad popped out and squatted on my chest. I sat bolt upright, banging my head on the pool table above me. "Ouch," I exclaimed, popping out another one. I rubbed the sore spot with one hand and brushed both toads away with the other. They hopped off under the sofa.

"Don't worry, I'll get them later," Rani whispered. "We have to hurry; it's almost six. Connor will be here any minute."

As Olivia and I crawled out from underneath the pool table, she passed us each some clothes. "Rajit and I talked it over, and we think you both should wear disguises." She gave Olivia a Seattle Mariners jacket. "Rajit's a big fan, and you two are about the same height," she told her, then plopped a matching Mariners baseball cap on her head. "Stick your hair up under this, okay? It's a dead giveaway otherwise. And you," she added, turning to me, "are going to be Olivia's little brother." She passed me a faded Red Hawk Elementary School hoodie and a pair of round glasses. "They're fake—no prescription. I wore them last year for Halloween. I went as a famous wizard."

I stood in the bathroom a few minutes later, looking at myself glumly in the mirror. It was depressing to think that I could pass for a boy. Olivia would never be able to pull off my disguise—she was already starting to develop a figure. Not me, though. I could pass for an ironing board. A vertically challenged ironing board, at that. I looked like a taller version of Geoffrey, only with glasses.

Might as well go whole hog, I thought. Rummaging through

the drawers, I managed to find a pair of nail scissors and started snipping off my hair.

"Whoa," said Juliet when I emerged a few minutes later.

Rani circled me, eyeing my close-cropped head with a critical eye. "It's a good look for you, actually. A little raggedy, but I like it. Short and sweet."

"You'll definitely pass for a boy now," added Juliet. Across the room, Olivia smirked. I resisted the urge to launch a toad at her.

Rajit had come downstairs now too. He spotted me and grinned. "Hey, bro," he said, punching me on the arm.

I scowled at him, and he laughed.

Even with her curly blond hair twisted up under the baseball cap, Olivia still looked like a girl. A cute one. She knew it too, and she gave Rajit her most dazzling smile.

A tap at the side door signaled Connor's arrival. He did a double take when he saw me, but at least he didn't say anything.

Rajit had printed out our bus tickets. He gave them to us, and then he and Rani and Connor shoved a bunch of money at us.

"It's all we have," Rani told us. "Sorry it isn't more."

"I don't know how we can ever thank you," Oliva told them.

"Are you kidding?" Rajit replied. "With the diamonds you gave us last night, we'll be able to pay for college." He grinned. "I'm just not sure how we'll explain it to our parents, though."

"You can tell them the truth once this is over," Olivia told him.

Connor passed me his cell phone. "All charged up," he said.

I nodded silently. I wasn't in the mood for more toads this morning.

I shouldered my backpack, and we gathered up our instrument cases and slipped outside. It was still dark out as we walked to the city bus stop at the top of the hill. The bus arrived a few minutes later, and we climbed aboard. My heart was racing like a metronome set to *prestissimo,* but I needn't have worried. The other passengers were just a bunch of yawning commuters heading to their jobs downtown. Nobody paid us the slightest bit of attention on the short ride, even though two of our pictures were plastered on the front page of the newspapers they were reading.

Rani was right; word of our disappearance had leaked to the press. Connor was right too, though. People were looking for a pair of kids, not five.

The bus station, though, wasn't quite so easy.

"Policeman approaching from the left," said Rajit. "Let's go over here for a minute."

We followed him to a doughnut kiosk and waited as he ordered half a dozen to go. The policeman glanced at us briefly as he walked by, but Rani and Connor started talking loudly about the all-state woodwind competition we were supposedly heading to, and tossing around terms like "aperture" and "tempo" and "glissando." Olivia and I stayed completely silent. This was not the time for a spontaneous eruption of any kind. The policeman's gaze dropped to our instrument cases, then slid right over Olivia and me as he walked on.

"That was close," said Connor after he left. "Stick together, now."

Moving as a unit, we made our way across the station to where the bus for Grants Pass was waiting. Connor and Rani and Rajit crowded forward with Olivia and me toward the line of passengers.

"See that family there?" Rajit whispered, and I nodded. "Go stand close to them. The driver will think you're their kids too."

I grabbed Olivia's arm and steered her toward a harried-looking couple with a baby and a pair of toddlers. Rajit's plan went off without a hitch; the driver barely looked up as we handed over our tickets and boarded the bus.

My stomach gave a little lurch as we pulled out of the station a few minutes later and our friends waved good-bye to us from the curb. We were on our own now. As I waved back, I wondered if we were doing the right thing. What if we couldn't find Great-Aunt Abyssinia? And even if we did, would she be able to fix the muddle she'd caused? We had less than twenty-seven hours left until the rendezvous at the zoo. If there even was one.

Only one thing was certain. It was too late to turn back now. Olivia and I were officially on the lam.

CHAPTER 19

Have you ever tried to pay for a cheeseburger with a diamond?

"You have got to be kidding me," said the lady behind the counter at the Pie-in-the-Sky Diner. She squinted at the sparkling stone that Olivia had just handed to her. "Honey, we take Visa, MasterCard, American Express, and cash. No rhinestones."

I took my notepad and pen out of my backpack. *It's not a rhinestone,* I wrote. *It's real.* I tore off the piece of paper and gave it to her.

She looked at it and plunked the gem down on the countertop. "Right. And I'm the queen of England."

I sized her up. The name tag on her blindingly pink uniform read PEARL, but it might as well have read ONE TOUGH COOKIE. Her fingernails, which were tapping the formica countertop impatiently, were the same bright shade as her lipstick and dress, and that sky-high updo of hers looked like she'd set her hair dryer control to "stun."

I elbowed Olivia and emptied my pockets. I had fifty-seven cents left. Olivia had two crumpled dollar bills and a quarter. We'd spent the rest of the money our friends had given us on granola bars, yogurt, and juice at one of the earlier stops. I shoved the pile of coins and bills across the counter and pointed to the picture of the cheeseburger on the laminated menu. We had almost enough money for one, and we could split it.

Pearl sucked her teeth as she counted up our money. "Sorry, kids. You're still a little short."

Please, I wrote on the pad. My stomach had the good sense to rumble just then. It was two thirty in the afternoon. Breakfast had been a long time ago.

She looked at me sharply and frowned. "What's with the notebook, young man? Are you mute or something?"

I nodded. She jerked her thumb at Olivia. "How about her?"

Also mute, I wrote.

"Let me get this straight. You're telling me you're both mute?"

I passed her another piece of paper. *It's genetic. It runs in the family.*

Her expression softened. "Oh, you poor little things."

You have no idea, I wanted to say, but I kept my mouth closed and did my best to look like a poor little thing. Which, when you haven't had a hot meal in over twenty-four hours, isn't all that difficult.

"Cheeseburger, is it?"

Olivia and I nodded hungrily. Pearl sighed. "Well, I guess we'll call it close enough," she told us, scooping up our money. She leaned over the counter and lowered her voice. "Go find a booth. And don't breathe a word to Frank. He's the owner." She looked over her shoulder at the man at the grill behind her, then straightened up again and gave a short bark of laughter. "Not that you could anyway," she added. "Breathe a word, I mean. You two being mute and all."

When she showed up with our order a few minutes later, she brought us not one but two cheeseburgers, plus two huge helpings of fries, two chocolate milk shakes, and two pieces of cherry pie. "Getting close to closing time," she said, scowling. "No point leaving all this food sitting around going to waste."

Olivia kicked me under the table, and I grabbed my notepad. *Thank you!* I wrote.

The waitress sniffed and trundled off. The diner was empty except for a lone customer on the far side of the room. Pearl refilled his coffee, patted her beehive hairdo as she chatted with him a bit, then came back to our table and looked us over. "So where are your parents?"

Olivia stopped midbite and glanced anxiously at me. It hadn't occurred to us that someone might ask this question, and I didn't have an answer ready. Grabbing my pen, I wrote the first thing that popped into my mind: *Bolivia.*

Pearl's painted-on eyebrows shot up beneath her stiff blond bangs.

Olivia glared at me and reached for the notebook. *They put us on the bus this morning before they left,* she wrote. *We're staying with our grandparents in Ashland while they're out of the country.*

My grandparents, not yours, I thought, but I had to give my stepsister credit for quick thinking. It was a pretty decent answer.

Pearl thought so too, apparently. "Well, that's good," she said, sounding relieved. "You had me worried there for a minute. We get runaways coming through here every now and again."

She went back over to the counter and busied herself refilling ketchup bottles.

Olivia leaned over the table. "Bolivia? What the heck did you say that for?" she whispered furiously, brushing a fistful of dandelions and another diamond off her cheeseburger.

"It just came out!" I replied indignantly.

"Yeah, like that stupid toad," whispered Olivia again, flicking a french fry at the amphibian on my plate. She flicked one at me, too, for good measure.

I grabbed the toad and stuffed it into my backpack. I'd release it outside later, before we got on the bus to Crescent City.

"You kids need anything else?" Pearl called from the counter.

We shook our heads.

"Croak," went my backpack.

Pearl looked up and frowned. Olivia kicked me under the table again. I glared at her and shoved my backpack onto the floor.

Do you think she saw anything? Olivia wrote on my notepad.
No.

How about that other guy?

I glanced over at the customer on the other side of the room. He seemed engrossed in his newspaper.

I don't think so.

No more talking, Olivia wrote, underlining the words sternly.

Like I don't know that, I scribbled back, underlining mine just as sternly.

Shut up, she wrote.

You shut up!

"You're not eating," said Pearl, materializing by our table. She put her hands on her hips. "What's the matter, don't you like our cooking here at Pie-in-the-Sky? Best breakfast-and-lunch spot on the I-5 corridor, bar none."

Olivia picked up her cheeseburger and took a bite. I stuffed a handful of french fries in my mouth. We both smiled at her.

Pearl nodded. "That's more like it."

Croak.

She cocked her head. "What was that?" she asked suspiciously.

I shrugged, feigning innocence.

Croak.

"There it is again," she repeated sternly. "It's coming from under the table."

Olivia reached for the notebook. *My little brother has a pet frog in his backpack. Sorry.*

I hung my head, trying to look sheepish.

Pearl sighed. "What is it about boys and frogs?" she said, shaking her head. "I had me a couple of little boys, back in the day. They're grown men now, but when they were young, they were just like your brother here. They loved critters—snakes, frogs, even a baby squirrel once—I was forever finding things stashed in their rooms." She patted my head. "Well, I guess it can't harm anything, as long as it stays put and Frank doesn't find out. Better not let the bus driver catch you with it, though. He won't like a frog aboard, no sirree."

She left and went over to check on the other customer.

Olivia and I ate in silence for a while. Then Olivia picked up the pen again. *That man is staring at us.*

Who, Frank?

Duh. The other customer.

This time I was the one to kick her.

Quit it! she scribbled. *I'm serious! He's watching us.*

It was probably her imagination, but I sneaked a peek anyway. It wasn't her imagination. He was definitely staring at us. So was the headline on the front page of his newspaper: NO LEADS YET ON DIAMOND GIRL AND HER SISTER!

My heart sank. I didn't realize they got the Portland paper down here in Grants Pass! I grabbed the pencil and paper from her. *We need to get out of here, NOW!*

Olivia nodded and started to pull on her jacket. Before we could get up from the table, though, the man on the other side of the diner stood up, threw some money down by his empty plate, and strode out the door.

Olivia and I exchanged a glance. Now what?

I slipped Connor's cell phone out of my pocket and sent A.J. a text, telling him what had just happened.

Might be your imagination, he texted back. **Advise staying put until the last minute, then making a run for the bus.**

Olivia took her jacket back off and we sat there warily, sipping our milk shakes. I expected to hear sirens any minute.

"Quitting time, Frank!" called Pearl a few minutes later. "You go on home to that new grandbaby of yours, and I'll finish up here."

The owner of Pie-in-the-Sky emerged from the kitchen, murmured a few instructions as he said good-bye to Pearl, then left. Once he was gone, Pearl turned the sign on the door to CLOSED, crossed the room to where Olivia and I were sitting, and threw the newspaper and its screaming headline down on the table in front of us.

She folded her arms across her bright pink uniform. "Now I think it's time you two girls told me what's going on."

CHAPTER 20

If anyone had ever told me I'd find myself holding hands with my stepsister someday, I'd have said they were crazy.

But that was before I met the Red Rocket.

Pearl patted its dashboard. "That's my girl," she said. "Don't you let anybody tell you you're over the hill. You keep this up and we'll be at Redwood National Park by dinnertime."

Pearl had been talking to her car ever since we hightailed it out of Grants Pass half an hour ago. She treated it like some kind of pet.

"Not every day you get to ride in a classic Ford Thunderbird convertible, is it, girls?" she said, glancing over the back of her seat to where Olivia and I were sitting, clutching each other for dear life. Pearl drove fast. *Really* fast.

Getting out of town had been an adventure. We'd just finished telling Pearl everything—well, everything except the fact that Great-Aunt Abyssinia was actually my fairy godmother—when a police cruiser pulled into the parking lot.

"Uh-oh," Pearl had said, "looks like we've got company." She drummed her flamingo pink fingernails briefly on the tabletop. "Tell you what, girls. I don't know why I believe your wild tale, but for some reason I do, and my radar's never let me down yet. You have to get up pretty dang early in the morning to pull the wool over Pearl Slocum's eyes, yes sirree." She crossed to the counter and rummaged briefly in her purse. "Here's what I want you to do," she said, passing a key to Olivia. "I'm going to distract Officer Norris with a piece of cherry pie—that's his favorite—while you two slip out the back door and hide in the Red Rocket."

We must have looked at her blankly, because she added, "My car. You can't miss it. Get in the backseat and cover up. You'll find a blanket there. I'll be out as soon as I can."

We did as she asked, and a few minutes later she slid in behind the wheel. "You were right," she murmured. "That customer who was in earlier went and blabbed to the police."

So much for my disguise. I should have saved myself the trouble of cutting my hair.

Pearl put the key in the ignition and switched on the engine, then leaned over the seat and adjusted our blanket. "It took two pieces of pie and a lot of smooth talk to convince Officer Norris that the fellow was just another greedy fool trying to make a quick buck," she told us. "I swore on my grandmother's knitting basket that you were a boy, Cat."

I grimaced. "Thanks, I think."

Olivia squealed as the inevitable toad popped out. It was trapped under the blanket with us.

Pearl lifted a corner of the fabric. "Hush," she told my stepsister, scooping the toad up and tossing it out the window into the bushes. She eyed us thoughtfully. "I hope I know what I'm getting myself into here. There's quite a hefty reward being offered for you two, you know."

We must have looked scared, because she quickly gave us a reassuring smile. "Don't you worry, though. My lips are sealed. Just make sure yours are too. No more toads until we're out of town!"

The blanket went down again and she revved the engine, then backed out of her parking spot. As we began to pull forward, I felt myself start to breathe a little easier.

Then the car rumbled to a halt.

"Say, Pearl," said a deep male voice. Officer Norris? I tensed, hoping he wouldn't look in the backseat and spot the two girl-shaped lumps under the blanket.

"Yes, Charlie?"

"I just wanted to thank you again for the pie."

"Anytime," Pearl replied sweetly.

The Red Rocket rolled forward again, and we drove sedately out of town. Once we reached the freeway, Pearl twitched the blanket away.

"You can sit up now," she told us, glancing in the rearview mirror. "Buckle up, please, we're on a deadline here!"

I'd barely shoved my seat belt into the slot before she floored it. That was half an hour ago, and since then we'd been barreling down the Redwood Highway, a twisty road that snaked through the forests and mountains of southern Oregon toward the California border. I had a cast-iron stomach, but even I was feeling a little queasy, and as much as

I missed him, I was really, really glad that Geoffrey wasn't along for the ride.

"Yep," said Pearl proudly, patting the dashboard again, "1966 was a very good year."

We flew around another corner, and Olivia's fingernails dug into my hand. I craned to see the speedometer. We were going seventy, but on this winding road it felt more like ninety. Probably because at the same time that she'd told us to buckle up, Pearl had pressed a button on the dashboard and the Red Rocket's roof had retracted and disappeared into the trunk.

"No point wasting good sunshine," she'd said. "Besides, I want you girls to have the full convertible experience."

Thanks to the "full convertible experience," Olivia had lost her Mariners cap somewhere back around mile marker twelve. Her curly blond hair flew out behind her like a flag until Pearl spotted it in the rearview mirror. She reached into the glove compartment and pulled out a scarf identical to the one holding her own bleached-blond updo in place. Not that there was any chance of it escaping, what with all that hair spray.

Pearl handed the scarf to Olivia and motioned to her to put it on, which my stepsister did reluctantly. She shot me a look, daring me to say anything.

"Life doesn't get any better than this, does it, ladies?" Pearl hollered, her words whipped away by the wind.

"Actually, it does," Olivia whispered to me through clenched teeth.

I looked over at her, startled. My stepsister had a sense of humor! "No kidding," I whispered back.

The poor toad didn't stand a chance. The wind swept it overboard practically before I'd finished speaking.

The sun was sinking lower in the sky, and as the car sped through the shadows of the towering fir trees that lined the highway, Olivia and I wrapped ourselves in the blanket and huddled closer together. Pearl finally took pity on us.

"Just wanted to give you a taste of real freedom on the road," she said, pulling over and raising the Red Rocket's roof again. As it snapped into place, she turned around to face us, her forehead puckered under the scarf. "Now, tell me again about this great-aunt of yours. How exactly is she going to help fix this mess you're in?"

Olivia and I exchanged a glance.

"Um . . . ," I began.

"Lean out the window when you talk, dear," Pearl told me. "I'm not partial to toads. No offense or anything."

I stuck my head out the window as the Red Rocket pulled off the shoulder and back onto the highway. "My great-aunt is kind of eccentric, but she's really smart," I replied, hoping that would satisfy Pearl's curiosity. "She's faced this kind of thing before."

Pearl's eyebrows did their disappearing act. "Really? Does this, uh, condition run in your family?"

"Not exactly," I said, watching the toads bounce onto the grass by the side of the road as we picked up speed.

"I should think not." She made the sucking noise with her teeth again, then shrugged. "Oh well. Probably best we find her anyway, her being family and all."

As I sat back in my seat, Pearl popped a cassette tape into the slot on the dash. She grinned at us in the rearview mirror.

"Perfect song for our getaway, don't you think?" she shouted as the opening notes of the Beach Boys' "Fun, Fun, Fun" came blasting over the speakers. Pearl joined in gustily at the refrain: "'And she'll have fun, fun, fun 'til her daddy takes the T-Bird aw-a-a-a-y.'"

Olivia looked over at me and shook her head in disbelief.

I slid Connor's cell phone out of my pocket. **Coming up on Cave Junction**, I texted to A.J. I'd been keeping him posted on our progress ever since we left Grants Pass.

ETA one hour, he texted back. **GAA still at Jedediah Smith Campground, campsite 50.**

I showed the phone to Olivia, who relayed the message to Pearl. Pearl didn't mind flowers and gems inside her T-Bird. Just no toads. I guess I couldn't blame her.

"And how does your friend A.J. know this?" she asked.

"Cat's mom is an astronaut," Olivia explained. "Fiona MacLeod Starr—maybe you're heard of her? A.J. is working with her to help track Cat's great-aunt from outer space."

"You don't say," said Pearl, digesting this new information. She glanced at me in the rearview mirror. "Well now, isn't that something. I watch all the launches, you know. Always have, ever since I was a little girl. I'll never forget that first moon walk." She stuck her head out the window and looked up at the sky. "So is NASA tracking us, too?"

I shook my head. "Nope."

"Toad!" shouted Olivia.

Pearl pulled her head back in as the creature tumbled over the back of her seat. The car swerved, sending me flying into my stepsister.

"Sorry," I blurted out before I could help myself.

Now there were two on the loose. Pearl flipped the one in the front seat over her shoulder. It landed on Olivia, who shrieked and batted at it with her hands. She managed to knock it onto the floor, where the second one was hopping around, then whisked her knees up to her chin as I scrambled to capture them both.

When I finally had things under control again and the pair of toads wrapped in my hoodie, I gave Pearl a thumbs-up.

"Thank goodness," she said with a shudder. "Pipe down now, okay?"

I kept very quiet for the rest of the trip.

An hour later, just as A.J. had predicted, we pulled into the Jedediah Smith Campground.

"What campsite did you say she's at again?" asked Pearl.

"Fifty," Olivia replied, with a spray of carnations and a large diamond. She handed the gem to Pearl. "Here," she said. "Maybe this will help pay for gas."

Pearl held it up and squinted at it. "Honey, if what you're telling me is true, this here stone will not only pay for gas, it'll fund my retirement. Thanks."

She hit the button to retract the roof again now that we were off the highway and into the national park. Olivia and I gaped up at the trees. They soared far above us, reaching for the dwindling spring daylight. I'd been to a lot of places, but I'd never seen trees like these.

"Really something, aren't they?" said Pearl. "I've always loved the redwoods. Did you know some of them are taller than the Statue of Liberty?"

"No way!" I said, then clapped my hands together in front of me, trapping my quarry. *Cat Starr, Toad Huntress scores again.*

Pearl pulled over for a second so I could toss it to safety.

"Isn't there a tree you can drive through?" Olivia asked, and the waitress nodded. "Can you take us to it?"

"If we have time."

The T-Bird drew a lot of attention as we made our way slowly through the campground.

"Stay down, girls," Pearl murmured, switching off the Beach Boys. She punched a button on the dashboard and the mechanism whirred as the rooftop slid back into place. We were going into stealth mode again.

A few minutes later we spotted Great-Aunt Abyssinia's RV, and Pearl pulled in beside it.

"Nice wheels," called Great-Aunt Abyssinia from her folding chair by the campfire.

She didn't look the least bit surprised to see us. So much for stealth mode.

"The Rocket gets me where I need to go, on time and in style," Pearl replied. She switched off the engine and gave the dashboard one last pat. "Yes sirree, baby, you did real good."

She untied her scarf, checked her lipstick and hair in the rearview mirror, then got out of the car and crossed to where Great-Aunt Abyssinia was waiting.

"Howdy, Pearl," said my great-aunt.

Pearl's eyebrows fled under her stiff blond bangs again. "How did you know my name?"

Great-Aunt Abyssinia grinned. "Says so on your uniform."

Pearl glanced down at her name tag and laughed. "So it does. Sorry, I'm a little jumpy. This day has been a little, uh, left of normal." She extended her hand. "Pearl Slocum of the world-famous Pie-in-the-Sky Diner. Well, maybe not world-famous, but we do okay. And you must be the great-aunt these girls are so eager to find."

"I guess I must be," said Great-Aunt Aby, rising to her feet. Like the redwoods, she towered over all three of us. Unlike the redwoods, she was dressed from head to toe in fleece. Purple fleece. I caught sight of her hiking boots and nearly laughed. They were sporting matching purple laces. Great-Aunt Aby had accessorized.

My great-aunt shook Pearl's hand. "Pie-in-the-Sky Diner, huh? Sounds like my kind of place."

"It is if you like pie," Pearl replied. "We serve seven kinds, one for every day of the week."

"I'll have to stop by sometime. I'm much obliged to you for bringing the girls to me." She glanced over in my direction and ran a big hand over her own short locks. "Nice 'do, by the way, Catriona. Give it a shot of color and we could almost be twins."

Olivia snorted, and I stepped on her foot.

"These two are in a heap of trouble," Pearl told her. "But I guess you know that, what with them being all over the news and everything."

Great-Aunt Aby stared at her blankly. She hadn't heard! My heart sank. What kind of a fairy godmother had I been saddled with? One that didn't even watch the news?

Pearl glanced back over her shoulder and lowered her voice. "Perhaps we'd better go inside, Mrs., uh—"

"Just call me Aby," said Great-Aunt Abyssinia. She lumbered over to her RV and opened the door. "Come on in, then."

Olivia wrinkled her nose as we followed her inside. The remains of my great-aunt's dinner—in a pan containing a blackened mess that looked like it might have been some sort of stir-fry—were petrifying on the stove.

"You three hungry?" asked Great-Aunt Abyssinia.

Olivia and I shook our heads vigorously.

"Starved," said Pearl.

"Have a seat," my great-aunt told us.

The three of us squeezed in around the little dining table while Great-Aunt Aby took the pan and stuffed it inside the RV's tiny oven, then rummaged in her cupboards and teeny refrigerator. *Right,* I thought scornfully. *Like she really watches the Food Network.* A few minutes later, though, she set down three plates of completely normal-looking bacon and eggs in front of us. Better than normal-looking, in fact.

"Breakfast-for-dinner night," she announced, cracking open a bottle of her green gloop and taking a big slurp.

"I'd give you a job any day of the week," Pearl told her, picking up her fork. "This looks mighty fine."

My great-aunt pulled up a stool and perched at the end of the table, like a circus elephant doing a balancing act. "So, fill me in."

I opened my mouth to speak, but before I could say anything, Pearl held up a warning finger. "Not at the dinner table."

I nodded, and nudged Olivia with my elbow.

"So it all began right after you visited us, Mrs., uh, Aby," my stepsister explained. "I woke up doing this"—she pointed to the buttercups and diamonds that littered her plate—"and Cat woke up doing, um . . ."

"This," I said, cupping my hands in front of my mouth to catch the inevitable toad.

Croak.

Pearl shuddered. "Puh-leez," she said. "Some of us are trying to eat."

"I see," said Great-Aunt Aby, her eyes glinting behind her glasses. She plucked the toad from my hand and inspected it, then opened the door of the RV and released it gently onto the step. As it hopped off toward the woods, Archibald twitched his tail and leaped down from his perch on the bookshelf. "No, Archie," said my great-aunt, quickly shutting the door of her RV again. "Toad would definitely disagree with you."

She flicked a glance at Pearl and Olivia, who were plowing their way happily through their bacon and eggs. She plucked a book from her shelf and flipped through its pages, muttering to herself. Then she turned to me. "Could I have a word in private with you, Catriona?"

I followed her outside.

"I take it you've spoken with your mother," she whispered.

I nodded again.

"Good. Not exactly the way we meant to tell you, but it couldn't be helped, what with the space mission and all interfering with our schedule."

I lifted a shoulder.

"How much does Pearl know?"

"I just told her that you're my great-aunt," I replied, prodding with the toe of my sneaker at the toad my answer produced.

"Good. Let's keep it that way for now. How about Olivia?"

"Uh . . ."

"I see. Well, couldn't be helped either, I suppose. Not under the circumstances." Great-Aunt Aby laid one of her large hands on my shoulder. "I'm sorry that we were never properly introduced," she said. "There's actually rather a lovely ceremony involved." She slipped a finger through the chain of my necklace and tugged it from its resting place under my hoodie. "Your mother and I would have presented you with this together," she said, "and explained its history, and yours."

I looked at her expectantly.

She blinked at me with her enormous, magnified eyes. "Not just yet," she replied to my unspoken question. "Your mother's been looking forward to the ceremony for many years, and I don't wish to deprive her of her part in it. And it's completely irrelevant information at the moment."

I must have looked disappointed, because she paused, then sighed. "Well, I guess I can explain one thing." She opened the book that she'd brought outside with her. I recognized the emerald green cover and worn binding—it was the same book she'd consulted the day she visited us back in Portland.

"Here," she said, passing it to me and tapping her finger against one of its pages. "I meant to help, truly I did."

I quickly scanned the page. It was an old fairy tale about two stepsisters. The nice one got the gift of diamonds and flowers, and the rude one got stuck with the toads.

"But that's not what happened," I told her, frowning. "You messed up, big-time."

"It happens occasionally," admitted Great-Aunt Abyssinia. "No real harm done, though."

"No harm done?! Great-Aunt Aby, *look* at me!" I pointed to the pile of toads at my feet. "Do you have any idea what I'm going through here? Thanks to your stupid mix-up, I'll probably never be able to go back to school again. And I'll have to give up the bassoon!" I paced around the campfire angrily, heedless of the toads I was scattering under the giant trees. "Olivia will be fine, of course. She and her diamonds will be welcomed with open arms wherever she goes. The school will probably build a new gym or library in her honor or something." I stopped and looked at my great-aunt accusingly. "There's been a whole bunch of harm done, Great-Aunt Aby—and the worst of it is, my little brother has been kidnapped!"

"I know," said my great-aunt sadly, hanging her head. She looked like a remorseful Saint Bernard caught swiping a steak off the grill. "That wasn't part of the plan."

"What is the plan, then? I say it's time to wave your wand, or whatever it is you do, and hurry up and fix this!"

"That's not exactly the way it works."

"Well, make it work!" I told her. "I want Geoffrey back, and I want my life back!" I stalked back inside and slid into my seat. Olivia and Pearl were smearing jam—or what looked like jam, though it was an odd brown color—onto their toast.

"So, we have diamonds, toads, and a missing brother," said Great-Aunt Aby, following me inside. "Got it. I think I'm up to speed."

"Do you think we should call their parents and let them know that the girls are safe?" asked Pearl.

I shook my head. "Nope," I said, heedless of what else came out of my mouth besides words. I was done worrying about toads. "The FBI is tapping our phones, trying to trace calls from the kidnapppers." I explained briefly about the note I'd given Connor, too. There'd been nothing on the news yet to make me think my father had received it, though.

"I can get a message through if need be," said Great-Aunt Aby, and I knew she was referring to the FGPS. She reached for her broom, and for a moment I thought she was going to mount it and fly away, but she merely began sweeping up toads. "Connor strikes me as a resourceful boy, though. Let's be patient a while longer." She emptied the dustpan out the RV's door. "We need to hit the road for Portland soon. Long drive ahead of us."

"Would you like to borrow the Red Rocket?" said Pearl.

"Nice of you to offer, but you'd be surprised at the speed I can coax out of this RV," my great-aunt replied. "I can't thank you enough for all that you've done for the girls, Pearl. I don't want to impose on your generosity any longer."

"Oh, you're not imposing," said Pearl.

"Nevertheless, you're free to leave," insisted my great-aunt.

Pearl laughed. "You aren't going to get rid of me that easy, Abyssinia," she told her. "This is more excitement than I've had in decades. Besides, now that I'm in it this far, I have to stick around and see how everything turns out." She winked at Olivia and me, then turned back to my great-aunt. "So," she said. "Where do we go from here?"

CHAPTER 21

Las Vegas, apparently.

"Omigosh!" I said, sitting up and staring out the big picture window of the RV. I'd been asleep on one of its dining benches when the sound of a car backfiring woke me up.

My exclamation sent a toad flying across the table to the bench on the other side, where Olivia was sleeping. It landed on her pillow, right by her face.

Croak.

My stepsister cracked open an eyelid and screamed. Diamonds and daffodils scattered in every direction as she flopped around in her sleeping bag like a beached seal. In her panic to get away from the toad, she slid off the bench and onto the floor of the RV with a thud.

"Girls!" scolded Pearl, hoisting herself up onto her elbow and scowling at us from her makeshift bed on the sofa a few feet away. "What in tarnation is going on?"

"Toad!" cried Olivia, pointing frantically at the creature that was still squatting on her pillow.

"LOOK!" I cried, popping out another one as I pointed frantically at the window.

The two of them turned and gasped. The giant redwood trees had completely vanished. In their place a vast cityscape of neon sprawled out before us, blinking and flashing against the night sky. Hotels and casinos, billboards and pyramids, the Statue of Liberty and the Eiffel Tower—I even spotted a pirate ship in a lake-size fountain, and a roller coaster atop a high-rise. Every single square inch was bathed in garish light. I wondered fleetingly how many lightbulbs it took to run a city like this. Millions? Billions? It was as over the top and eye-boggling as Olivia's gem-encrusted version of Geoffrey's bedroom.

"Holy sweet whistling Annie," whispered Pearl. "What are we doing in Vegas?"

Great-Aunt Abyssinia poked her head around the half wall that separated the driver's seat from the rest of the RV. "Ah, sorry, girls—just a little detour," she said sheepishly, wrestling with a large map. "I made a wrong turn a ways back."

Wrong turn? We were in *Nevada*! Great-Aunt Aby had messed up again!

"Where's my car?" asked Pearl, sounding anxious.

"Safe and sound," my great-aunt replied, jerking her thumb toward the back of the RV. "I hitched her to the back."

Someone behind us honked, and my great-aunt stuck her spiky orange head out the window. "Hey!" she boomed. "Cut me some slack! Senior citizen here!"

I fished around under the table for my backpack, unzipped

its outside pocket, and grabbed my cell phone. I didn't care if he was sleeping—A.J. needed to know about this. We were in serious trouble here.

Woke up in Las Vegas! I texted.

Waaaaaaaa? he texted back a moment later.

Occupationally challenged FG. I added a frowny face.

Maybe we should chip in and get her a new wand.

Ha, ha, I texted back. **She doesn't use one. Just a map from AAA. How far away from Portland are we, anyway?**

Lemme check. There was a short pause, and then: **A thousand miles. You have to be at the zoo in six hours. You'll never make it!**

"We're a thousand miles from Portland," I announced, flipping the cell phone shut and returning it to the pocket of my backpack. "We have to be at the zoo in six hours. We'll never make it."

"That's the spirit!" said Great-Aunt Aby sarcastically. "Where's your sense of adventure, Catriona?"

"Adventure!" I cried, my voice rising along with the toad count. "The clock is ticking! Have you forgotten about Geoffrey?" I wondered if I should call NASA again and get them to patch me through to my mother. But what could she do besides yell at Great-Aunt Aby from outer space?

"How could anyone forget the G-Man?" my great-aunt replied. "Charming boy." She glanced back over her shoulder again and gave me a stern look. "Now, clean up those toads and let me drive."

As the RV lurched down the Las Vegas Strip—the back-firing was coming from us, I soon realized—Olivia and Pearl rushed to the big picture window in the living-room area to gawk at the sights. I unzipped my sleeping bag in a fury, climbed out, and began tracking down my latest crop of toads. *If anything happens to my little brother because of Great-Aunt Aby's bungling,* I thought, stuffing them in my backpack because the trash was full, *I'll . . . I'll . . .* I sat back on my heels. Just exactly what would I do? What *could* I do, after all? I was just a twelve-year-old toad spitter, when it came right down to it.

The thought was sobering. Not only was I just a toad spitter, but I was a toad spitter stuck in the middle of the desert with a waitress named Pearl, an incompetent fairy godmother, and a stepsister who was on Area 51's most-wanted list. Plus one enormous cat. I glanced at Archibald, who was regarding me with his unblinking green eyes.

The odds of this being a successful rescue attempt were not good.

"Look!" cried Olivia. "Gondolas!"

A diamond clinked against the window as we lurched to a stop outside a hotel that looked like it belonged someplace in Italy. The RV backfired again, and I wondered gloomily if I should add "engine trouble" to our long list of handicaps.

I looked over at Olivia as Great-Aunt Aby consulted her map for the umpteenth time. My stepsister was still gaping out the window. She was actually enjoying this! *Lamebrain.*

Struck by a wild idea, I reached down and picked up the diamond on the floor by the window, then slipped it into the pocket of my jeans. What if I were to make a dash for the airport? Surely someone would fly me to Portland in exchange for something as valuable as this. I could easily get to the zoo in time if they did, and surely I could dig up a blond wig and pass for Olivia. At least one of us would have a chance at rescuing Geoffrey that way.

Time to improvise! As soon as this thought flashed through my head, there was a sharp movement from the driver's seat. I turned to see Great-Aunt Aby adjusting the rearview mirror. *Maybe she really can read my thoughts,* I thought as I caught a glimpse of her magnified eyes staring at me.

Before she or anyone else could stop me, I grabbed my backpack, opened the side door of the RV, and sprinted into the night.

CHAPTER 22

I ran back down the Strip in the opposite direction from the RV, then turned onto a side path that crossed an open expanse of lawn. It felt good to run. I'd been feeling cooped up for days: in my room at home, on the bus, and then in the Red Rocket and the RV. My backpack jounced as I sped down the sidewalk, causing the toads it contained to croak wildly in protest. I ignored them and ran on.

I hurdled a hedge and cut across a manicured garden, ran through an archway, and found myself indoors. It was unlike any place I'd ever seen indoors, though. It was more like being outdoors—only a fake outdoors. The large, open plaza was surrounded on all four sides by the high walls of a fake Italian building. Graceful arched windows looked down on the restaurant tables spilling out onto the cobblestones below. All of it was spread under a soaring, painted blue sky.

This is a hotel? I thought. *Whoa.*

I slowed to a walk. The plaza was thronged with people,

and I figured I could blend in with the crowd, then look for a taxi to the airport once I was sure I'd thrown Great-Aunt Aby off my trail. As long as I kept a low profile and didn't spill any toads, I'd probably be all right.

I felt a flicker of guilt at having ditched Great-Aunt Aby. I knew my mother definitely wouldn't approve. But I thrust the feeling firmly away. Getting back to Portland and saving Geoffrey was the only thing that mattered now.

I was warm from running, so I peeled back the hood of my sweatshirt. I took the glasses from the pocket of my backpack and put them back on, though, just in case. My picture was still plastered all over the news alongside Olivia's, after all.

You'd have never known it was the middle of the night by the number of people who were out. There were college students and retirees, businessmen in suits, people in shorts and swimsuits, and a few in glamorous evening wear. There were even people in costumes, including an Elvis impersonator.

I ducked into a doorway for a moment to text A.J., watching as a couple in a wedding dress and a tuxedo posed for pictures on the bridge that arched over a phony canal at the far end of the plaza. Were they for real, or just models? I wondered. It was hard to tell in a city like this, where so many things were fake. They sure seemed like a real couple, though. The groom said something to the bride and she laughed, tossing back her curly blond hair. From a distance she looked like Iz.

All of a sudden I was struck by a pang of homesickness so strong I nearly keeled over. Dad and Iz had been married on a bridge too—the one in Portland's Japanese Garden. They'd called the wedding their "bridge to a new life." One that included me and Olivia, and one that would expand to include our little brother a year later.

I would have given anything at that moment to see them again, or at least to be able to call and talk to them. I knew they must be worried sick about us. First Geoffrey, then Olivia and me. All three of us had vanished! My mother, too, must be frantic by now. I hoped that Great-Aunt Aby had somehow been able to get a message through to her.

Great-Aunt Aby.

I snapped Connor's cell phone shut and returned it to the pocket of my backpack. A.J. would have to wait. I peered out from the doorway, scanning the crowd. There was no sign of my great-aunt yet, but I doubted she was far behind. I stood there for a moment, trying to clear my mind of anything that might tip her off as to where I was—*Don't think about the big bell tower you passed, Cat, and don't think about the plaza or the canal or the gondolas or the fancy shops or strolling musicians*—and tried instead to think of something entirely different.

Something like fast-food restaurants.

I'd been to a zillion in my lifetime, and I quickly flipped through my mental photo album of them, pausing at one in particular. I conjured up as clearly as I could the red booths and jukeboxes, the smell of french fries, the menu board on the wall behind the cash registers. *There,* I thought. *That should throw her off track.*

Then I dashed out of hiding and began to zigzag through the crowd.

I paused briefly by a kiosk displaying a map of the hotel and its grounds. After quickly locating the YOU ARE HERE dot (I was someplace called Saint Mark's Square), I tracked down the valet parking area. There were bound to be taxis there.

Calculating the quickest route, I was surprised to find that it looked to be by gondola. Turning around, I stood on my tippy-toes, craning to see across the crowded plaza to the stairs that led down to the pretend canal. Were there any boats available?

There were. One was pulling alongside just now, in fact.

I made a dash for it and arrived breathless, just behind the bride and groom.

"That'll be sixteen dollars," said the gondolier. He was wearing a costume too—black pants, red sash, black and white striped T-shirt, red neck scarf, and a straw boater hat with a matching red ribbon wound around it.

I drooped. All I had was Olivia's diamond, and I wasn't about to waste that on a boat ride. It was my ticket home to Portland.

Sometimes it helps to be vertically challenged. The bride and groom turned and saw me, then exchanged a glance.

"Poor little boy," said the bride. "He just wants to have some fun!"

"That'll be sixteen dollars," the gondolier repeated, unmoved.

"Tell you what, kid—I'll pay your fare if you'll take some pictures of us," said the groom, holding out his camera.

I gave him an enthusiastic smile and a thumbs-up in return, and the three of us stepped into the crescent-shaped boat. The bride settled into her seat in a whoosh of white chiffon, like a marshmallow collapsing in a campfire.

"My name is Marco and I'll be your gondolier tonight," said the man in the black pants. He sounded bored. As he thrust his oar into the water and started to sing (something in Italian, of course), I tossed my backpack into the bottom of the boat, hoping that any stray croaks would be drowned out by the music. I needed to dump the toads at some point, but this was neither the time nor the place. Then I switched on the camera and began holding up my end of the bargain.

Late-night visitors lined the wrought-iron railings of the shopping promenade, whistling and cheering as we passed, and I snapped a picture of the bride and groom as they waved like visiting royalty.

I got pictures of them pretending to sing along with the gondolier, and smooching under one of the bridges, and holding hands and gazing deeply into each other's eyes. It was a little embarrassing, and silly, really, in this place that was so obviously fake, and yet there was something romantic about it too, floating under the arched bridges, past the brightly lit shops and the Elvis impersonator and the woman in the bright pink dress with the beehive hairdo—

Wait a minute, I thought, zooming in through the camera viewfinder. That wasn't a dress, it was a uniform. Pearl Slocum's uniform!

I slumped down in the boat, hoping she wouldn't see me.

"Are you okay?" asked the bride, looking concerned.

I shook my head and leaned abruptly over the opposite side, away from where Pearl was standing. The gondolier stopped singing.

"Gimme a break," he said in disgust. "See if you can hold it in, kid, while I get you to dry land."

He maneuvered the gondola swiftly to the next landing,

where I hopped out and handed the groom his camera back. Giving him and his brand-new wife another thumbs-up, I shouldered my backpack and melted into the crowd, hoping Pearl hadn't spotted me.

No such luck.

"Catriona!" Great-Aunt Aby's booming voice echoed across the canal like a megaphone. She and Pearl began to trot toward me. I pulled my hood up and made a run for it, darting down the corridor toward the valet parking and, I hoped, taxis.

"Catriona!" my great-aunt hollered again. She was moving pretty fast for such a big woman.

Ignoring her, I sprinted around a corner and through the first open door I saw.

"Whoa there, little fella," whinnied a deep male voice as I slammed into a glass wall.

Ding! A bell rang and the door slid closed behind us.

"Dang!" I blurted, bending over and spitting a toad onto the floor.

I was trapped in an elevator with Elvis.

CHAPTER 23

Croak.

I grabbed the toad and stuffed it quickly into my back-pack, hoping that the Elvis impersonator hadn't spotted it. He hadn't; he was too busy waving to the crowd of people below us as the glass elevator rose in the air.

A crowd that included my Great-Aunt Abyssinia. She stood with her hands on her hips, glaring up at me.

There was no sign of Olivia. They must have left her back in the RV. I leaned back against the wall and took a deep breath, closing my eyes. I'd bought myself a little time. My eyes flew open again as I realized that I'd also backed myself into a corner. All my great-aunt had to do was catch the next elevator and the jig would be up.

Ding! The elevator slowed to a stop and the doors opened to reveal a fancy restaurant.

"Getting out?" whinnied Fake Elvis. I hesitated. "Or are you going to the helipad, too?"

Helipad? Maybe I still had a chance to get back to Portland! A helipad meant helicopters, and surely there'd be somebody willing to give me a ride in exchange for a diamond. I nodded enthusiastically, and Fake Elvis punched the button to close the doors again.

When we reached the top and got out, though, there was no sign of a helicopter. The Elvis impersonator glanced at his watch, shrugged, and strolled over to a bench in the gated waiting area. I paced anxiously back and forth, too nervous to take a seat. I hoped the chopper would get here soon; I couldn't have very much time before Great-Aunt Aby showed up.

Croak.

The toads! I'd forgotten about them. This would probably be a good time to ditch my amphibian companions. Slipping behind a sandwich board announcing helicopter tours of the city, I squatted down and opened my backpack. The toads were wedged sullenly in the bottom, and it took some coaxing to get them out. Just as the last one hopped off into the shadows, I heard a loud *whip-whip-whip* overhead, and Elvis stood up expectantly in the waiting area as a helicopter came in for a landing. I hurried to join him.

"Usual routine, right? Dropping in on the Tunnel of Love?" the pilot said to Fake Elvis, who nodded. "I see you brought your son with you this time."

Fake Elvis peered at me over his tinted sunglasses. "Son? Never seen him before in my life." He strode across the helipad and climbed aboard the chopper.

The pilot frowned. "What are you doing out here all by yourself, young man?" he demanded. "This is a dangerous place to be in the middle of the night." He glanced around, probably looking for security.

I whipped out my notepad and paper. Time to put my plan into action. *I need to get to Portland by morning,* I wrote.

"Fat chance," he said with a laugh.

I glanced over my shoulder, certain that the elevator doors would open any minute now to reveal a wrathful Great-Aunt Abyssinia.

I'm serious. I'm prepared to pay well.

He looked at me sharply. "I'm listening."

I slipped my hand into my pocket, pulled out the diamond, and held it up.

The pilot shook his head in disgust. "You think I was born yesterday? This is Vegas, haven't you heard? Crossroad of phony and fake." He started to turn away.

I grabbed his arm. *It's real,* I wrote, digging in my backpack for the clincher. I pulled out Iz's black drawstring bag. I'd stuffed it in there after emptying the jewels out, and there was a piece of paper inside. It was from the jeweler who'd examined Olivia's first gems and certified their authenticity. I passed it to the pilot. I was practically jumping out of my skin by now. Great-Aunt Aby would be here any minute!

He glanced at it, then took the gemstone from my hand. He gave me a long, hard look. "Okay, then," he said. "You've got yourself a deal." He checked his watch and rubbed his chin. "We'll drop Elvis off at his gig, and afterward I'll take you to the little airfield where I keep my charter plane. I could have you in Portland by, say, eight a.m. That work for you?"

It was cutting it close, but what choice did I have? I nodded.

I followed him across the helipad, climbed aboard, and strapped myself into the seat next to Fake Elvis. He raised his eyebrows when he saw me, but didn't say anything.

The pilot seemed to be taking a ridiculous amount of time getting seated and checking his instruments. I jiggled nervously in my seat. I'd never flown in a helicopter before, plus I was sure Great-Aunt Aby would be arriving any second.

The engine finally whined to life. We were off! And not a moment too soon. As the helicopter lifted into the air, I saw the elevator doors slide open and my great-aunt come staggering out. Pearl was right behind her, clutching her updo with one hand and Great-Aunt Abyssinia with the other as the backdraft from the helicopter blades kicked up a sharp gust of wind.

I barely had time to glance in their direction before we angled steeply to the side and dropped over the edge of the hotel roof.

My stomach lurched, and to my intense embarrassment, I clutched Fake Elvis's arm and only just managed to squelch a scream. This was worse than a roller coaster! Way worse. Was this what it was like for my mother when she blasted into space? I closed my eyes, hoping I wouldn't pull a Geoffrey. We swooped down in what felt like a freefall, leaving my stomach up in the air—and then suddenly we straightened and the ride smoothed and we were floating effortlessly over Las Vegas.

After a few moments I felt brave enough to open my eyes. I gazed out at the city below us. It was beautiful from up here, not garish at all. The lights glowed like, well, gems. As we floated along over the Strip, I searched for the RV. There was no sign of it. Maybe my great-aunt had given up on me. I hoped so.

I didn't need any more of her "help." I didn't care if she was my fairy godmother, she'd meddled—and muddled— enough already.

We dropped lower, and the pilot pointed to a neon sign below, whose flashing red hearts announced the Tunnel of Love wedding chapel. Fake Elvis gave him a thumbs-up.

Who gets married in the middle of the night? I wondered, count- ing three wedding parties waiting in the parking lot. One couple was on a motorcycle. My mouth dropped open as I realized that the Tunnel of Love was a drive-thru chapel. Only in Las Vegas.

The brides' dresses and veils started flapping like crazy as the helicopter whirred lower and lower. No one seemed to mind, though—they all just laughed and grabbed at the bil- lowing fabric, waving their hems like flags.

The helicopter came to rest on the roof of the Tunnel of Love. As it whined to a stop, Fake Elvis opened the door, flung out a rope that was clipped at one end to a metal loop inside the helicopter, then clipped a carabiner on the belt of his white sequined jumpsuit to it. Waving to his audience, he leaped out.

This was obviously a well-practiced grand entrance.

I watched as he slid down the rope to the parking lot below, then grabbed the waiting microphone and launched into "Burning Love." The partygoers went wild, twisting and gyrating along with him to the lively beat. *Definitely not Bach,* I thought, wincing slightly as he hit a wrong note. *But catchy.*

The helicopter pilot took off his headset and turned

around. I knew the minute I saw the look on his face that the game was up.

"You're Diamond Girl's sister." It was a statement, not a question. "Did you think I wouldn't put two and two together? The gem, the receipt—it was from a jewelry store in Portland, Oregon!" He smiled at me. It was not a nice smile. "Guess this is my lucky day."

His hand clamped down onto my wrist in a viselike grip. "Here's what's going to happen," he told me. "When Elvis there is done sweatin' to the oldies, we're going to drop him back at the hotel. Not a word out of you, or I'll drop you there too. Only from a lot higher up, understand? Then we'll head to the airport and take my plane to Portland. Let's just say I want a whole lot more than one lousy diamond if your family wants you back."

My plan had backfired worse than Great-Aunt Aby's RV.

There was only one thing to do.

Leaning toward him in order to give the inevitable toad maximum propulsion, I yelled, "FAT CHANCE!"

The pilot yelped, recoiling. I wrenched my wrist free, and while he swatted at the toad, I unbuckled my seat belt, grabbed my backpack, and lunged for the open door. Before I could shimmy down the rope and make my escape, however, the pilot leaned over and grabbed the waistband of my jeans.

"You're not going anywhere," he said as I dangled there, half in and half out of the helicopter.

I reached for the landing skid—the long metal runner that the helicopter had instead of wheels—and wrapped my arms around it tightly as he tried to pull me back inside.

"Yoo-hoo! Catriona!"

I looked down in disbelief. A familiar RV was pulling into the Tunnel of Love's parking lot below. Great-Aunt Abyssinia's bright orange head was sticking out of the driver's window. She honked and waved at me.

"Who the heck is that?" asked the pilot, hollering to be heard above the soulful warbling of "A hunk, a hunka buuuuuurning love."

"The cavalry," I hollered back, dropping a toad on Fake Elvis. He sang on, oblivious, his eyes shut tight.

Great-Aunt Aby climbed out of the RV and looked up at us, the flashing hearts of the neon sign reflecting in her glasses. The wedding parties fell silent at the sight of all that purple fleece.

I heard the helicopter's engine roar to life, and a breeze kicked up as the rotor blades began to spin. I began to struggle, but the pilot still had tight hold of me with one hand.

"Do something!" I hollered at my great-aunt, launching another toad. The rotors were whipping around now at full speed, and Fake Elvis reached up to grab his black pompadour wig as it was knocked askew.

As the helicopter lifted skyward, I shrieked, spattering the rooftop of the Tunnel of Love with terrified toads. The chopper gave a lurch and I finally managed to twist free, but at the same time I lost my grip on the landing skid. I flailed wildly for a second, then somehow managed to grab hold of Fake Elvis's grand entrance rope. In a flash I found myself swinging wildly back and forth at the end of it as the helicopter continued to rise into the air.

So much for improvising, I thought. I'd gotten myself into a real fix this time.

"Hold fast, Catriona!" Great-Aunt Abyssinia shouted up at me. "Hold fast!"

My birthday necklace had slipped out from under my T-shirt, and I clutched instinctively at its golden charm. *Hold fast.* What exactly did those engraved words mean, anyway? Just what was I supposed to hold fast to? And why didn't Great-Aunt Aby hurry up and turn this stupid helicopter into a pumpkin or something?

"That's a great idea!" she bellowed, her front teeth making their own grand entrance as she grinned up at me.

I was directly above her now. I took a deep breath. Maybe Great-Aunt Aby was occupationally challenged, and maybe she was scatterbrained and unreliable and really, really odd, but she was my fairy godmother and she was family, and it was time to take a leap of faith and trust her.

Holding fast to my necklace, I let go of the rope.

CHAPTER 24

I opened my eyes and lay still for a long moment, trying to get my bearings.

There wasn't a speck of neon in sight; just ordinary daylight. I sat up and looked out the window, rubbing my eyes. Outside lay a familiar expanse of green, with the snow-capped peak of Mount Hood hovering on the far horizon. Just beyond the curb where the RV was parked was row upon row of lush, colorful blooms.

"The Rose Garden," I whispered, my hand automatically cupping my chin to catch the unavoidable toad.

We were home!

Maybe last night's wild ride in Vegas was all a dream, I thought. Then I turned and saw Elvis asleep in Great-Aunt Aby's armchair.

Or not.

"Well, whaddya know," Pearl exclaimed as she, too, opened her eyes and sat up. "We're back in Oregon."

The door to the RV flew open and Great-Aunt Abyssinia breezed in carrying a bag of doughnuts and a cardboard tray with five steaming paper cups. "Rise and shine, ladies and Elvis," she said cheerily. "Busy day ahead. Let's see here, I have two hot chocolates"—she passed Olivia and me each a cup—"and a double cappuccino for you, Pearl. Your favorite, right?"

"How did you know?"

Great-Aunt Aby flapped her hand dismissively. "You talk in your sleep." She nudged the sleeping Elvis impersonator's shoulder, and he jolted upright, regarding her with reproachful eyes.

"You kidnapped me!" he said as she took off his gag.

"Nonsense," Great-Aunt Aby replied. "Consider it a free vacation. Who wouldn't want to travel to beautiful Portland, Oregon?" She thrust a paper cup into his bound hands. "Nonfat half-caff caramel macchiato, extra hot, extra foam."

He blinked at her, speechless.

"You can thank me later." Pulling the stool out from under the table, my great-aunt lowered her giant frame onto it and took a sip from her own cup. "And for me, a soy latte." She grinned at the four of us. "Full house this morning. I can't remember the last time we had this much company, can you, Archie?"

Archibald, who hadn't taken his eyes off the toad I was holding in my hand since it appeared, twitched his tail.

"Catriona, honey, why don't you pass me that critter so I can put it outside," said my great-aunt, putting her finger to her lips. Her big teeth were nowhere in sight. "Safer for the little thing that way."

"And for the rest of us," said Pearl with a shudder. "Toads

are definitely not my favorite thing to wake up to in the morning. How about you, Elvis?"

Our sequin-spangled visitor looked from her to Great-Aunt Aby to me and back again in bewilderment. "All shook up," he said.

"Of course you are," said Great-Aunt Aby soothingly. "Don't worry, this is a round-trip vacation. We'll be sending you home again to Las Vegas shortly."

Pearl swung her legs over the edge of the RV's sofa and stood up. "Did you—I mean did we—"

"Yep," said Great-Aunt Abyssinia. "You four slept through the whole trip."

"What about my car?"

"The Red Rocket is safe and sound," my great-aunt assured her. "She's still hooked to my trailer hitch."

Pearl went over to the window to check. "Well, whaddya know," she said again.

I had the distinct feeling that my great-aunt wasn't telling the whole truth. I didn't recall driving anywhere last night. In fact, except for the showdown at the Tunnel of Love Wedding Chapel—especially the part where Great-Aunt Aby caught me after I let go of the rope—I didn't recall much of anything about last night. From the look on his face, I didn't think Fake Elvis did either.

"Switch on that TV, would you, Pearl?" said Great-Aunt Aby.

Pearl did as she was asked, and a familiar face flashed onscreen. It was the reporter who'd turned up on our doorstep the night Olivia spit out the diamond after the talent show.

"Good news this morning, folks! Diamond Girl has been found!"

I leaped to my feet, spilling my hot chocolate. My father had gotten my note!

"She and her sister were discovered last night hiding in Forest Park. Apparently the poor things had been rattled by all the, uh, media attention"—she had the grace to look a little sheepish at this—"but all's well that ends well, and they're safe and sound again at home with their parents."

"Clock's a-ticking, everyone," said Great-Aunt Abyssinia. "The mission is a go and we're at T minus one hour and counting." She crooked her finger at Fake Elvis. "You—come with me. How would you like to earn some real bling to go with that outfit?"

He glanced down at his white jumpsuit, looking confused. My great-aunt held out her hand, and Olivia obligingly sang the alphabet, filling her palm with glittering gems.

"You're Diamond Girl!" Fake Elvis said, staring at her in amazement.

My stepsister curtsied primly.

"And you're her sister," he said, taking a closer look at me and putting two and two together. "I thought you were a boy."

Olivia grinned and I stuck my tongue out at her.

"Well, she's not," said Pearl. "This here's Cat, and that there's Olivia, and their little brother has been kidnapped. We're fixing to get him back."

Fake Elvis looked confused. "But the TV just said—"

My great-aunt flapped a big hand at him. "It's a ruse," she explained. "All part of the plan—Catriona's plan, that is." She beamed at me. "If the kidnappers thought the girls were still missing, they wouldn't bother showing up at the rendezvous this morning."

He frowned.

"We could use some extra help," Great-Aunt Aby contin-ued. "We're heading for the zoo in an hour." She pointed at his feet. "You'll want to change out of those nice blue suede shoes, though. There may be some penguin poo involved."

Fake Elvis looked alarmed at this news, and Great-Aunt Abby patted his arm consolingly.

"I have a pair of hiking boots I think will fit you," she told him, which only seemed to confuse him further.

Playing her winning card, my great-aunt stretched out her palm. The sparkling stones made a tantalizing pile. "They're yours if you care to join us."

Her offer seemed to clear our guest's head. He got to his feet, nodding vigorously.

"Thought so," Great-Aunt Aby replied, a note of triumph in her voice.

As we all scattered to get dressed, I sent a text to A.J.: **Back in Portland. Not sure how.**

Me neither, he texted back. **According to FGPS, U made the trip from Vegas in 12.3 seconds.**

I stared at the cell phone screen. Great-Aunt Abyssinia defi-nitely wasn't telling the whole truth. There had to have been a wand involved here somewhere. No way had we gone a thou-sand miles in 12.3 seconds. Not even if this RV had wings.

Did u see the news this morning?

Apparently you've been found. Congratulations. ☺

Yep. Connor came through, I replied. **Did u let Hawkwinds know the plan?**

Yes, A.J. replied. **All systems go.**

Back at the campground yesterday, before the unscheduled

Vegas detour and our apparently near-instantaneous return trip to Portland, Great-Aunt Aby and Pearl and Olivia and I had worked out a strategy for this morning. I'd texted the details to A.J. and asked him to arrange some backup at the penguin exhibit. We all agreed that the Hawkwinds, plus Connor, were our best bet, since they already knew what was going on, and since they'd already be at the zoo on the field trip.

I slipped Connor's cell phone into my pocket and waited my turn for the bathroom, where I changed back into my Olivia's-little-brother disguise. It probably wouldn't fool anybody for too long—especially not the FBI agents who would be crawling all over the zoo—but it was better than nothing.

When I was finished, I knocked on the door to my great-aunt's bedroom.

"Come in!" she said.

Great-Aunt Abyssinia was standing in front of the mirror, holding up earrings and turning her head this way and that. "Parrots or pineapples?"

"Uh," I said. They were both hideous. Thrift-store finds, most likely.

"Yep," she said, putting both pairs away. "You're right." She bent down and grabbed my latest toad, then popped it out the window. "They wouldn't go with my outfit anyway."

She'd traded her purple fleece for a large navy blue one-piece coverall. It looked like something a mechanic might wear, especially with the hiking boots.

"You all need to see this," called Pearl from the RV's living room.

We joined her in front of the TV, where she was watching a news update. She pointed wordlessly at the screen. On it was a picture of a giant pumpkin.

My eyes widened as I realized that the pumpkin was perched on the roof of the Tunnel of Love. A white rat ran frantic circles around the base of it.

I gave my great-aunt an admiring look. This was more like it!

"Sometimes I get things right," she whispered smugly.

"No one knows just how the pumpkin got here," said the reporter as the camera zoomed in for a closer look. "The Tunnel of Love is temporarily closed until city workers finish clearing it away, but as a thank-you to any wedding parties who rebook, the management is offering free pumpkin pies while supplies last."

"Mighty odd happenings last night, yes sirree," said Pearl, sliding her eyes over to my great-aunt.

Great-Aunt Aby winked at me. "Mighty odd place, Las Vegas."

Pearl frowned. "Sure wish I could remember more of what happened."

My great-aunt nodded sympathetically. "Vegas tends to have that effect on people."

The picture on-screen switched to something closer to home. A little too close to home, in fact. The news crew was standing right outside in the Rose Garden.

"A pair of burst water mains have all but cut off access to the zoo this morning," announced the local reporter. "Kingston Road between the Rose Garden and the zoo parking lot is closed completely for the time being, and there's quite a bottleneck on Highway Twenty-six at the zoo exit as well, as school buses from all over the city converge for Portland's annual 'Field Trip Friday.' Northbound and south-bound lanes are partially blocked, with road crews working feverishly to make the necessary repairs. Commuters may want to look for alternate routes."

"That's the FBI's doing," said Pearl. "They're establishing a perimeter and limiting access."

"How do you know?" asked Fake Elvis.

"I watch a lot of cop shows on TV." She shot my great-aunt a worried look. "How will we get there if we can't drive? We don't have a whole lot of time left."

"Too bad the zoo train isn't running yet," Olivia said. "It doesn't start until Memorial Day, though."

Great-Aunt Abyssinia's eyes glinted behind her glasses. "Doesn't it? That's funny, I could swear I heard it just now."

She opened the door, and sure enough, in the distance we heard the hoot of a steam engine's whistle.

"What are you waiting for?" she said, grinning at our astonishment and setting an engineer's cap at a jaunty angle atop her bright orange hair. "All aboard!"

CHAPTER 25

"Best vacation I've had in years!" hollered Fake Elvis, sticking his head out the window of the zoo train's passenger car and lifting his nose to the wind like a retriever. He looked different in the full light of day. The only thing left of his costume from last night was his tinted sunglasses. Along with the white sequined jumpsuit and blue suede shoes, he'd left his black pompadour wig back in the RV, and it turned out that underneath he was as hairless as a Ping-Pong ball. I decided to think of him as Bald Elvis from now on. "You girls sure know how to have fun!"

Pearl grinned at him. In the engine cab ahead of us, Great-Aunt Abyssinia tootled the whistle again. The train sped along the narrow tracks that skirted the edge of the steep, forested canyon between the Rose Garden and the zoo. It was a little spooky under the canopy of trees, especially since we were the only passengers. I still wasn't exactly sure how Great-Aunt Aby had arranged to have the train waiting for us, but I guessed there were some perks to being a fairy god-mother, even a slightly defective one.

Bald Elvis was clearly enjoying himself, but my stomach was in knots. What if Dr. Dalton was there and spotted Olivia? She was the key to our plan for getting Geoffrey back. What if we bungled things somehow?

Beside me, Olivia looked equally nervous.

"Do you think Hawk Creek will make it?" she whispered with an anxious flurry of crocuses.

I shrugged. The dismal traffic report made it sound like getting to the zoo would be a nightmare. The only good thing Field Trip Friday had going for it was that Mrs. Bonneville was in charge, and Mrs. Bonneville didn't like delays. They were on her list of rules.

We chugged to a crawl near the perimeter of the zoo, then came to a stop just outside the wolf enclosure.

"This is as far as she goes," my great-aunt told us. "Can't afford to have anyone spot the train, so you'll have to go on foot along the tracks from here."

I leaned forward. "Aren't you coming?" I whispered, risking a toad. I flicked it into the shrubbery alongside the track. Bald Elvis still didn't know about my affliction, and I figured I might as well keep it that way.

She shook her head. "I'm going to try and bring the RV around. Good luck, and whatever you do, try to blend in."

Fat chance of that, I thought. We looked like a bunch of hillbillies. Bald Elvis was wearing a coverall just like Great-Aunt Aby's and chewing a toothpick; Pearl and her updo were swaddled in the bright orange poncho she'd borrowed from my great-aunt; and my stepsister had replaced her lost

Mariner's cap with a straw sun hat she'd dredged up from a storage cupboard in the RV. It was obviously one of Great-Aunt Abyssinia's thrift-store finds and looked like Archie had used it as a chew toy. And then there was me: aspiring toad huntress disguised as a small boy, but really just Catriona Skye Starr, twelve-year-old toad spitter.

I shook my head as we trudged off down the tracks.

I would have felt better with my great-aunt along for backup, but what with her unpredictable skills and all, maybe it was better this way. The zoo could be a dangerous place for an occupationally challenged fairy godmother. If she messed up here, who knew what could happen. I didn't want to end up as a penguin. Or lunch for one.

"Hey!" shouted a uniformed man a few minutes later as the four of us stepped from the train tracks onto the deserted platform. "What are you doing over there? The tracks are off-limits!"

"Just looking for the little boys' room," Pearl replied brightly. She tucked her arm through Bald Elvis's and pointed at me. "Our grandson had to go, and since we couldn't find it, we headed for the woods. Any port in a storm, right?" She laughed a tinkling little laugh, and I hung my head and scuffed my feet, pretending to be embarrassed.

Which I was. We were a freak show.

It was quick thinking on Pearl's part, though, I had to admit. Still, why did I always have to be the butt of every joke? Beside me, Olivia suppressed a laugh. I shot her the stink eye.

The zoo employee pointed wordlessly across the platform to the door clearly marked MEN'S ROOM.

"Well, whaddya know," exclaimed Pearl, pretending to be astonished. "Can you believe that, kids?"

Shaking his head in disgust, the employee walked off.

"That was a close one," whispered Pearl. Letting go of Bald Elvis's arm, she took my hand and put her arm around Olivia's shoulders. "Stay close, kids, and remember, girls—no diamonds and no toads."

"Huh?" said Bald Elvis, who was still clueless in the toad department.

"Nothing," said Pearl.

The four of us made our way to the penguin exhibit and got in line outside. The plan was to keep a low profile, avoid Dr. Dalton at all costs, and see what we could do to help grab Geoffrey back in case the FBI's plan went awry. Two heads were always better than one, so we figured, why not two plans?

Now that everyone thought my stepsister and I were safe and sound, the FBI would be bringing along a stand-in for Olivia. At least that's what I'd suggested. We'd be there in case anything went wrong with Plan A.

Bald Elvis had agreed to be the muscle for Plan B. He was middle-aged and a little pudgy, but the bald head kind of made him look like a boxer. He was going to act as Olivia's bodyguard and, if needed, run interference with the kidnappers while Pearl and I grabbed my little brother. Great-Aunt Aby's job was to bring the RV around to the zoo entrance. I'd been skeptical about using it as the getaway vehicle, but now that I knew it could make it from Las Vegas to Portland in 12.3 seconds, I was willing to give the RV a little more respect. If Great-Aunt Aby couldn't get around the roadblock, we'd have to improvise. There was always public transportation. My dad is forever bragging about how great it is in Portland. I hoped we wouldn't have to put it to the test, though.

We'd also eventually have to sort out the whole diamond and toad mess. Right now, though, the main thing was to get Geoffrey back and keep Olivia out of Dr. Dalton's clutches, and a lifetime of captivity in Area 51.

I regarded the line of people in front of the penguin exhibit. Which ones were FBI? Police? Plain old zoo visitors? Were the kidnappers here too? It was impossible to tell. There was no sign of Dad and Iz yet, nor did I see my little brother anywhere. And so far there weren't any Hawk Creek students, either.

All of a sudden Olivia stiffened. I looked to see what had caught her attention, and sucked in my breath sharply. Dr. Dalton was sitting on a bench across from the exhibit entrance. He was reading a newspaper and trying to look casual in a sweatshirt and baseball cap, but I'd know him anywhere. He looked up from his reading, his intense eyes scanning the crowd. Olivia turned her back to him, her face drained of color.

We both stood motionless, until his gaze passed over us, then sagged with relief. I grabbed Pearl and pointed him out surreptitiously.

"Dalton?" she whispered, frowning.

I nodded, and she relayed the message to Bald Elvis, who sized him up. "He's the one who wants to take you to Area Fifty-one?" he asked my stepsister.

She nodded.

"Not on my watch," Bald Elvis told her stoutly. He looked at me. "And he can't have you, either."

I became an Elvis fan right then and there.

The exhibit doors opened and the line moved forward. As we descended the long hallway that led into the Penguinarium, I heard a familiar voice behind me.

"Mrs. Bonneville wants everyone to stay with their assigned partners! No wandering off!"

Hawk Creek Middle School had made it!

Olivia's face lit up and she started to turn around—to look for Connor Dixon, no doubt. I elbowed her sharply. She glared at me, then faced forward again and jammed her sun hat down more firmly on her head. We filed into the exhibit's warm, humid interior, wrinkling our noses. The Oregon Zoo's penguins are Humboldts from the coast of Peru, not the arctic kind. The temperature in the exhibit always fools people who expect it to be glacial.

"P-U," said Pearl. "It's stinky in here."

"You said it, sister," agreed Bald Elvis, fanning the air in front of his face.

The crowd began milling around, and the large, dimly lit room soon echoed with the shouts of excited middle school students. As planned, Pearl, Bald Elvis, Olivia, and I made our way to the wall across from the glass tank, where we pretended to examine the informational placards.

"'Found only in the Southern Hemisphere, Humboldt penguins are agile and can swim at speeds of up to thirty miles per hour,'" Pearl read aloud, keeping one eye on the crowd. "Well, whaddya know."

All systems go, I texted A.J.

He texted me right back: **Hawkwinds in place.**

I glanced over to where Rani and her brother and Juliet Rodriguez were setting down their backpacks. Connor was with them too. Their mission was to provide a diversion if one proved necessary. I wasn't sure exactly what they were going to do, but I had a pretty good idea.

Olivia, who was wedged securely between Bald Elvis and the map of the Humboldt penguin's natural habitat, reached over and poked me in the arm, jerking her chin toward the entrance. My father and Iz had just walked in. I glanced at the cell phone in my hand: 9:00 a.m. on the dot—right on time. My heart did a somersault at the sight of them, and I would have given anything at that moment to be able to run across the room and fling myself into their arms.

But if I did that, Dr. Dalton would step in and snag Olivia, and our bargaining chip would be gone. We might not get Geoffrey back. *Suck it up, Cat,* I told myself sternly. *Pull up your socks. Hold fast.*

My father and stepmother had a girl between them with curly blond hair just like Olivia's. Or at least at first glance I thought she was a girl. On closer look I could see that she was actually a vertically challenged adult—an FBI agent, probably—dressed like a middle schooler.

Would she fool the kidnappers? I certainly hoped so. If she didn't, we'd have to step in.

I saw my father tense as he spotted Dr. Dalton. He clearly didn't like the government scientist. I doubted anyone did. If Dr. Dalton had a dog, I'd bet even his dog didn't like him.

A moment later a door in the wall just to the left of us that read STAFF ONLY opened, and a tall, skinny man in a zoo employee uniform appeared. He was carrying a jani-tor's broom. He started sweeping, scanning the room all the while. His gaze settled on my father, Iz, and the female FBI agent standing between them.

Here we go, I thought. *Showtime.*

A few yards away on the other side of us, I noticed a woman with a stroller lean down and speak directly into her baby's sippy cup. *Odd,* I thought, then realized that it was actually Agent Reynolds—and that the "baby" in the stroller was just a bundle of blankets. She'd spotted the kidnapper too.

I nudged Pearl and Bald Elvis, pointing at the janitor.

"Got him," Pearl whispered. "Where's your little brother?"

There was no sign of Geoffrey.

Olivia peeked out from behind Bald Elvis. Her eyes wid-ened when she saw the man we were talking about. "I've seen him somewhere before!" she exclaimed, quickly covering her mouth with her hand to hide the inevitable result of her words.

Pearl frowned. "Who is he, honey?"

Olivia scrutinized him as he began sweeping his way toward my father and Iz. She shook her head. "I'm not sure," she told us, covering her mouth again.

Suddenly a female voice cried, "Hey, look, there's Olivia!"

I whirled around to see Piper Philbin waving at my step-sister. Olivia ducked back behind Bald Elvis, but it was too late. The janitor paused, alert as a hawk. He watched as Piper ran over to us.

"Why are you hiding?" she asked my stepsister. "And what's with that ugly hat?"

"You stupid—," I began to say, before Pearl clamped her

hand over my mouth. I gagged as I felt my mouth fill with toad.

"Fleabrain!" Olivia finished for me, launching a sharp-edged diamond at her.

Everything happened really fast after that. The janitor spotted the gemstone. His eyes lit up. So did Dr. Dalton's. As Piper stood there looking bewildered, they both started for us. Out of the corner of my eye I saw Agent Reynolds grab the sippy cup off the stroller. She spoke into it again as she sprinted in our direction.

The janitor reached us first. Pushing Piper aside, he lunged for Olivia. Bald Elvis stepped forward to block him, but the janitor tripped him with his broom, sending him sprawling. Pearl let go of me and started smacking the janitor with her purse as he grabbed Olivia's wrist and dragged her toward the door that read STAFF ONLY.

My eyes were watering. I couldn't hold the toad in any longer. "Bleah!" I cried, spitting it into my hands and hoping no one saw me.

Piper did. She shrieked and backed into Dr. Dalton, who stared at the toad, then at me, riveted.

Great, I thought. *Area 51, here I come.*

At least the janitor hadn't seen me. He was too intent on capturing my stepsister. Hoping to distract him, I pitched the toad at the back of his head. Unfortunately, it missed and hit Pearl instead, who yelped and dropped her purse. The Hawkwinds mistook this for the signal to create a diversion, and in a flash the Penguinarium echoed with the strains of Mozart's *Eine kleine Nachtmusik.* I resisted the urge to cover my delicate, shell-like ears. Connor was *terrible* on the saxophone.

"Where's my little brother?" I hollered at the man in the zoo uniform, heedless now of toads, Piper Philbin, Dr. Dalton, or anyone else. All I could think of was Geoffrey. "You promised to give him back!"

He didn't even pause to turn around and look at me as toads streamed from my lips, dropping to the floor and scattering in every direction. One landed on Piper Philbin's foot. She fainted, and Dr. Dalton caught her just before she hit the ground.

As the toads hopped off in a panic, people screamed and ran for the exit doors. Agent Reynolds was swept away in the stampede, and so were Pearl and Bald Elvis and my father and Iz.

Things had gone terribly, horribly wrong. Plan A, Plan B, all of it. I looked around wildly, hoping to spot the cavalry again, but Great-Aunt Abyssinia was nowhere in sight. *Really,* I thought with disgust. What was the point of a fairy godmother if she didn't show up when you needed her?

I had no choice.

It was up to me to try and rescue Olivia and Geoffrey.

I dived for the man in the zoo janitor's uniform, latching on to his leg as he hauled my shrieking stepsister through the open door in the wall. The last thing I heard before it slammed shut behind us was my homeroom teacher wailing, "Mrs. Bonneville doesn't like toads!"

CHAPTER 26

Before I could even open my mouth to scream for help, a gag was stuffed into it and my hands were bound in front of me. Something scratchy—a burlap bag, maybe?—was pulled over my head.

A second later I was dumped into something soft and squishy. One of my hands brushed up against whatever it was, and I recoiled. The something was *slimy,* too. And what was that awful smell?

I nearly gagged on my gag when I realized that I was sitting in a cart full of dead fish.

"Mmmf mmmf!" Olivia was trussed up beside me, struggling wildly. I felt a brief flash of sympathy—Miss Prissy Pants, who hated nature when it was alive, must be even more grossed out to find herself sitting in the middle of the penguins' lunch.

The cart surged forward, one of its wheels squeaking loudly as our captor pushed it down a dimly lit corridor.

Panting heavily, he steered us around a sharp corner. Olivia rolled into me. Another stretch of corridor, then the cart suddenly picked up speed. We were heading downhill.

Where the heck were we going?

I got my answer a minute later when the cart angled up again and I felt a blast of fresh air. The trumpet of an elephant and a whole new set of smells announced that we were halfway across the zoo, behind the elephant enclosure.

I remembered my dad telling me once, when he brought me here with Olivia before Geoffrey was born, that the exhibits were connected by underground tunnels. My heart sank as I realized the FBI would be looking for us in the wrong place. They'd be searching outside the penguin exhibit, not way over here.

I squeezed my eyes shut and tried sending Great-Aunt Abyssinia a mental SOS, hoping that fairy godmothers were equipped with some kind of radar that could pick up a distress signal.

If she heard me, though, she didn't respond.

Now that we were outside in the daylight, I could make out a tiny bit of my surroundings through the burlap bag's rough mesh. The cart was heading for a white zoo van. Its rear door was wide open, and when we reached it, our captor picked me up and tossed me inside. A second later I heard a thud as Olivia was dumped in too. Then the door slammed shut.

Where were the police and the FBI? Why weren't they stopping us? Where were Dad and Iz and Pearl and Bald Elvis? *Where was Great-Aunt Abyssinia?*

The van's engine roared to life, and a split second later

there was a crunch of gravel as we pulled forward onto a driveway or a road. I tried to make as much noise as possible as we drove on, hoping someone would hear me. I didn't dare holler—no point choking myself on a toad—but I did lash out with my feet, kicking as hard as I could against the side of the van.

Unfortunately, I also kicked Olivia.

She grunted and kicked me back.

"Keep it down back there, for crying out loud!" snapped the driver, making another sharp turn that sent Olivia rolling into me.

We lay there side by side, breathing heavily. The van made its way along what must have been some kind of a back road, from the way we were bumping and jolting. Were we in the canyon?

We lurched again, and then I felt the hum of smooth pavement. We were back on a main road. Had we left the zoo? Before long I heard the rush of cars on the freeway. The kidnappers were getting away with it!

Olivia grabbed my hand and squeezed. She must have had the same thought. I squeezed back, just as scared as she was. Where, oh, where was Great-Aunt Abyssinia?

Life lessons, my mother had said. Our family's fairy godmother was all about teaching life lessons.

What kind of a life lesson is this? I wondered bitterly. All of a sudden Great-Aunt Abyssinia's words came floating into my mind. "What you two need is to find some common ground," she'd told me that first night she came to visit, right before this whole stupid diamond and toad business started.

What did Olivia and I have in common, though? We were

so completely, utterly different. I racked my brain trying to think of an answer. And then it hit me.

Geoffrey.

Of course! Our little brother was what we had in common. We both loved Geoffrey, and we both wanted him back.

But how was knowing this supposed to help? I mulled it over as we sped along the freeway.

A short time later we pulled off. Another stretch of road, a few more sharp turns, and then the van slowed as I heard the rumble of a garage door. We eased forward and came to a halt, the garage door rumbling shut again behind us.

My stepsister and I were rapidly bundled out of the van and set on our feet. As the burlap sacks were whisked off our heads, we blinked in the harsh glare of the overhead light.

"Two of them?" said a gravelly voice—the same gravelly voice we'd heard on the speakerphone after Geoffrey first vanished. It belonged to a short, pudgy man who was standing in front of us. Very short, in fact. The two of us stood eye to eye. "You were only supposed to bring me one." He pointed to Olivia. "Diamond Girl here."

"Yeah, boss," our captor replied. "But I couldn't shake the other one, and I just thought—well, I figured I'd better not leave her behind."

"*You* thought? *You* figured? You shouldn't think so much. It gets us in trouble when you think. And whaddya mean you couldn't shake her? She's a pipsqueak."

Who's calling who a pipsqueak? I thought, scowling at him.

He ignored me. Leaning in for a closer inspection, he grimaced. "What is that nasty smell?"

"Sorry, boss," said the janitor. "It was feeding time at the zoo. Only way to get them out."

The pudgy man flicked his pudgy fingers at me dismissively. "Get rid of her. No point dragging along dead weight."

My heart nearly stopped at his words. Olivia shot me a glance, then started hopping up and down and squealing behind her gag. The pudgy man brightened.

"Quick," he said. "Untie her! Not her *hands*, you moron, her *mouth*! She might be making diamonds!"

She was. Lots of them.

"Keep your hands off her!" she sputtered. "She's my sister!"

I take back every mean thing I ever said about you, I thought. *Well, almost every mean thing.*

The pudgy man stooped down to gather up the glittering stones she'd dropped, then straightened again and looked at me with renewed interest. "Sister, huh? That's right, I read about how there were two of you." He extended a fat finger and poked me in the ribs, then looked over at Olivia. "So what you're telling me is, if we squeeze her, she might make diamonds too?"

He doesn't know, I realized with a sudden burst of clarity. He didn't know about the toads! Neither of them did.

I had a secret weapon.

I edged a little closer to Olivia, hoping she'd catch my drift. If she could just untie my gag somehow—

Instead she stepped on my foot.

"That's right," she told the pudgy man, shooting me a warning look.

"Really? Lemme see." He motioned to the janitor to remove my gag.

As the man in the zoo uniform moved to do his bidding, his cell phone rang. He answered it. "Uh-huh," he said, listening to the voice on the other end. "Uh-oh. I see. I'll tell him."

"Tell me what?" snapped the pudgy man as the janitor hung up.

"Our transport is ready," he replied, and Olivia and I exchanged a glance. Transport? That didn't sound good.

"Captain says there's a complication, though," he continued. The pudgy man frowned. "What complication?"

"The harbor is crawling with FBI," the janitor told him unhappily. "They've shut down the airport and the train station and set up roadblocks on all the freeways, too. It's all over the news."

The pudgy man threw his hands up in the air. "I should have known better than to listen to you!" he cried, waddling back and forth in agitation. "If we'd made the trade the day after we grabbed the kid, like I wanted, this never would have happened. They wouldn't have had time to get organized. But noooo, you had to talk me into your stupid 'my cousin who works at the zoo and is out of town' scheme. Your stupid 'I can borrow his ID' scheme." He stopped and shook his head in disgust. "And Field Trip Friday—what was that all about? I don't care if the zoo *was* crawling with kids. Waiting for that extra cover you wanted was a disaster!" He started pacing again. "'Piece of cake,' you told me. Some cake! What'd you do back there, leave a bread crumb trail leading to our door?"

The janitor looked like he was hoping the floor would open up and swallow him.

"Call him back," the pudgy man ordered, snapping his fingers. "I'm not getting this close and giving up. Tell him to move the boat downriver. Far enough away where the feds won't be watching. St. Helens, maybe. We'll meet him there."

The janitor nodded.

"And get these two in the car," added the pudgy man, snapping his fingers. "We're leaving now."

We were going on a boat? I could feel panic welling up inside. It would be much, much harder for the FBI, and probably even for Great-Aunt Abyssinia, to rescue us if we were on the river, or worse, at sea. I doubted the RV could float.

"I have to go to the bathroom," Olivia announced as the janitor started for us.

"Oh, for crying out loud," said the pudgy man.

"Well, I do," she told him, spitting out another diamond.

He picked it up, mollified. "Fine, then," he said, motioning to the janitor. "Take her inside. But make it quick."

Olivia disappeared, leaving me in the garage with Mr. I'm Not Vertically Challenged. For the first time in my life I was sorry to see her go.

"Get in the car," he told me, opening the rear door of the black SUV that was parked next to the zoo van.

I climbed awkwardly inside. It wasn't an easy thing to do with my hands tied, and I fell on my face. I managed to squirm into place, and he buckled me in. "Gotta protect the valuables," he said with an unpleasant smile. He removed my gag. "Now let's see what you can do."

I could hardly wait to show him. It was high time for a demonstration of toad power.

"Cat!" cried Olivia just as I sucked in a lungful of air and prepared to unload. "Cat, look!"

Something in her voice made me pause. Holding my breath, I turned around to see her emerging from the house with the janitor. Our little brother was in her arms.

"Geoffrey's safe!" Olivia cried, and burst into tears.

CHAPTER 27

I whooshed out my breath.

In all the excitement of the last few minutes I'd completely forgotten about our little brother!

"Cat!" he hollered, spotting me in the back of the car. He waved, and I held up my bound hands and waved back, wanting to laugh for joy and at the same time blinking back tears.

A few seconds later he and Olivia were bundled into the backseat alongside me. The janitor put Geoffrey between us, and my stepsister and I bumped heads as we both leaned down at the same time to kiss him. Olivia sat up. "You first," she said in a low voice, scattering bluebells. Geoffrey's favorite flower. "He likes you best." She turned away to face the window, and I heard her mutter, "He doesn't even know my name."

Geoffrey heard her too. He pulled his finger out of his mouth. "Livy," he said.

Olivia turned around again. "G-Man!" she cried, showering

him in a drift of rosy apple blossoms. "You know my name!"

"Any diamonds from the short one yet?" asked the pudgy man, hurrying across the garage. "Lotta talking going on in there."

"Not that I can tell," the janitor replied

Olivia shot me a warning look as the two men searched the seat around me.

"We need some water first before my sister can make diamonds," she said quickly. "That's the only way it works. Gotta keep hydrated."

The pudgy man looked at her suspiciously. "Okay, then. Water it is." He snapped his fingers at the janitor again. "You get the luggage; I'll get the water." Turning to us, he added, "No funny business, though, or you get the bags-over-the-head routine again, understand? Him, too." He pointed to Geoffrey, who stuck his finger in his mouth and started sucking on it with vigor.

The two men headed back inside. I didn't care what Mr. I'm Not Vertically Challenged said, I wasn't just going to sit here and do nothing. I fumbled for the door handle.

"Cat, wait, listen to me," said Olivia, her voice low and urgent. "We don't have much time before they come back."

I looked over at her, irritated. "What?" A toad popped out and landed on my knee. I brushed it to the floor.

"Cat! No toads!"

What was she talking about?

"It's my secret weapon!" I protested. "Our ticket to freedom!"

She shook her head. "We have to make them think that you and Geoffrey make diamonds too, and quick. Otherwise . . ."

234

She paused, then added, "I heard the janitor guy on the phone in there. You have to trust me on this. I know what you're thinking, but you can't use the toads. It's gotta be diamonds, okay? Please, Cat? Trust me?"

I looked at her. Trust Olivia? The one who'd called me "Catbox" in front of the entire school? The one who'd given me the cold shoulder all these years and resented every scrap of attention Iz gave me, and always made sure I never felt welcome? The one who'd stuck duct tape down the middle of our bedroom?

I glanced down at the empty ring finger on her right hand. Olivia couldn't even bear to keep her "Sisters are forever friends" ring on for a single week, and now she wanted me to trust her?

"Please," she said again.

A pure white rose fluttered from her lips like a peace offering. I sighed. Olivia'd had to trust me a lot these past couple of days, what with me dragging her out of the house in the middle of a rainstorm, forcing her to come with me to find Great-Aunt Aby, and then abandoning her last night in Las Vegas. Maybe it was my turn to return the favor.

Between us, Geoffrey was watching, round eyed, as toads and gems flew back and forth across the backseat of the car. What choice did I have, really? Our little brother's safety was at stake. The only way we had even a sliver of a chance of getting ourselves out of this mess was if we worked together as a team.

"Okay," I said slowly. "But if the right moment comes along, you have to let me improvise."

She nodded, and I wondered if I'd regret the bargain we'd

just struck. When musicians improvise—make it up as they go along—they have to trust their fellow musicians. Could I really trust my stepsister?

"Here," she said, stuffing my hands with gems. "I made these when I was in the bathroom."

"Eew," I replied, and she grinned.

"Shut up—you know what I mean. You get rid of the toads; I'll pick up the rest."

By the time our two captors returned, my pockets were full of diamonds and the backseat was cleared of toads—well, all except for one, which had retreated way under the driver's seat and wouldn't budge. I was still bent over trying to coax it out when the men got into the car.

I sprang upright the minute the driver's door opened.

"What are you doing back there?" said the pudgy man, looking at me with suspicion. "You're not up to something, are you?"

I extended my bound hands slowly and opened one of them. He looked at the pile of gems it contained with greedy delight.

"About time!" He snatched them from me, then suddenly his eyes narrowed and darted from me to Olivia and back again. "Hey—you two aren't trying to pull a fast one, are you?"

I'd been expecting this. I shook my head, then ventured the slightest of coughs, hoping it wouldn't spark a toad. I was in luck; it didn't. Delicately I plucked out the diamond I'd popped into my mouth a minute ago and held it up smugly.

"Holy cow, we hit the jackpot!" he crowed. "Two for the price of one!"

"I told you so," said the janitor. "The research specialists thought maybe it ran in the family."

Olivia's eyes widened.

"What?" I mouthed.

She shook her head at me. "Later," she whispered.

The pudgy man turned around again. "So, what about the kid, then?" he demanded. "When does he start cranking them out?"

Croak.

He frowned. "Did you hear that?" he asked the janitor.

"Hear what, boss?"

Croak.

Olivia and I sat rooted to our seats, aghast. This was not good. If our captors found the toad, there would be questions, and eventually they'd get the truth out of us. The pudgy man opened the driver's side door and started to get out.

"Frog!" said Geoffrey happily, pointing to the floor.

Thinking quickly, I leaned over and slipped another diamond out of the cuff of my hoodie. Then I sat up again, holding it in the air triumphantly, as if I'd just picked it up off the floor.

"Hey, check it out, boss, the little guy makes 'em too," said the janitor.

"Looks like this is my lucky day," said the pudgy man, forgetting all about the croaking toad. "Runs in the family, eh?" He closed the SUV door again. "Then we're just gonna be one big happy family." He whistled as he started the engine.

"Are we there yet?" asked Geoffrey hopefully.

"For Pete's sake, kid, we haven't even left yet," said the janitor.

As we backed out of the garage, Geoffrey started looking anxious, as he always does on car trips. Olivia gave his hand a reassuring pat.

"You might want to roll the windows down a little," she told our captors. "Our little brother gets carsick."

"Great," muttered the pudgy man, pressing a button up front. The tinted rear windows each descended an inch.

Olivia started to sing. She actually had a good voice, and I wondered why she wasn't in the Hawk Creek Chorus. That would be so much better than her lame tap dance troupe.

She sang the theme song to *Robo Rooster*, and as she sang, Geoffrey stuck his finger back in his mouth and started swinging his chubby legs in time to the music. I shot her a grateful look. She was doing her best to keep our little brother calm and happy.

"How come you're not singing?" the pudgy man asked, frowning at me in the rearview mirror as we got onto the freeway again.

I grabbed my throat, miming thirst.

"Oh, yeah, right." He snapped his fingers at his companion. "She needs more water."

The janitor opened a bottle and passed it over the back of his seat to me. I took it and sipped slowly, stalling for time. This was going to be tricky. Olivia sang louder, as if to make up for my silence.

"So sing already," said the pudgy man, still watching me.

What on earth was I going to do? I couldn't keep stalling forever. Olivia shot me a worried look. Then I remembered—whistling didn't produce toads! I took one more sip of water, managing to slurp up another diamond from inside my cuff as I did so.

I started to whistle. I whistled along for about a minute, then stopped, as if in surprise.

"Did you make one?" he asked, looking at me keenly.

I nodded and opened my mouth, extending my tongue. On the end of it was the diamond.

"That's more like it." His fat little hand whipped back and grabbed it.

Pipsqueak, I thought, scowling out the window.

I heard the rapid click of the blinker, and the SUV slowed as we approached a four-way stop. I looked at the street sign. Skyline. My heart sank. Skyline led to Cornelius Pass Road, the cutoff from Portland's West Hills down to the river, where our "transport" was waiting—the boat that would spirit us away from our family forever.

Wasn't this also the road that led to Iz's favorite berry farm, though, the one she took us to every summer to help pick berries for pies and jam? It was—I was sure of it! The people there were so nice—maybe this was the break I'd been hoping for. What if we could get our captors to pull over near it somehow? Could we take a chance and make a run for it?

It's not like we had anything to lose. Not with a voyage to permanent exile on the horizon.

All we needed was a diversion.

No problem, I thought. *Time to break out the toads.*

I glanced over at Olivia, trying to catch her eye.

"'Robo Rooster, he's the one,'" she sang, heedless of my frantic hand motions. With all this singing, she was nearly up to her knees in flowers and gems. "'He makes sure we all have fun!'" She rested her fingers on the top of the open window as she sang.

In the front seat the pudgy man's head bobbed in time to the music.

I flicked a glance out the window. We were getting closer. The sun had come out; it was turning into a beautiful day. The suburbs melted away as the road pushed deeper into the countryside, and soon we were winding through a patchwork of fields and forest. Up ahead I saw a homemade sign nailed to a tree that proclaimed FRESH BERRIES—ONE MILE AHEAD!

Ahead in the distance I could see the roof of the berry farm's red barn. I prodded Olivia with my foot. She looked over at me, and I motioned with my chin toward the sign, then mimed picking berries and eating them. She watched me, puzzled. I jerked my chin at the pudgy man behind the wheel, pantomiming him steering off the side of the road, then pointed at the berry farm again. My stepsister's face clouded with confusion as she looked from one to the other, trying to decipher what I was telling her. This wasn't working! I pointed frantically at the toad still crouched under the passenger seat ahead of me then back at myself, and light finally dawned in her eyes.

She gave me a thumbs-up with her bound hands and started singing again.

The mission was on! *Toad minus one mile and counting.*

The SUV slowed as we approached a series of switchbacks that led down the hill to the farm. As we swerved first one way and then the other, I glanced at Geoffrey. He was pale as milk, and his face had that pinched, anxious expression it always gets right before he barfs.

Suddenly I had a better idea. Forget the toads. The real secret weapon was my little brother.

I stuck my leg out and prodded Olivia again, then pointed to Geoffrey. Our eyes met over the top of his head and we both smiled.

"How come you stopped singing?" demanded the pudgy man.

My stepsister swung into yet another chorus of "Robo Rooster," and I whistled along, biding my time. Any minute now for sure. The barn ahead was calling me like a beacon, a lighthouse in a field of green. We slowed to a crawl, and with each hairpin turn, we grew closer to our destination, and Geoffrey grew slightly greener around the gills.

The farm was just ahead now, and the SUV swerved again sharply as it made the final turn. Geoffrey pulled his finger out of his mouth. "Are we there yet?" he asked weakly.

"Now!" I cried.

Olivia and I held Geoffrey by the shoulders and leaned him forward, pointing him at the pudgy man behind the wheel.

Right on cue, the Barf Bucket delivered.

CHAPTER 28

Both of our captors let out a howl as Geoffrey doused them thoroughly.

"That's disgusting!" cried the pudgy man behind the wheel.

Wait until you see this, I thought as I took a deep breath and launched into the first thing that popped into my mind—a rousing chorus of the national anthem.

"'Oh, say, can you SEE by the DAWN'S early LIGHT!'" I sang at the top of my lungs, leaning forward and unleashing a torrent of toads over the back of the seat. "'What so PROUDLY we HAILED at the twilight's last GLEAMING!'"

I bellowed my way through the anthem's first stanza, toads gushing from me like water from Old Faithful on one of Great-Aunt Aby's Yellowstone postcards. By the time I reached the end, there were amphibians everywhere.

Our captors didn't stand a chance against toad power.

The SUV swerved wildly as the pudgy man lost control of

the wheel. We twisted this way and that, then lurched off the road and into a ditch, hissing to a stop. Our captors sat there for a moment, dazed. They were covered in barf—and toads. The man in the zoo janitor's uniform was whimpering.

"Run for it!" I told Olivia.

Unbuckling Geoffrey, I popped my bound hands over his head and scooped him off the seat. Somehow I managed to get the door open and the two of us outside. Several cars had pulled over behind us, and concerned passersby were starting to get out and make their way in our direction. I saw one woman on a cell phone and hoped she was calling 911. I didn't wait to find out, though. Intent only on reaching the barn—and safety—I started across the field.

Behind me, Olivia gave a cry of frustration.

"Oh, no you don't," said the pudgy man, and I turned to see that he was leaning over the back of his seat, holding on to the sleeve of her hoodie.

I hesitated. "Olivia?"

"Forget it, Cat!" she called back, waving me on. "Get Geoffrey out of here!"

I thought fleetingly of her diorama back home, the one of Geoffrey's room with the gem-covered arrow that led to her door. She was going to sacrifice herself to try to put things right.

My little brother stirred in my arms. He was covered in barf and smelled almost as bad as I did, thanks to my ride in the Penguinarium lunch cart. Should I just cut my losses and try and get him to safety?

Geoffrey looked up at me, his greenish blue eyes huge in his pale face. "Livy," he said.

I sighed. "You're right, G-Man," I told him. "We can't leave Livy. You wait here." I set him down at the edge of the field, then I ran back to the SUV. "Let her go, pipsqueak!" I hollered at the pudgy man. And taking hold of both of my stepsister's hands, I pulled with all my might.

The silver ring on my right hand gleamed in the sunlight, its aquamarines sparkling between the words "Sisters are forever friends." *Maybe,* I thought. *Or maybe not.* But one thing was for sure: There were some things worth holding fast to, and family was one of them. I knew that now. Olivia and I might be as different as night and day, and we might never like the same things or even the same people. But deep down we were family. And it was time for me to accept her, warts and all. I braced my feet against the doorjamb of the SUV and hung on stubbornly.

"Hold fast, Olivia!" I shouted, popping out a particularly large toad.

Croak.

I looked at it, startled. Had it just winked at me?

As it hopped away, Olivia's hoodie sleeve tore loose and the two of us popped out of the car like a cork out of a bottle. We scrambled to our feet, ignoring the pudgy man's angry shouts. I scooped Geoffrey up again and the three of us started to run. Across the field we flew, never once looking back until we reached the safety of the barn. We rounded its corner, breathless.

The Red Rocket was parked on the other side. The top was down and Pearl was in the driver's seat, her bright pink fingernails drumming on the steering wheel. Bald Elvis was beside her, fiddling with the radio. I could hear the strains of "Jailhouse Rock."

"There you are," said Great-Aunt Abyssinia, who was lounging against the hood. Her orange hair flashed in the sun as she stood up and opened the door for us. "Right on time."

CHAPTER 29

"P-U!" said Pearl as the three of us piled into the backseat. Bald Elvis reached over to untie our hands. "What the heck kind of perfume are you kids wearing?"

"Eau de barf," I told her, shoving over to make room for my great-aunt. "With a side of Chicken of the Sea."

G-Man climbed straight into Great-Aunt Aby's lap. She buckled the seat belt firmly around them both, then tapped Pearl on the shoulder. "Hit it, Pearl. Let's see what this baby can do."

In a flash we were on the road, sailing back up Cornelius Pass Road toward Portland, and home. We passed the disabled SUV as we sped up the switchback. A police cruiser was parked behind it with its lights flashing. I caught a glimpse of the pudgy man and the zoo janitor, trussed up like Thanksgiving turkeys. They were still covered in barf.

"Hey! How did they . . . Where did that rope come from?"

Great-Aunt Aby's big front teeth peeked out as she gave

me a sly smile. "Sometimes I get things right."

"I finally remembered where I saw that janitor guy before," Olivia told us. "He was at the hospital the day I went in for tests. He was the lab assistant who tried to steal one of my diamonds."

So Iz had been right about him!

"There's one thing I still don't understand, though," I said a few minutes later as we merged onto the freeway. I had to holler to be heard, as the wind was whipping my words away now. Pearl had taken Great-Aunt Aby's challenge and floored it. "How did you find us?"

Bald Elvis glanced back at me. "We just followed the diamond trail."

I looked at him blankly. "What diamond trail?"

"The one I left," said Olivia. "After I got them to roll the windows down, remember? I just kept tossing them out." She smiled at me. "You were the one who said to improvise."

Maybe my stepsister was smarter than I'd given her credit for. It turns out Olivia's diamonds gave off a lot of light. More, even, than regular ones. A.J. and Mom had picked them up on the FGPS and relayed our location to Great-Aunt Aby.

"Your great-aunt may not have a cell phone, but I do," said Pearl, fishing it out of her purse. It was bright pink, naturally. "That friend of yours in Houston is one smart kid. He tracked me down somehow and had us on your trail in no time."

Fifteen minutes later we were home. Dad and Iz burst out the front door and came flying down the porch steps when they saw the Red Rocket pull into the driveway. The FBI was right behind them.

"You're safe!" they kept repeating, hugging and kissing us despite our collective odor.

"Congratulations, girls," said Agent Salgado. "You did an amazing job today."

Agent Reynolds nodded. "Foolhardy but brave. Your kidnappers are both in custody."

"As well they should be," said Pearl, tucking her arm through Bald Elvis's.

"Warden'll be throwing a party in the county jail," he added in agreement.

"Do you mind if we ask you a few questions?" asked Agent Salgado, taking out his notebook.

"Sure," I replied. "Go right ahead."

Everyone stared at me.

"What?" I said defensively.

Olivia poked me in the back. I turned around and she pointed to my mouth. "You're not—you stopped—there aren't any—"

"Toads?" I looked at the ground in surprise. She was right. There wasn't an amphibian in sight. "Hey, wait a sec," I said, looking back at her. "No diamonds, either."

Nothing was coming out of either of our mouths but words.

"When did it stop?" I asked her.

She shrugged. "We were so busy escaping I didn't notice."

"Me neither." I tried to think back. Were there toads in the Red Rocket? I wasn't entirely sure, but I didn't think so. I did remember that big one at the SUV, though, when I pulled Olivia out, the one that I thought maybe had—

I looked over at Great-Aunt Aby. She spread her big hands wide, the picture of innocence.

"Let's get you kids cleaned up," said Iz. "G-Man, you're going straight into the tub."

As we started up the front steps, a taxi screeched around the corner of our dead-end street and pulled into our driveway behind the Red Rocket. The door opened and Dr. Dalton leaped out. Olivia froze. So did I.

"Which one of you let the air out of my tires back at the zoo?" he screeched.

Agent Reynolds edged quietly behind her partner.

"Never mind," the government scientist continued. "Olivia Haggerty, you are hereby ordered to accompany me to Area Fifty-one!" He flapped a document at her. "You, too, Catriona Starr."

Olivia and I exchanged a glance. I folded my arms across my chest. "You're not taking us anywhere," I told him flatly.

Olivia folded her arms too. "Not today, not ever." She opened her mouth and stuck out her tongue. "Check it out—no diamonds."

"And no toads, either," I said, hooking my fingers around the edges of my mouth and stretching it wide to show him. Cat Starr, Toad Huntress was gone for good.

"Looks like the girls are cured, Dr. Dalton," said my father, putting his arms around our shoulders. "Not much use to you now, are they?"

The government scientist's face got very red. He started to sputter. "It's some kind of a trick."

"No trick," said Agent Salgado. "It's true. They're back to normal."

Bald Elvis advanced toward him. "You ain't nothing but a hound dog," he told Dr. Dalton.

"You can say that again," said Great-Aunt Abyssinia, lumbering up behind the two of them. Dr. Dalton had to tip his head back to look up at her. "If I were you," she said, glowering down at him, "I'd leave before someone plays a real trick and turns you into a toad—or worse."

Dr. Dalton quailed. Clutching his now-useless document, he backed away, muttering to himself as he climbed into the taxi. As it pulled out of the driveway, he rolled down the window and leaned out. "You haven't seen the last of me!" he warned.

My little brother pulled his finger out of his mouth. "Go away," he said distinctly. "Nobody likes you."

We all turned to gape at him, and Iz burst into delighted laughter. She swung him up in the air and kissed the top of his head, which was about the only barf-free spot on him. "Well said, Geoffrey."

"With a G!" he crowed.

"You bet, buddy," said my father, putting his arm around me. "Come on, Kit-Cat, let's go inside."

EPILOGUE

A ripple of excitement ran through the crowded auditorium at Hawk Creek Middle School. Mr. Morgan rapped his baton on his music stand, then raised it in the air.

The other four Hawkwinds and I sat poised, awaiting his signal. We were a quintet now, instead of a quartet. Connor Dixon had been practicing like crazy ever since what he called our Woodwinds to the Rescue adventure, and Mr. Morgan had finally relented and let him join. Connor still wasn't all that great, but at the rate he was improving, he soon would be.

Out of the corner of my eye I spotted my family in the front row. Great-Aunt Aby was seated at the end, taking up two chairs and blocking the view for several rows behind her. Geoffrey was on her lap, clutching his blanket with one hand and playing with the rhinestone cactus links of her eyeglass chain with the other. Iz beamed at me proudly, and Olivia waggled her ring finger. She'd gotten the silver and aquamarine band back from her mother the day we rescued Geoffrey and hadn't taken it off since. I waggled mine back at her. We might never see eye to eye on everything, but the two of us were getting along a whole lot better these days.

Mr. Morgan's baton came down, and my friends and I launched into the opening bars of "Sheep May Safely Graze," part of my favorite Bach cantata. It was one of the first pieces I ever played with the Houston Youth Symphony. As the first dreamy notes of its melody floated out over our audience, I actually heard a few sighs of delight. It has that effect on people.

My father held up his cell phone. Back in Houston, my friend A.J. D'Angelo was relaying our final recital of the year—via a legitimate NASA satellite link, not the FGPS—to the International Space Station.

This time next week my mother and I would both be home in Texas. I couldn't believe my stay here in Oregon was almost over. Three months had seemed like an eternity when I'd first arrived, but the rest of the school year had flown by after what had indisputably been the strangest week of my life.

It had been a relief to settle back into a normal routine. Olivia and I were in the spotlight for a while in the news and around Portland, but everyone gradually lost interest when they realized there was nothing to see but us—just two ordinary middle school stepsisters.

Eventually most people stopped believing anything had ever happened. "Publicity stunt," some called it. "An elaborate hoax, like Sasquatch," said others. "Spontaneous adolescent aberration" was the final verdict from the specialists at the research hospital, who'd poked and prodded at us a bit, but in the end were completely baffled. With no evidence of diamonds or toads, the only diagnosis they could offer was "perfectly normal."

Even my Hawkwinds friends weren't convinced that Great-Aunt Aby was really my fairy godmother. I was pretty sure they thought I'd made that part up, in spite of the diamonds and toads, and I'd decided not to try and convince them otherwise. It was better that way. A.J. knew the truth, of course, and so did Olivia, but my great-aunt's secret was safe with them. Especially Olivia. She was still a little intimidated by Great-Aunt Aby, particularly after I told her what had happened with my mother and the feathers.

After her short, disastrous career as Diamond Girl, Olivia was heartily sick of the limelight. Especially once she'd gotten an up-close-and-personal look at the downside of being a celebrity. No "Photo Shoot Barbie" or "Magazine Cover Barbie" dioramas for her. She even traded in her spangled Hawk Creek Tappers costume for a spot in our middle school's chorus instead.

Her friendship with Piper Philbin cooled as well, thanks to Piper's boneheaded move at the Penguinarium, and the fact that she made the mistake of calling me Catbox on our first day back at school. Olivia really lit into her for that.

"She saved my life, you fleabrain!" she told her.

There was no more duct tape on the bedroom floor or hints about me going home to Houston, either, and Olivia even made room for my clothes in her closet.

From time to time my stepsister still got out her glue gun and Barbies, but she had bigger projects to focus on. The diamonds had seen to that. Not only were all of our college savings accounts fully funded now, but a construction crew had also started on the new master bedroom suite in the attic. Olivia and her mom were spending a lot of time together these days looking at paint chips and fabric samples and stuff like that, and Olivia even offered to help me redecorate my new bedroom, once Dad and Iz moved upstairs.

Funny thing about the diamonds, though—most of them had disappeared. I don't mean stolen, I mean disappeared as in vanished! Poof! Gone!

The ones in the SUV were never found, nor were the ones that Dr. Dalton had confiscated. It was as if they'd melted into thin air. The only ones that stuck around were the ones in Olivia's diorama of Geoffrey's room and the ones we'd given to our friends.

"They were the only ones created with a truly generous spirit," Great-Aunt Abyssinia told us, with a significant look at my stepsister.

My great-aunt had hit the road again the day after Olivia and Geoffrey and I returned home. So had Bald Elvis, who hitched a ride back to Las Vegas with Pearl.

"We promised you a round-trip vacation, remember?" she told him, patting her beehive. They'd left in a cloud of dust and with the strains of "It's Now or Never" blaring on the Red Rocket's radio.

Three weeks later we got a postcard from them. On the front was a picture of the Tunnel of Love Wedding Chapel. On the back was a note: "Just married! Thanks for the wedding present. Love, Pearl and Herman."

Herman? I'll always think of him as Bald Elvis.

The two of them bought the Pie-in-the-Sky Diner from

Frank with the diamonds we'd given them, and last we heard, they'd added an eighth pie to the menu in honor of Great-Aunt Abyssinia. It's called the SuperGloop Special. Pearl had grown fond of my great-aunt's disgusting green breakfast drink on that wild road trip.

I took another, more sedate road trip when Great-Aunt Aby showed up again on Memorial Day weekend and whisked me back to the redwoods.

"Can't have you cheated out of a proper look at one of our nation's finest parks," she told me.

The two of us had a great time. We hiked all over and went to ranger programs and saw Roosevelt elk and made s'mores every single night. The best part, though, was what happened on our last morning together.

Great-Aunt Aby woke me early, just before dawn. "Shhhh!" she whispered. "Don't wake Archibald."

As if anything could, I thought darkly. It turns out Archie snores almost as loudly as my little brother.

We dressed quietly and crept out of the RV, then onto a trail I didn't recall seeing before. The forest was quiet, except for the occasional birdcall, and its thick carpet of pine needles muffled the sound of our footsteps as we walked along. I didn't know when I'd seen anything prettier, what with the trees shrouded in the early-morning mist and the rhododendrons in full bloom, their bright blossoms glowing like gems.

The trail grew steeper, and soon we were huffing and puffing. After a while Great-Aunt Aby turned off onto a side path I would have passed right by if she hadn't spotted it. She sure had sharp eyes for someone who called herself a senior citizen.

Again we climbed. Finally the path leveled off, and a few minutes later we emerged into a clearing. There was a flat tree stump in the center of it. I followed my great-aunt over to it and sat down, panting.

I reached for my water bottle and took a sip, then looked at my surroundings. Redwoods, taller than any I'd seen the entire weekend, ringed the clearing like a circle of silent guardians. The grass underfoot still glistened with dew, but the sun was rising higher now, melting away the mist, and shafts of light streamed through the canopy of green overhead like sunlight pouring through the stained-glass windows of a cathedral. The branches of the redwoods stretched so high they seemed to touch the clouds, and I wondered idly if my mother could see them from outer space.

"You bet," said Great-Aunt Aby, reading my mind again, a practice I still found kind of unnerving. "And in a minute she'll be able to see you, too."

She rummaged in her day pack and pulled out her new laptop. After the fiasco with Geoffrey, my mother had insisted she get one. Plus an e-mail address too: ABYCNU@FGmail.com. No more going completely off the grid.

"A.J. helped me with this," she explained as she booted it up and clicked away at the keyboard. Suddenly a familiar face appeared on-screen.

"Mom!" I exclaimed.

"Surprise!" she replied. "Happy belated birthday, honey!"

We waved at each other, beaming.

"You cut your hair!" my mother said, and I nodded, running my fingers through it. Iz had taken me to her salon after the kidnapping to fix the mess I'd made of it with the nail scissors. It looked a little better, but I still didn't like it very much. "It looks cute, honey."

I shrugged.

"We decided we didn't want to delay the ceremony any longer," Great-Aunt Aby told me, her big teeth peeking out and looking particularly pleased with themselves.

She was right; the ceremony was lovely. Solemn, but joyous at the same time. I'd been half expecting something weird, but it wasn't at all. In fact, the only weird thing in the clearing was the sight of my great-aunt in hiking shorts and kneesocks.

At her request I unclasped my necklace and held it in my upturned palm. Then my mother began to speak, and her voice had that same oddly formal tone as the note she'd left behind under my pillow.

"Juniper for the protection of Catriona Skye Starr," she said as Great-Aunt Aby ran her finger over the etched image on the front of the charm. "Gold for strength and wisdom. A circle to keep her from ever straying far"—my great-aunt traced her finger around the edge of the gold disk—"and a chain to forever bind her."

"Bind her to my heart and keep her safe from harm; help her learn the value of this ancient golden charm," said Great-Aunt Aby, picking up the necklace, which flashed in the sun. "Each link in the chain will hold her fast, as it has for a thousand suns; each link in the chain will hold me, too, from now till our time is done."

"Hold fast!" said my mother, smiling at me as Great-Aunt Aby replaced my necklace and took me by the hands, giving them a reassuring squeeze.

"Hold fast!" she echoed.

"You are linked forever to your family, now, Catriona Skye," my mother continued.

And then she blew me a kiss from outer space and Great-Aunt Aby hugged me, and that was that. No wand, no flying sparks, no fairy dust.

After we said good-bye to my mother, my great-aunt put her laptop away and we hiked back down to the RV, where she made me a special belated-birthday breakfast.

"I got the recipe from one of those shows on the Food Network," she told me, whipping up a perfectly normal—and delicious—coffee cake. "Figured if we're going to be spending more time together, I'd better step up my culinary game."

We toasted each other over generous slices, me with a glass of orange juice and Great-Aunt Aby with—what else?—SuperGloop. As I fed a piece of coffee cake to Archibald, I happened to glance up at the shelf above the table. There was a new addition to the snow globe collection.

"Hey!" I said, spotting a tiny gold plaque on the front of it that read DIAMOND GIRL AND TOAD SISTER.

"Never mind that for now," Great-Aunt Aby replied, reaching for it with a large hand. She shoved it behind the Red Riding Hood one, but I managed to catch a glimpse of the two figures inside. I frowned. The tall one had curly blond hair and the smaller one was dark-haired. She was holding something lumpy and green, while the taller one held something that glittered.

Archibald blinked at me and twitched his tail.

"Have some more coffee cake," said Great-Aunt Aby, passing me the platter.

Later that night, as we sat around our final campfire toasting a few last marshmallows, I ran my fingers idly through my hair. "I wish I had my long hair back," I said with a sigh. "I'm sick of looking like a boy."

My great-aunt's eyes glinted behind her glasses. "Are you now?" she said softly. "Be careful what you wish for, Catriona. Very careful. Beauty is as beauty does."

I snorted. "That's what mom always says."

"A wise woman, your mother."

"So, what was all that about me being linked to my family?" I asked, changing the subject. "During the ceremony, I mean. Mom always told me she didn't have any family except for you."

"Did she, now?" replied Great-Aunt Aby mildly.

"I mean, I get the feeling there's more to the story."

She looked amused. "There's always more to the story, Catriona," she replied. "That's the wonderful thing about stories. But your mother needs to tell you this one."

That was nearly a month ago, and I'd been waiting for the rest of the story ever since. As Mr. Morgan pointed his baton at me and I raised my bassoon to my lips for the cantata's final movement, I reminded myself to ask my mother about it next week, when I saw her back in Houston.

"I'm going to miss you," said Rani after the concert as we gathered in the cafeteria for brownie sundaes. She gave me a hug.

I hugged her back. "I'll miss you, too," I told her. "Maybe you can come visit me in Texas sometime."

"That would be cool!"

"No fair! I want to come too!" said Rajit.

I looked up at him. When had he gotten so tall? He must have gone through a growth spurt this spring. And had his eyelashes always been so thick?

"Why are you staring at me?" he asked.

I gave a start, then blushed. "Sorry. Yeah, sure, of course you can come to Texas. That would be really fun. I'll get my mom to call your mom once I get home. My other home, I mean."

The thing was, Oregon felt like home now too.

I glanced across the cafeteria. Mrs. Kumar was talking to Iz and Great-Aunt Aby. She was wearing one of her prettiest saris—a bright orange one with lots of intricate embroidery. I noticed my great-aunt fingering the edge of it.

Uh-oh, I thought. I could only imagine what Great-Aunt Aby would look like in a sari.

Later, when we got back to my dad's house, I went upstairs to change out of my concert clothes.

"Hey," said Olivia, trailing into our room after me. She flopped down on her stomach on her bed.

"Hey yourself. What's up?"

"Um, can I ask you a favor?" she said.

I shrugged. "Sure."

"I was, uh, wondering if maybe you could put in a good word for me with your fair—with your great-aunt and see if she could, you know, wave her wand or something and make Connor Dixon like me."

I snorted. "Fat chance."

Olivia reddened, and I sighed. "I didn't mean it that way," I told her. "I didn't mean fat chance Connor would ever like you, all I meant was fat chance Great-Aunt Aby would agree to help. For one thing, I don't think she even owns a wand, and for another, Mom says she's more into life lessons than magic and spells and stuff."

"Oh," said Olivia, deflated.

"Plus, what if she got in a muddle again? Things could be a whole lot worse next time around."

"I hadn't thought of that."

I pointed out our bedroom window. It was a beautiful June evening, and the Dixon brothers were in their driveway making the most of it. "Connor's right there," I told her.

She lifted a shoulder. "Yeah, I know."

"You like basketball, right?"

"I guess."

"So, what are you waiting for?" I asked. "Go on out there and play a game with him! Boys can be friends, too, you know, not just crushes." That reminded me, I'd promised to call A.J. after the concert.

"I guess," she said again, still sounding uncertain, but she didn't put up a fight when I propelled her through the door and toward the stairs.

Iz poked her head out of Geoffrey's room when she heard us. My little brother was lying flat on his back on his Traffic Tyme rug again, apparently afflicted with another case of spaghetti leg. It still happened occasionally at bathtime. "Your great-aunt is getting ready to leave, Cat," my stepmother told me. "The rest of us have all said our good-byes. I thought maybe the two of you would like a private moment." She smiled at me, and I smiled back.

"Yes, ma'am," I said, and went downstairs. I found my great-aunt on the porch swing, watching Olivia.

"So, what do you think?" she asked. "Happily ever after?"

"Um, I don't know if I'd say that, exactly," I replied. Olivia was standing in the Dixons' driveway, giggling hysterically at something Connor had just said. She sounded like a chicken about to lay an egg.

My great-aunt laughed. "She does, doesn't she?"

I didn't know if I was ever going to get used to her reading my thoughts.

"Sure you will," she said, heaving herself to her feet and slipping her large arm through mine. "Walk me to my RV? I don't want to keep Archibald waiting, and I know he'd like to say good-bye before we hit the road."

"I wish you didn't have to go," I said. I really meant it too. I felt like I was just getting to know her.

"Oh, don't worry," she told me. "I'll be back. That's the thing with fairy godmothers—we're like yo-yos, or Velcro. You're stuck with me."

Archibald was sitting on the step by the RV's door. I picked him up and gave him a snuggle—well, if you can call hefting a twenty-pound cat a snuggle—then set him down again. He disappeared inside, twitching his tail. Great-Aunt Aby gave me a hug, then followed after him, shutting the door behind her.

A few seconds later, as the RV's engine roared to life, I suddenly remembered the little good-bye ritual that my great-aunt and my mother always shared.

"Abysinnia!" I cried, lifting my hand in farewell.

My great-aunt poked her head out the driver's window and grinned. "Not if I be seeing you first!" she called back, and tossed something at me. I caught it.

It was a toad.

As she pulled out of the driveway, I heard her RV backfire as usual.

And I swear it actually went, "Croak."